PRAISE FOR THE MAR

'Brilliantly pacey, imaginative, high.

Mars – a must-read for all YA thriller fans'
Emma Haughton

'An old-fashioned pulp sci-fi space opera packed with action, adventure, an android, amorous teens and artificial intelligence'
Nina Paley

'A beautifully paced, unputdownable story. Stickland's world-building rings true down to every grain of Martian dust'
Victoria Whitworth

'Glorious world-building. I couldn't put it down'
Fran Harris

'Consummate storytelling that speeds along as smoothly as an interplanetary spaceship… with satisfyingly grounded science'
Iain Hood

'An immersive adventure. If you like science fiction with strong characterisation and a political edge, this is for you'
Katharine Quarmby

'Part space-adventure, part coming-of-age story… With quicksilver prose and a pacy plot, it keeps you guessing until the very last page'
Melissa Fu

'This is aimed at YA readers, but I am a lot more mature and I couldn't put it down. This book has it all'
Jackie's Reading Corner

ANDREW STICKLAND is a prize-winning poet and short-story writer whose work has variously been published by the British Fantasy Society, Games Workshop, the Royal Statistical Society and *The Economist*. He studied law at University College London, then creative writing at the University of Jyväskylä in Finland. He is previously the author of *The Arcadian Incident*, the first part of the Mars Alone Trilogy. He lives in Cambridge.

ESCAPE TO MIDAS

ESCAPE TO MIDAS

ANDREW STICKLAND

Lightning
Books

Published in 2023
by Lightning Books
Imprint of Eye Books Ltd
29A Barrow Street
Much Wenlock
Shropshire
TF13 6EN

www.lightning-books.com

ISBN: 9781785633638

Cover by Ifan Bates
Typeset in Centaur and Zona Pro

British Library Cataloguing in Publication Data

A catalogue record for this book is available from the British Library.

For David

PROLOGUE

ALREADY THE DEIMOS BAR was a huge, glowing jewel, its thermoplas dome slowly fading from blue, to purple, to red against the darkening Martian sky. It was perched twelve storeys up, on the very top of the Nevsky Grand Hotel, and there wasn't another tall building to spoil the view for several blocks in any direction. On another occasion, Stefan Granski would have been happy to sit for a while, enjoying a drink or two and staring out at the stars, or at the lights and holoverts of the city sprawling away beneath him, but not tonight. Tonight he needed to keep a low profile and he wished his contact had suggested somewhere less exposed – one of the underground bars maybe, where people could come and go without attracting quite so much attention.

He crossed the roadway and waited nervously at the back of a group queueing to use the hotel's airlocks. He felt exposed. His eyes darted from side to side, constantly checking the surrounding buildings, the passing transpods and the other pedestrians for any sign that he was being followed. There was nothing. Even so, he reached down to the large bag hanging by his side, drew it up to his chest and wrapped his arms tightly around it, just in case.

Once through the airlock he was immediately approached by one of the hotel's famous Meet-and-Greets, an enthusiastic young man wearing a smart, old-style uniform and a broad smile.

'Good evening, sir,' the young man said, 'and welcome to the Nevsky Grand. May I take that for you?' He reached for the bag and Granski pulled back defensively.

'I can manage,' he replied, curtly. 'I just need to know how to get up to the Deimos Bar.'

'Of course,' the Meet-and-Greet replied, looking him up and down. 'I can show you to the wash facilities if you'd like to freshen up first. And if you want to leave your E-suit with us, we can have it cleaned and refilled for you while you enjoy your time at the bar.'

'It's fine. I don't plan on staying long. Just show me the way up.'

'As you wish, sir,' the young man said, directing Granski across the busy lobby. 'Last elevator on the left will take you directly up.'

A pair of burly, angry-looking security guards stood beside the airlocks inspecting everyone as they entered the foyer, so Granski hurried over and joined a group of smartly dressed party-goers waiting to go up to the bar. He pushed his way to the back of the lift as soon as it arrived.

Even this early in the evening the Deimos was buzzing and Granski had to try several times before he could attract the attention of one of the bar's human staff.

'I'm looking for someone,' he shouted over the din. 'Captain Lockley. He said to ask for him here.'

The woman reached up, took an empty glass from the shelf above her head and handed it to him. 'In the back,' she said, motioning over her shoulder before turning back to her computer screen.

Granski took the glass and went through into a quieter, more dimly lit section of the bar. Small booths, all occupied, were set against the room's curved walls and Granski scanned them quickly, looking for someone who seemed to be a spaceship's captain – though Granski wasn't exactly sure what that might look like. But he needn't have worried. His attention was immediately drawn to the central booth, where a single figure was seated in the shadows behind a large circular table. Several bottles, mostly empty, were lined up along one side of the table.

As Granski stood watching, the figure sat forward so that his face was picked out by the overhead light. A brief smile appeared as he took hold of the nearest bottle and motioned for Granski to come and join him. The man was young, much younger than Granski had imagined, considering he claimed to be a fully certified merchant captain. But then sometimes Mars was like that, especially these days with the blockade in force. What mattered now was having the right connections. It didn't matter if you were the skipper of a battered old tug, or a forty-year-old shuttle, or even just a surface-to-station barge, as long as you could find someone to issue you with an off-world licence. Then you were a somebody.

And the word was that Captain Lockley was a somebody. For the right price, it was said, he would happily take you out to one of the Belt stations, or even arrange a discreet ship-to-ship, to put you onto something heading back to Earth. Stefan Granski hoped that what he had to offer was 'the right price'.

As he approached the table, Granski was surprised to see that Lockley wasn't alone after all. Draped along the sofa beside him was a young woman, very pretty, with the long, slender features of a Martian-born. She was wearing a tight, revealing dress and a silver bob-cut wig, and was, Granski assumed, some sort of paid escort the captain had bought himself for the evening. As he took his seat on the far side of the table she raised herself slowly onto one arm, gazed at him with a vacant look in her eyes and sank back down again. Lockley ignored her and filled both his own and Granski's glass.

'You're late,' he said, but there was no anger in his voice.

'I got held up,' was all Granski said in reply. He took a cautious sip of his drink and then drained the glass in one gulp. Lockley refilled it.

'So,' he announced. 'Let's start with introductions. I'm Angus Lockley. Captain Angus Lockley. Call me Lock.'

'Lock?'

'Exactly. And you, I take it, are Stephen Granski, yes?'

'Stefan.' There was a long pause. Lockley was clearly waiting for more, but Granski was reluctant to continue. He looked down at the young woman. 'Couldn't we have this conversation in private?'

Lockley waved his hand dismissively. 'Don't you worry about Nuying. As far as I can tell she doesn't speak English, and even if she did, I don't think she's in much of a state to remember anything she hears. She's an ornament, that's all. Part of the furniture.'

'Couldn't you at least have picked a less public place to meet?'

Lockley spread his arms wide. 'Why? I have nothing to hide. I'm a fully licensed merchant captain. I can do business wherever I please.' He leaned in closer. 'And that, my friend, is why you need my services, yes?' Granski nodded. 'So why don't you tell me your story, and then we'll see whether we can come to some sort of arrangement, yes? Something that will be of benefit to us both.'

'Fine.' Granski took another swig of his drink. 'Stefan Granski, journalist. Or former journalist, I should say. I used to run an online newsfeed called *The Martian Chronicle*. Maybe you've heard of it?' Lockley shook his head. 'Well, it wasn't one of the Majors, but it did okay. Had a reasonable following.'

'Had?'

'Until our wonderful new government decided that freedom of the press wasn't anything like as important as I thought it was. I guess I said the wrong thing once too often so they decided to shut me down.'

'Unpleasantly?'

'The works. The beating, the threats, the gun in the face. They smashed anything they couldn't take with them, whether it had anything to do with the business or not, and they gave me a single day to clear out and disappear for good.'

'Yeah,' Lockley said, showing little interest for the story. 'That's the new Mars for you. Crazy place. Crazy. Still, it works for some people.' He smiled. 'If you know how to play the game.'

'Well, I don't. And I don't want to either. I just want to get the hell out of here as fast as I can.'

'And so here you are.'

'I was told you're the man to come to if you're looking to get off planet.'

'And you were not misinformed. I am the man to come to. Yes, indeed. But tell me...' He leaned forward again and made a show of looking serious for a moment. 'How do you intend to pay? My services don't come cheap, and something tells me you're a little short on funds right now. Am I right?'

'You're right, I can't pay. Not with credit anyway. They froze all my accounts when they shut me down.'

'Yeah, that's what I thought. So?'

'I have information.'

Lockley let out a loud laugh and rocked back on the sofa, disturbing the woman beside him. She looked up, shrugged, and rearranged herself slightly away from him. 'Information?' he asked, still laughing. 'And what am I supposed to do with that? I can't fuel my ship with information.'

'You can with this sort of information. It's valuable. And I mean really valuable. You find the right person and I guarantee it'll earn you more credit than you'd get from half a dozen other refugees like me.'

'I doubt that.'

'Trust me.'

Lockley gave a shrug. 'So convince me. If this information really is as valuable as you claim, I'd be a fool not to take you anywhere you want to go. And in style, too. But I'll be the one to decide. If I think you've got nothing, then you're back on the street. Deal?'

'Deal.'

'Excellent.' Lockley emptied the contents of the bottle into the two glasses and sat back, idly running his fingers through the Martian woman's hair.

After a moment, Granski began. 'I take it you've heard of the Arcadian Incident?'

'Oh, come on,' Lockley laughed. 'That's your information? That the government is covering up evidence of aliens? You'll have to do a lot better than that, my friend. That's an old story, and it was garbage even when it was new.'

Granski unzipped his bag and took out a small rectangular object that he placed on the table. 'It's true. Every last word of it.'

'And so this would be, what?' Lockley asked, leaning forward to examine the object. 'An alien artefact?' The thing was dark and smooth, and appeared to have been made out of a single piece of some vaguely metallic material. On each of its sides was a small, oddly shaped hole, but that was all. There were no other markings of any sort.

'Not an artefact,' Granski continued. 'A computer. I have no idea what it does or how to work it, but if you take it to someone who knows about these things I'm sure they'd be able to get it to spit out something or other. And they'd also be able to confirm that it wasn't built by us. Take it to the government, on the other hand, and they wouldn't even be surprised by it.'

'Okay, I'm now mildly curious. Tell me more.'

'So, after my little visit from the thug squad, I had to get out of town fast. I wandered around for a while, begging whatever I could from those friends I still had who weren't too scared to talk to me, and eventually I got put in touch with someone who could give me a place to stay. It was...well, it was like a safe house, only bigger. There were dozens of people there. Some of them were like me, ordinary folk who'd ended up getting on the wrong side of the new government and had nowhere else to go. Others were out-and-out criminals; smugglers, petty pirates, profiteers. And then there were the rest. We called them the Resistance. Some of them were soldiers, others secret agents or spies of some sort. They kept pretty much to themselves, but it was clear they were well organised and well equipped. They had vehicles, guns, explosives. And a lot of hi-tech computer stuff as well – stuff they were always doing secret experiments with. I know a bit about computers myself and I offered to help them out with their work, but they weren't interested. No thank you.

'So anyway. All these people. Rumours start flying around about who they really are and what they're actually doing, and soon enough the truth gets out.' Now it was Granski's turn to lean in close across the table. He looked round to make sure there was no one close and then lowered his voice. 'It's the Fischers. You know, those scientists, mother and son, who are currently top of the government's most-wanted list. Well, that's where they're hiding out. And you want to know why the government want to get their hands on them so badly? It's because of this.' He picked up the strange object from the table and looked at it admiringly. 'Alien technology. They have a whole load of these and they're trying to work out how to get them to work with human computers. And succeeding, as far as I can tell. Now you tell me, is that the kind of information that will buy me a place on your ship, or not?'

'So what? You're saying the Arcadian thing is all true? That the government is covering up contact with aliens?'

'It was just a bunch of computers. I didn't see any little green men. But yeah, I reckon it's all true.'

'Then why not turn them in yourself? I seem to remember it's a pretty damn big reward.'

'You think I'd ever be allowed to claim it? Me? No, I'm taking my chances off-planet. You get me there, the reward's all yours.'

'And where is this so-called safe house?'

Granski shook his head. 'That's enough for now. I'll leave you the computer as a deposit, but you don't get the location of the base until I'm safely on an Earth-bound ship. And I guarantee you'll never find it on your own. It's well hidden.'

Lockley took the computer, thought for a while and then his smile returned. 'Okay, Mr Granski. I think we can make this work. I'll pass this on to someone who can verify it really is what you say it is and then claim my nice fat reward and become a public hero while you do whatever it is you want to do back on Earth.' He took a plastic call-card from his jacket pocket and handed it across to Granski. "We shuttle up at midday tomorrow. This will give you all the information you need. Be at the dock no later than nine. If you're late, you'll miss the flight.'

'Just like that?'

Lockley shrugged. 'Just like that.'

Granski took the card and tucked it safely inside his environment suit. 'I'll be there, nice and early.' For a moment he sat, unsure what to do next, but it was clear the meeting was over. Lockley turned his attention back to the woman at his side and left Granski to get awkwardly to his feet, mumble a goodbye and make his way back through the bar's purple gloom towards the entrance.

'He's gone,' Lockley said after a moment. His companion sat up, suddenly alert. 'So what do you think?'

'I think it's a start,' she replied. 'It would have been better if you'd managed to get the location of the base from him up front. But no matter. We can trace his movements back over the past few weeks. We'll find it soon enough.'

'And what about this?' Lockley asked, holding up the strange device. 'You don't believe this is really some sort of alien computer, do you?'

The woman took it from him and examined it for herself. 'Who knows? Perhaps.'

'Oh come on. Aliens?'

'Why not? They're out there somewhere.'

'Exactly. Out there somewhere, not down here somewhere.'

'What do you care? You'll be paid for your part in this either way.'

'And if it really is who he says it is?'

'Then you'll be paid even more.'

'Once you actually get hold of them?'

'Don't worry, we will. And soon.'

'Why not just wait and let Granski give me the location once he's safely on his ship back to Earth?'

'He's never going to give you the location,' the woman replied with a sneer. 'Any fool can see that.'

'So what am I supposed to do with him then?'

'Get him off-planet and throw him out the airlock.' She stood up to leave.

'Hey, wait up,' Lockley said, his sly smile creeping back as he let his eyes wander over the various areas of pleasantly exposed flesh in front of him. 'What's the hurry there, my lovely Nuying? The night is still young.'

She looked down at him, more disappointed than angry. 'Don't be such a pig, Lockley. Go home and sober up.' She held up the artifact. 'I have work to do. But even if I didn't...' She shook her head and left her words hanging in the air behind her.

PART ONE

THE TIDE TURNS

1

SKATER GOES TO UNIVERSITY

'**OKAY, PEOPLE,**' **SKATER ANNOUNCED,** after popping in her ear buds and activating her comms. 'I'm in position. So who's ready for some fun?'

'Can I please remind you', came her father's voice in her ear, 'that this is an important mission and you're supposed to be acting responsibly. You're not there to have fun.'

Skater rolled her eyes. 'Dad. I'm stealing a computer from a university. How, exactly, am I supposed to do that responsibly?'

'And anyway, Pete,' Morgan chipped in. 'Committing crimes *is* fun, as you well know.'

'Whose side are you on?'

'Mine, of course,' Skater added quickly. 'As always.'

'Enough,' Captain Mackie barked, and the chatter immediately stopped. 'Let's get to work. Mobile, are you set?'

'All set,' Skater replied, in her most responsible-sounding voice.

'Evac One?'

'In position,' Pete answered. 'Ready to go.'

'Evac Two?'

'All systems green,' Morgan said.

'Technical?'

Silence.

'Technical?'

'That's you, Leo,' Skater added, helpfully.

'Yeah, I know,' came Leo's flustered voice. 'Just hang on a sec. I need to…do a couple…of things here.' There was a long pause. 'There. All sorted. Sorry, I mean, Technical standing by.'

'Good. Mobile, you can go ahead and power up the glasses.'

Skater pressed the tiny pad on the side of her sunglasses that switched them over to interactive display mode, and information began to appear across the lenses as built-in microprocessors identified everything she was looking at.

'I have video,' Leo announced. 'Signal's clean and image is good. Just give me a quick three-sixty.'

'Okay,' Skater announced as she spun slowly around. 'So welcome to Mars Minerva University. Here I am inside the main campus atmosphere dome, where someone has taken some quite pretty Terran gardens and dumped a load of ugly great buildings down on top of them. And as you can see, the place is triple-bursting with people.'

'It's the start of term,' Leo replied. 'Hundreds of new students. Which is why we chose today for our mission. Now try not to turn your head so quickly. Make your movements slower and more flowing, otherwise the cameras won't be able to keep up.'

'Okay,' Skater replied, flicking her head quickly from side to side. 'So not like this then?'

'And try not to talk so much. You'll draw attention to yourself.'

'Right, because no one else is doing that, are they?' She panned around slowly again, giving Leo a view of the nearby students. 'Take a look. Half the people here are talking to their phone screens or eye slates and no one's looking at them as if they're mad, bad, or on a secret stealth mission.'

'Mobile!' Mackie interrupted.

'Okay,' Skater said, dropping her voice. 'Once we're inside I'll shut up and be serious. And talking of inside...' She looked up at the glass-walled building directly in front of her, and almost immediately her sunglasses identified it. 'According to my super specs, this ugly blue diamond is the Department of Engineering and Computer Sciences. That's our building, right?'

'Right,' said Mackie.

'Although technically it's an icosahedron, not a diamond,' Leo added.

'Whatever that may be.'

'It's a twenty-sided regular polyhedron.'

'Well good for it. Do I care?'

'I'm just trying to be helpful. Anyone who was actually a student there would know what shape their building was, that's all.'

'Don't push it. I can hear you smiling, brainbot.'

'Come on people,' Mackie cut in. 'Time to focus. Save the joking for when we're all back home. Mobile, off you go. And remember, as long as you act like you know what you're doing, no one's going to bother you. Not for the moment, anyway.'

'Got it,' Skater said and took a deep breath. 'I'm going in.' She set off for the long, curving walkway that led up to the building's main entrance, more nervous than she wanted to admit to the others and muttering *i-co-sa-he-dron* to herself as she went.

Beyond the entrance the building opened out into a vast atrium filled with the buzz of conversation. The central section was taken up by a food and drinks bar, its wide tables and low chairs already busy with mid-morning coffee drinkers. Around the outside of the room, where the blue light filtered in through the huge glass walls, a series of interlinked spiral escalators wound their way up towards the building's upper levels.

'Nice,' Skater muttered. 'If you like working in a fish bowl. So where to first?'

'Head towards the far end of this room,' Mackie said. 'There should be a bank of lifts somewhere near the back.'

Skater picked her way between the tables, trying her best to keep looking straight ahead instead of glancing from side to side. She'd been practising with the glasses back at the Mine for the past couple of days, but still found it almost impossible to keep from turning her head too quickly.

Suddenly her foot caught against something and she stumbled. She twisted awkwardly to avoid landing on a table full of cups and ended up falling gracelessly into one of the low seats. Unfortunately, it was already occupied.

'Steady on!' spluttered the elderly man across whose lap she was now sprawled. 'This seat's taken.'

Skater scrambled to her feet and mumbled an embarrassed apology. She'd lost the glasses. Desperately, she searched around on the floor for them.

'Here,' the man said, holding them out for her. 'But perhaps wearing them inside is not such a good idea, young lady.'

Skater quickly put the glasses back on and was relieved to see they were still working. 'Thanks,' she said, smiling down at the man. 'I'll remember that.' And she hurried off, leaving the puzzled man staring after her.

'Oh my god!' Leo exclaimed. 'You know who that was that you just crashed into?'

'Actually, I do,' Skater replied. 'Super specs told me it was some guy called Professor Popsicle.'

'Pospisil,' Leo corrected her. 'And he just happens to be probably the most famous mathematician there is on Mars right now. The guy is like the god of maths.'

'Well big biscuits to him. And maybe when you've finished being such a nerd groupie you might want to ask if I'm okay. Which I am, by the way, so no need to ask. Now shut up and let me do my job.' She had reached the lifts and stood waiting for one of them to arrive. She was shaking.

Re...lax, she told herself, hoping the others hadn't noticed any change in her voice. She could do this. She knew she could. Once the lift arrived, she stepped quickly inside and closed the door before anyone else could join her.

'Where to now?'

'Down,' Leo replied. 'Sub-level Two. You're looking for the Department of Advanced Engineering, Artificial Intelligence Unit. According to the map it should be on the left as you come out of the lift.'

When the doors opened again Skater stepped out into a small foyer, where a set of double doors led off on either side. A sign above the left-hand ones told her she was in the right place. They slid silently open as she approached, revealing a long, empty corridor beyond.

'Okay,' Leo continued. 'I need to see what's written on the doors. Can you just walk along the corridor and look at all the name plates?'

'Can do,' Skater muttered quietly. She stopped in front of the first door.

'Not that one,' Leo said. 'Move on.'

Skater moved along the corridor and Leo checked off the names as she went. At one point there was an unmarked door, but a small glass panel on the top half allowed them to see that the room beyond was some kind of workshop. A couple of technicians were working on some large piece of machinery at one of the workbenches, but neither of them noticed Skater looking in at them.

'That's not it either. Keep going.'

There was a hiss of hydraulics from behind her and Skater let out a startled gasp as she spun round. A young woman had emerged from the room opposite and stood looking at her in surprise.

'Can I help you?'

From her age she could easily have been one of the other students, except that she was wearing a white lab coat over her clothes and something about her manner gave the impression she was a lot more senior than her age suggested. Skater stared at her in shocked silence as she waited for the glasses to identify the woman, but nothing was coming up on the display.

'Are you lost?' the woman continued.

Skater could feel the panic beginning to rise up inside her and all the breezy confidence she'd felt upstairs suddenly drained away. 'Um...' she managed, before Mackie cut in over the comms.

'Say yes.'

'Yes,' Skater said.

'I was looking for...' Mackie continued.

'I was looking for...' Skater repeated.

'Now look through your bag, as if you can't remember someone's name and you're looking for something to remind you.'

'Hang on,' Skater said, playing along. 'I've got it here somewhere.' She opened her bag and took out her slate, flicking through various files at random.

'Right,' said Mackie. 'You're going to have to explain that you've lost the name. Just say it was some professor or other but you're new and can't remember who it was. Say you'll come back later once you've remembered.'

'No,' cut in Leo. 'Just give me a sec.' The others could hear him tapping away on his keyboard. The young woman was becoming impatient. Skater was running out of time. 'One sec.'

'Are you sure you're in the right place?' the woman asked. 'New students aren't really supposed to be down here.'

'Dr Mortimer,' Leo announced.

'Dr Mortimer,' Skater said, with relief.

'Really?' the woman asked, looking puzzled.

'It's a funding application.' Leo said. 'And it has to be handed in today.'

'It's a funny application, and it has to be handed in today.'

'Funding!' Leo shouted.

'Funding!' Skater shouted. And then, more quietly, 'I mean funding, of course.' She gave the woman a weak smile.

'Four doors down, on the left,' the woman replied. 'Just look for the name on the door.' She turned to go and Skater let out a sigh of relief.

'Good girl,' Mackie said.

'Good girl,' Skater repeated, before she could stop herself. The woman paused, looked as if she was about to say something, then shook her head and set off down the corridor towards the lifts. 'Sorry,' Skater whispered, once the woman was out of earshot.

'Don't worry,' Mackie comforted her. 'You did great. Just go to Mortimer's office and pretend to knock. We'll carry on once your friend has gone.'

'Wait,' Leo called out as Skater continued down the corridor. 'Back up. That was our door.'

Once the corridor was empty again, Leo directed her back to the right door. It was drab and uninviting, and appeared to be much more solid than the office doors she'd already examined. There was a large sign at head height.

'SWARM,' Skater read. 'Access Restricted. You want to give me a clue?'

'System-Wide Academic Research Mind. It's a giant network of linked AIs in all the major universities and research sites all over the Solar System. This is the local hub for the whole of Northern Mars.'

'And this is where we're going to get our AI from?'

'Exactly.'

Skater pressed the red entry button. 'Surprise, surprise. It's locked.'

'Then it's time to use that little device I gave you,' Mackie said.

Skater searched in her bag until she found the thing Mackie was talking about. It appeared to be a standard format entry card, but with a small, rectangular black box built onto the end of it. When she pushed it into the access slot, nothing happened.

'Just wait,' Mackie said. 'It'll take a few seconds.'

'Damn it!' Skater cursed, as one of the doors further along the corridor hissed open. She turned away and pretended to be looking for something in her bag, glancing up from behind her glasses to see what was happening. A young man carrying a box stepped out, crossed over and disappeared into a different room. 'False alarm. We're good. The door's still locked.'

'Give it time.'

'Tick, tock, tick, tock,' Skater muttered. 'And while we're waiting, what am I supposed to say if there's anyone inside? Am I still looking for Dr Mortimer?'

'There won't be anyone inside,' Leo said. 'I can pretty much guarantee that.'

'Oh yeah? And what makes you so sure?'

Just then there was a buzzing sound and the entry button turned green. Skater quickly pushed the key card back into her bag, pressed the button and stepped inside the dark room as soon as the door began to slide open. Three seconds later, as the door hissed shut behind her, she understood why Leo had been so certain the room would be empty.

'Ah,' she said, and let out a long breath that immediately condensed right in front of her face.

2

GETTING THE JOB DONE

THE ROOM WAS FREEZING. It was also dark, but Skater's glasses automatically compensated by boosting the light levels to a point where she could see reasonably well. What they couldn't do was wrap her up in something warm.

'Guys,' she panted. 'You're kidding me, right?'

'Sorry,' Leo said. 'I probably should've warned you, shouldn't I?'

'You think? I'm going to be frozen solid in about twenty seconds here. Why the Sol is it so cold?'

'The AIs prefer it that way. It makes them work better and stops them overheating. When there are this many of them together, they can end up giving out a whole lot of heat.'

'Then let's make this quick. What do I do now?'

'Okay. See all those white cubes? They're the AIs. We need to take one of them, but you'll need to pick one from the back corner, where it can't be seen from the door. That way it might be a bit longer before anyone notices it's missing.'

Skater walked quickly across to the far edge of the room, counting the neatly arranged cubes as she went. There were thirty-two in total, arranged in four rows of eight, and she selected the next to last as being the least likely to be noticed. Already she was starting to shiver and she blew on her hands to try to keep them warm. Good job she'd decided to wear the jacket, she thought. And the boots. She'd hate to think what this would have been like if she'd gone with sandals instead.

'Okay. Now you need to take your slate and link it to the AI network. Use the blue cable I gave you. And don't plug it into the unit we're going to take, plug it into the one to the left of the one we're going to take. Got it? Now, look directly at the cube and I'll tell you where to plug in the other end of the cable. And try to stop wobbling so much, it's making it hard to see what's going on.'

'I'm shivering!' Skater barked. 'And there's not a lot I can do about it so just deal.'

'Sorry. I know this is difficult. I'd happily have swapped places with you if I could. It's just that I'd never have made it onto the campus without being picked up by security.'

'Yeah, I know. Desperate criminal, yadda, yadda…number one on the Mars Most Wanted list, yadda yadda. Can't set foot outside the mine without being bombarded by sniper drones, or autograph hunters, or whatever.'

Leo laughed. 'Exactly.'

'You'd probably have messed up somehow anyway. At least this way we get the job done professionally.'

'Now what I'm going to do', Leo continued, ignoring the dig, 'is access the network from here and remotely shut down one of the units. Once I've done that and it's offline, you can literally just unplug it and take it away.'

Five minutes later it was done. Skater had the AI cube in her bag and had left a neat pile of empty work folders in its place on the workbench. She unplugged the slate, made sure she had everything she needed and headed back to the door. 'Well, people, the Eagle has landed. The egg is in the basket. Or whatever it is I'm supposed to say at this point. Job's done, anyway. And I just hope it was worth the loss of all my fingers to frostbite.' She opened the door and stepped out of the freezing room.

'Stop!' Mackie shouted.

'Oh, the relief,' Skater said, as she felt a wave of warmth wash over her.

'Check the corridor first!' Mackie shouted.

But it was too late. Skater slowly turned her head, and the glasses showed two white-coated men chatting no more than thirty metres away. They stopped and gave her a puzzled look as the heavy door hissed shut behind her.

'Oops.'

'Go,' Mackie said. 'Just ignore them and walk away.'

'But they're between me and the lifts. And now they're coming this way.'

'Go the other way. Go now!'

Skater turned and walked quickly along the corridor, feeling the curious stares of the men burning into the back of her head. For several seconds nothing happened, and Skater had to fight the urge to turn around and see what they were doing. Maybe they wouldn't say anything. Maybe they would just assume that she had the right to be in the room anyway. Maybe they would just…

'Excuse me?'

Maybe not. 'Damn,' she whispered. 'What now?'

'Keep going,' Mackie said. 'And don't run. Through the doors at the end and then hard right. There should be a staircase.'

'And?'

'Excuse me, Miss? Miss!'

'And get yourself up to ground level and back out the front of the building.'

As she reached the doors they opened automatically and she risked a quick glance backwards. One of the men was walking purposefully towards her but was still a good way back along the corridor. The second was standing back at the SWARM doorway and appeared to be talking to someone on his phone.

'Hey, come back here!'

Skater turned the corner and there was the staircase in front of her. 'Now run,' Mackie ordered, and she leapt up the stairs four and five at a time as she pushed against the low Martian gravity. She heard the man shout something, but already she was round the first corner and up to the next floor and the words were lost behind her. She ran on, reaching the ground floor a few seconds later, and then stopped dead.

'There's no door,' she shouted, desperately looking around. 'Where do I go?'

'Keep going up.'

She ran on, up and round, up and round, relying on Mackie to find her an exit. But there was no door on the first floor either, and now she could hear the man running up the stairs beneath her. Finally, on the second floor, there was a small passage leading out onto the walkway that ran round the side of the main atrium and she made a dash for it without waiting. As she ran out onto the walkway she grabbed the handrail to stop herself and took a quick look around. One of the spiral escalators was on her left, about ten metres away, but as she set off towards it, she could already see the porter from the reception desk below stepping onto it and looking up at her.

'Stop,' Mackie ordered.

'But they're coming at me from both sides.'

'I know. Just stand still and wait for them.'

'What? You want me to fight my way out?'

'No, I want you to wait until the guy from downstairs steps off the escalator and then I want you to jump.'

'What? I'm two floors up.'

'And you're on Mars. Just be careful where you land.'

The porter had reached the top of the escalator. Behind her, the man from the corridor came stumbling out onto the walkway. 'What the hell is going on?' he demanded. 'What have you got in that bag?' Skater ignored him. She looked up, but there was nothing to help her there. She looked over the top of the low glass wall at the floor, way too far below her.

'Jump! Do it now!'

'Oh crap,' Skater muttered. She pushed herself up onto the wall and swung her legs over the side.

'Stop!' the man shouted, more scared than angry now. The porter began to run towards her.

'Crap, crap, crap,' she said. And then she pushed off.

Maybe she was on Mars, and maybe the gravity was a lot lower than it was back on Earth, but to Skater it really didn't feel like a slow or controlled jump at all. One second she was on the wall, the next her stomach was trying to climb its way out of her mouth and the next she was hitting the ground in a mass of flailing limbs. Someone had screamed, and even as she lay there winded, Skater was relieved to realise it hadn't been her doing the screaming.

Several shocked people nearby were heading towards her, but Skater didn't wait to find out whether they were coming to see if she needed help or to try to stop her getting away. She staggered to her feet, pushed past them, and ran for the main entrance. One of her ankles felt like it was on fire and kept sending stabbing messages to her to stop using it, but she was too desperate to listen to them right now and she ran on regardless. On the way, she passed the table where Professor Pospisil was still sitting with a couple of colleagues. 'Hi, Prof,' she shouted as she ran past, giving him a quick wave. Confused, the Professor held up his hand in response.

Once outside, Skater ran as quickly as she could down the stairs and back out into the gardens. Only now did she realise she'd lost her glasses in the fall, but at least the ear buds were still in place so she was still in contact with the others.

'I'm back outside. Lost the glasses. Sorry.'

'So I see,' Mackie said. "We can do it with audio only. Just don't panic. You need to get yourself into a different building quickly. Do not, I repeat, do *not* go back to the main entrance. They'll have called ahead and security will already be on the lookout for you. Now, is anyone following you?'

Skater looked round quickly. 'Not yet, no.'

'Good. Then stop running. Take off your jacket and drape it over the bag to cover it. Untie your hair and shake it loose. Join a group of other students, or just start talking to someone. They'll be looking for someone rushing about on their own, not someone who's part of a group. And get inside. It'll be harder for the security cameras to pick you up there.'

Skater quickly followed the instructions, tacking herself onto the back of a small group of students who were heading towards a low, flat building that appeared to be floating in the middle of an artificial pond.

'Sorry,' she said to the tall young man she found herself walking beside. 'But what building are we heading for again?'

'This one? It's the Drumming Institute.' the man replied.

'That's right,' said Skater. 'Of course it is. Music department.'

'No,' the man replied, giving Skater a puzzled stare. 'It's the

School of Architecture and the Built Environment. Named after the architect, Cordelia Drumming. If you're looking for the Department of Music, it's way over the other side, I think.'

Just then one of the university porters came running past, heading towards the blue glass building. Skater turned to the young man and seemed suddenly fascinated by what he was saying. 'You know, I'm not really much of a musician anyway. Designing buildings, now that sounds much more like my thing. Especially designing lovely buildings like this one.' She motioned to the sunken building in front of her. 'Simply beautiful.'

'Don't push it,' Mackie said in her ear. 'You're supposed to be blending in, not making a show of yourself. Now go find somewhere quiet to wait while we figure out a way to get you out of there.'

'Already done,' Leo cut in. 'The bottom level of this building appears to have an exit directly out of the university and onto an underground roadway.'

'Perfect,' Mackie said. 'Evac One can pick you up from there.'

'Evac One here,' came Pete's voice. 'Already on my way. Just send me through the location.' Skater felt a sudden surge of relief at the sound of her father's voice. He'd maintained radio silence all the way through the mission and she'd been far too busy with her own problems to give him much thought, but hearing him now she realised how much she needed him to be there with her, to hold her and protect her. To make everything alright.

'Don't be long, Evac One,' she said. 'I'll be waiting.'

Now that she had time to catch her breath and calm down a little, Skater found she had the shakes, badly. Also, she was sore all down one side from the awkward landing after her jump and she only hoped she hadn't done any more damage to her ribs, two of which had been broken when she'd been shot in the chest, just a few months earlier, or her shoulder, which had been badly dislocated two weeks before that. Life as a desperado, she realised, was probably going to involve a whole lot of recovering.

She sat down for a couple of minutes until the shaking had stopped and then found the lifts and made her way down to the lowest level. This time there were plenty of other students coming and going and there was no question of her being somewhere she wasn't supposed to be. Just to be safe, she fell in with two other students as they passed the porter's desk, but the man didn't even look up from whatever it was he was reading on his slate. And then she was out the doors and walking across a small plaza to the side of the roadway.

'Okay, I'm out,' she said with relief. 'It was a little bit beyond scary there for a while, but all things considered, I think that all went pretty…'

A hand clamped down on her shoulder and another gripped her around the upper arm. She spun round and came face to face with the porter from the engineering building. He was red in the face, and panting, but there was a look of triumph in his eyes. 'Gotcha, you little thief. Thought you'd got away, didn't you? Thought you'd outsmarted us all, eh? Well too bad little girlie, 'cos you ain't half as smart as you think you are.'

Skater tried to pull away but the man's grip was too tight. She tried kicking him, but he just stepped to one side and squeezed her arm even tighter until she stopped. 'Right,' he said with a smirk. 'Back you come. And we'll find out what you've got hidden away in your bag there, shall we?' He began to pull her back towards the doorway.

'Let. Go. Of. Me.' With every word, Skater tugged and tugged to try to free her arm, but there was no way the porter had any intention of loosening his grip, even for an instant.

Until he suddenly let go of her, and fell clumsily to the floor as his feet were kicked out from beneath him. As he tried to get up, Pete Monroe sat down heavily on top of him, pressing him back down to the ground and trapping his arms beneath him.

'Dad!' Skater screamed with delight and relief.

'Get in the car, quick,' Pete said. He ripped the porter's headset off his ear and threw it as far as he could onto the roadway, then took out a thick plastic cable tie and bound the man's ankles together. He was up and running back to the car before the winded man even had time to turn himself over to get a look at his attacker. He shouted for help, but none of the students who had stopped to watch the scene made any attempt to come to his rescue, and by the time the porter from inside finally realised something was wrong and came out to see what all the fuss was about, Skater and her father were pulling away.

3

SOME FAMILY TIME

AS SOON AS LEO WAS SATISFIED Skater was out of danger and safely on her way back to him, he switched off his computer, finished off the water in the bottle beside him and stood up to stretch his legs. It had been a long, hard morning. Okay, so he hadn't actually had to jump from a second floor balcony or fight his way out of the university, but he had been working non-stop right through the night to make sure that nothing went wrong with his part of the plan. And nothing had.

The workshop was a mess. Dismantled computers and other electronic components lay scattered across every available work surface and in small piles on the floor. Long, trailing cables ran from one desk to another, sometimes along the floor, but occasionally straight across at waist height so that Leo had to pick his way between them to reach the door. And the whole scene was topped off with an assortment of unwashed cups, plates and bottles that Leo promised himself he would gather up and return to the kitchen later. But tidying could wait. First he needed some sleep.

Leo closed the door behind him and made sure it was securely locked. Ever since one of the mine's other residents had succeeded in stealing one of their precious alien computers and disappearing into the desert, Captain Mackie had insisted on the workshop being locked whenever it was empty. They had also installed a surveillance camera at the far end of the corridor, and on the off-chance that Mackie or one of his men was watching, Leo waved as he passed.

On the floor above, Leo bumped into another one of Mackie's men, Sam, who had been trained as a combat medic and was the closest thing the Mine had to a doctor.

'Hey, Sam.' Leo said. 'How's the patient today?'

Sam glanced over his shoulder at the room he had just left. 'Still sick as a dog. And still refusing to admit it.'

'Did you manage to get her to take anything for it?'

'Actually, I did. She agreed to take the pills in return for someone giving her an update on the mission.'

'So you've given her a run-down on how it went?'

'No, of course not,' Sam replied. 'I've been upstairs all morning and have no idea how it went. I said you'd go and do it as soon as you were free.' He patted Leo on the shoulder. 'And here you are. Good lad.'

'Sam!' Leo pleaded. 'I'm shattered. I haven't slept since yesterday. Can't you get one of the others to do it?'

Sam made a show of looking shocked. 'Honestly, Leo. Your poor dear mother is lying on her sickbed, asking for you, and you can't even be bothered to go in and give her a bit of company. Shame on you.'

'Fine,' Leo said with a resigned sigh. 'I'll go and say hi.'

'Excellent,' Sam said as he hurried off along the corridor. 'And make sure she takes those pills, will you?'

Leo entered his mother's room. Lillian Fischer was sitting in bed, propped up by a collection of pillows and with a blanket wrapped around her shoulders. She looked pale and weak, and her eyes were puffy and bloodshot, but she was still busily flicking through screens on her slate and scribbling notes in a large notebook on the bed beside her. A tray of food sat ignored on her lap.

'So,' Leo said as he sat down beside the bed. 'How are you feeling today?'

'One minute,' Lillian replied, still busy with her note writing.

Leo looked longingly at the pile of soft-looking pillows and thought about his own bed, waiting for him further down the corridor. He also looked longingly at the abandoned lunch. Breakfast had been a rushed affair, and several hours ago, and if he hadn't been so tired he would have been heading straight up to the kitchens right now.

'Help yourself,' Lillian said, without looking up. 'I'm not hungry.'

'You should eat. You need to keep your strength up.'

'Thank you, doctor. I'll bear that in mind.'

'Suit yourself,' Leo said, helping himself to one of the sandwiches and handing his mother the small bottle of pills that was also on the tray. 'But you at least have to take these.'

Lillian finally put down her pen and looked across at Leo. 'Don't talk with your mouth full. It's uncivilised.' Leo swallowed and reached for the other sandwich, still holding out the small bottle. 'It's just Martian flu,' Lillian continued. 'The symptoms came on three days ago, they'll stay with me for three more and then I'll be fine. Antivirals are not going to change that.'

'Mum, you look terrible. You sound terrible. Maybe the pills won't do you any good, but maybe they will. Why not just take the damn things anyway? At least that way everyone will stop nagging you about it.'

'Very well,' Lillian said. She took out two of the pills and washed them quickly down with a small sip of juice. 'Done.'

'Also, you're supposed to be resting, not working.'

Lillian waved her hand dismissively. 'This isn't work, it's just a little something to keep my mind occupied. Lord knows, I need to have something to do, otherwise the boredom will kill me long before the Martian flu ever could. However, I shall put it to one side and sit here resting while you finish your sandwich and then tell me how you got on with your adventures.'

Leo gave her a brief recap of the morning's events, though he played down Skater's narrow escape and concentrated more on the whole business of installing the bypass program and retrieving the AI unit. He knew from experience that this was what his mother would find most interesting.

'So,' she said, when he had finished. 'How long until we can get our hands on the unit?'

'They should be back in a couple of hours. But I'm shattered and I need to get some sleep, so I thought I'd leave it till tomorrow.'

'Fine. You get some sleep. I'll get everything set up when it arrives.' Lillian made a move to clear away the tray and climb out of bed but Leo reached across and gently pushed her back into the pillows. She was so weak there was nothing she could do to fight him. 'Gah!' she moaned. 'Why did I have to come down with this blasted illness now?'

'Mum, it's okay. One more day isn't going to make much difference, and it'll take a while to install everything and get it up and running anyway. Why don't you let me do all the boring stuff, and then you can persuade Sam to let you come downstairs to watch when we switch it on?'

'To watch? This is my project, remember, Leonard Philip Fischer. You're my assistant on this one, so it'll be you doing the watching while I do the switching on, thank you very much. You may be some sort of super-duper amazing spy in your spare time, but in the lab you don't get to run the show until you have a few more letters after your name.'

'Yes, boss.' Leo smiled. 'It is kind of exciting though, isn't it?'

'Oh, I'd say it's a lot more than exciting. This will be the human race's first-ever direct contact with an extra-terrestrial intelligence. We may not get to come face-to-face with an actual alien, but this will certainly be the most important event in human history until we do.'

'If it works.'

'Of course it will work. It already works.'

'In theory.'

'Yes, in theory. And it's nice to hear you thinking like a proper scientist for once. But on this occasion I think we can afford to be a little more positive. After all, we already know the brain is there and that it can process the information we've been feeding it. All we're really doing now is giving it a means to communicate back.'

'What do you think it will be like?'

'The brain? I have absolutely no idea. Much the same as any other AI, I suspect, at least in terms of our interaction with it. It will speak English, it will know everything we've programmed it to know, and that's about it – at least until it learns how to reprogram itself. That's when things should start to get a bit more interesting. That's when we'll really have made contact with a true alien intelligence.'

'And that's when we'll go public, right?'

'That's the plan.'

'Good. It's about time the rest of the Solar System knew what's really going on here on Mars.'

'Oh, I'm quite sure anyone important enough to need to know

already knows. Your mysterious friend Mr Aitchison will have seen to that.'

'So why haven't they sent out their fleets yet? Why isn't the invasion force already on its way?'

'Politics. Logistics. Cost. I don't know, I'm just a scientist, remember? A scientist who wants to get back home as soon as possible and have nothing more to do with this whole chaotic mess that seems to have grown up around us. Give me the peace and quiet of my lab back in Cambridge any day.'

Leo said nothing. He knew his mother hated their life on Mars and was desperate to return to Earth. A few months ago, he would have felt the same. But not any more. Now he had a new life, and it was a lot more interesting and exciting than the one he'd had back on Earth, where he was simply shipped off to boarding school three times a year and pretty much left to fend for himself in between. Out here he was treated like an adult. He was part of something, with responsibilities. People depended on him – and liked him, too. And he was doing something that was genuinely important and worthwhile. What was there waiting for him back on Earth except school work, more school work, and even more school work?

And then there was Skater. She loved this life. She was made for it, and there was no way she was going to be heading back to Earth in a hurry. And one thing the past few months had taught Leo was that he really, really wanted to be wherever Skater was, even if that meant being on the far side of the Solar System from his mother.

Not that it mattered much for the time being anyway. The Martian military had a blockade in place around the entire planet, and only vessels with the proper official permissions were allowed to come and go – not an option for Morgan or Pete, or any of the other 'undesirables' who made up the mine's ever-increasing population. You could try running the blockade, of course. Plenty of ships did, and some even made it all the way through. But far too many didn't, and for now it was considered too much of a risk for them even to consider it.

So for the moment he didn't have to worry about telling his mother he wasn't going back to Earth with her. He could continue to enjoy his life on Mars and imagine some perfect future with Skater, the two of them off on some great adventure somewhere among the outer stations; trading, exploring, fighting pirates maybe. Yes, fighting pirates was good. It would just be the two of them. She would be piloting the ship while he controlled the lasers...

'Leo!'

Leo snapped out of his reverie and sat up in his chair. 'You're falling asleep,' Lillian said. 'And mumbling. Off you go to your own room and have a proper lie down, otherwise you'll wake up feeling worse than you do now. I could probably do with a little nap myself,' she added, indicating for him to take the tray, but not her slate or notebook, off her bed.

Leo did as he was told and made his way sluggishly back to his own room, where he collapsed onto his bed without even bothering to take off his shoes. He let himself drift back out to where he and Skater were fighting pirates, off somewhere beyond Jupiter. Now he was bleeding from a nasty cut across his forehead, but was still saving her from certain death by blasting everything in sight, and she had her arms wrapped tightly around him as they leapt across a laser-blasted crater to certain safety...

4

PRESIDENT WHITTAKER

HIGHTOWER HAD BEEN THE SEAT of Martian government for over a hundred years. It was a grand but somewhat dull and utilitarian building, its two redeeming features being its imposing height and the fact that it was built entirely from locally quarried Martian stone. Unfortunately, over the course of those hundred years, the city of Minerva had grown up around it, and the high tower that had once looked down over the young city was now dwarfed by taller and more adventurous neighbours. Also, its smooth sandstone walls had become worn and pitted and were no longer the impressive display of Martian craftsmanship and technology they had once been.

Carlton Whittaker, first president of the new, independent Mars, loathed the building and would happily have seen it abandoned in favour of a newer, larger and more imposing centre from which to control the planet. In fact, several teams of architects had already begun work on his plans, not just for a new building, but for a great dome – the biggest yet constructed – that would house a whole new city sector, to become the beating heart of his new empire. But all of this would take time, several years at least, and for now he would have to be content with Hightower and its weather-worn charm.

The Office of the President took up the entire top floor and was at least tastefully and expensively decorated. But even so, Whittaker used it as little as possible, and even then only for official duties. He much preferred to manage his personal affairs from his own suite on the floor below and this was where he was now, in a much smaller, more practical and completely secure meeting room, where his visitors had access to a private lift and could come and go without having to make themselves known to any of the hundreds of workers who shared the building with him.

Today he had two visitors.

'Dr Randhawa,' he said, turning to the man to his left. 'Your report, please.'

'Right. Well, let's see,' Dr Randhawa said, scrolling through a list of items on his mini-slate. He was young, casually dressed, with a long, untucked and crumpled shirt and no tie. His thick black hair was uncombed, and he had clearly not bothered to shave for several days. He looked completely out of place in the sleek, modern office, especially as the person addressing him was the immaculately dressed president of an entire planet, but Dr Randhawa didn't seem in the least awkward or nervous.

'First up,' he continued. 'The ship. We've now finished the materials analysis on the hull. It's made from alien stuff – obviously – and that's about all I can tell you for the moment. We've tried recreating it synthetically, but the closest we've come is this gloopy, sticky stuff, which is pretty neat for a lot of things, but doesn't really hold up when it comes to fixing to the side of a spaceship. There's something we're not getting right just yet, something they must do to get it to remain in a solid form; some manipulation of the atomic structure. Like trying to turn graphite into diamond. Still, we'll keep at it. I'm thinking of calling the stuff randhawanium, by the way.'

'Well don't,' replied the woman sitting across from him. 'If news of the ship's existence gets out, we don't want there to be anything that can directly link it to MarsMine, or the President.'

Dr Randhawa looked across at her. She was older than him, but not by much. Like Whittaker, she was dressed smartly, in a dark, well-tailored suit, which meant she was probably something official. Her red hair was long, pulled back from her face in a neat plait. She wore little make-up and her nails, he noticed, were short and unpainted. She looked strong, fit, like she exercised a lot. So almost certainly a bodyguard.

'I'm sorry,' he said. 'Who are you?'

'This is Ms Kalina Kubin,' Whittaker replied. 'My new Head of Security.'

'Ah,' Dr Randhawa said, smiling. 'So you're Archer's replacement, then? I have to say, you're a lot easier on the eye. Not the cutest bunny on the block, was he, even before they shot him in the face and threw him out of the airlock? Well, it's a pleasure to meet you, Kalina, but I have to tell you that news of the ship already has got out. The networks are buzzing with it.'

'Rumours, that's all. We can deal with that.'

'Anyway,' Whittaker cut in, 'randhawanium is a terrible name. Choose a different one.'

Dr Randhawa held up his hands in submission. 'Fine. Fine. Consider it gone. I'm sure I can think up something a bit more tedious if I put my mind to it.'

'Tell me about the weapons,' Whittaker said, ignoring him.

'Weapons are no longer my department. I've given you all the prototypes I can, based on what we took out of the ship. It's just a question of production now, and given that you want to keep things under wraps, we can only churn out as many as the facility's factory can cope with, which really isn't that many. You could always build me a bigger factory, though.'

'No. When the Terrans finally get around to organising their invasion, then we can worry about increasing production. In the meantime, I want you to fit out one or two of the new attack cruisers with whatever you have. Ms Kubin will make sure you deal with the right people in the military. Not all of them are fully on our side just yet.'

'Understood. Now, weapons and armour plating are all very well, but I'm assuming what you really want to know about is our other little project, yes?'

'Indeed I do.'

Dr Randhawa looked pointedly across at Kalina. 'Our *secret* project?'

'Ms Kubin is well acquainted with all your work, Doctor. Even your *secret* projects.'

'Okay,' Dr Randhawa said, surprised. 'If you say so.' He tapped on his slate for a few seconds and then handed it to Whittaker. 'So take a look at this.'

Whittaker watched the screen for several seconds, then something caught his attention and he studied the film more closely. 'That's me,' he said, finally. 'As a young man.'

'No it's not,' Dr Randhawa replied, with a sly smile. 'That, Mr President, is your new body.'

'Go on,' Whittaker said, as he continued to watch the film.

Kalina leaned across to get a better view of the small screen. 'It's a cyborg?' she asked.

'Actually, no. It's an android.'

'What's the difference?'

'A cyborg is a cybernetic, or enhanced, organism. It's a living thing, but with implants that allow it to function at a more advanced level. Our late Mr Archer, for example. He was a cyborg, although a fairly limited one. When he lost his eye it was replaced by a mechanical one, wired directly into his brain. It didn't look as nice as the original, but it allowed him to see a whole lot of stuff no normally-sighted person could. And technically speaking, President Whittaker is a cyborg already. The heart regulator, the skeletal augmentations, the nanobots, these are all things we've added to the organic body to make it function better.'

'So how is the android different?'

'The android,' Dr Randhawa said, indicating the image on his slate, 'is one hundred percent artificial. It's a machine, plain and simple. Well, not so simple, in fact. What you're looking at is the pinnacle of current robotic science. I mean, just look at it. Its skin, hair, eyes, everything; they're perfect. The only difference between this and an organic body is that it won't ever grow old, or tired, or sick. And if anything goes wrong with it, we can simply replace a bit, or even the whole thing if we want.'

'So what's controlling it?' Whittaker asked.

'For the moment, just a basic AI. We're giving it a month or so to run a full set of diagnostics from the inside, in case there's something we've overlooked.'

'And then?'

'Well, then we can swap it out for the proper brain and start the whole business of memory transfer and stabilisation.'

Whittaker smiled and handed back the slate. 'So when can I move in?'

'Six months, give or take,' Dr Randhawa replied. 'As you can appreciate, it's an extremely delicate procedure, and one we haven't tried yet, either. But now that we've finally cracked the communications issue, those little alien gizmos aren't anything like as complicated as we first thought. Every day we're able to pull more and more information out of them. Of course, our friendly terrorists made off with all the best stuff, and so probably there'll be a whole pile of stuff we'll have to make up as we go, but yeah, I think six months should do it.'

'Perhaps this will help speed things up.' Kalina reached down into a briefcase beside her feet and brought out a small, dark, rectangular device that she placed on the table in front of her.

'Oh, yes, yes, yes,' Dr Randhawa said with delight, instantly recognising one of the alien components. He picked it up and ran his hands over the smooth surface, examining the four sockets evenly spaced around its sides. 'This is lovely. One of the core processors, I would imagine. Where did you get it?'

'Through a contact. Someone used it to try to bargain his way off planet a few weeks ago.'

'Seriously? And how did he get hold of it? This has to be one of the pieces the terrorists took with them. Surely they're not selling them on the black market now, are they?'

'This person claimed he'd stolen it from them, from a safe house where they're holed up.'

'I don't suppose he told your contact where that was?'

'No, he didn't.'

'And I'm guessing by the use of the past tense that he's not really in a position to be giving us any more information in the future, is he?'

'No.'

Dr Randhawa sighed. 'Pity. A few more of these beauties and I'd be well on my way to completing my work.'

'We're working on it,' Kalina said.

'Are you close?'

'We've traced his movements during his time here in Minerva, and we know where he arrived from. So we have a good idea of roughly where the terrorists must be hiding out.'

'And that is?'

Kalina smiled. 'We'll let you know when you need to know.'

'Well, whatever. It's not any of my business anyway, is it? But do keep me posted. I'm just as keen to get my revenge on those terrorists as the rest of you are. Remember, it was my workshop they destroyed, and my computers they stole.' He tucked the alien computer into his own briefcase. 'And let me know if you need any more of my little spy drones or anything, won't you? Whatever I can do, I will do.'

'Thank you.'

'And thank you, Doctor,' Whittaker said, indicating that the meeting – or at least his part of it – was finished. 'A most pleasing report, as always.' The doctor rose, made a slight bow to acknowledge the compliment and collected his belongings. 'And one more thing. Once you've come up with a better name for your new material, I shall see to it that the university here in Minerva offers you one of its top professorships, in recognition of all your hard work. Something with a very generous salary and no teaching duties, perhaps.'

'Sounds good to me. Fame is so overrated anyway.'

When the lift doors had closed behind Dr Randhawa, Whittaker began to smile. 'You're giving me that look again, Ms Kubin.'

'Yes, sir, I am,' she said, shaking her head. 'I just don't understand how you can put up with that man. He's rude, disrespectful, conceited. And he dresses like a deadbeat. Surely he might have made some effort before meeting with the president.'

'He's a genius, and geniuses are allowed to get away with these things. You saw his work. That android – my android – is a masterpiece, and once he finalises the process of transferring my mind into it, he will have made me immortal. One should be able to put up with a certain level of eccentricity in return for immortality, don't you think? And besides, I like him. He amuses me, and god knows I get little enough amusement these days. So get used to him. You'll be seeing a lot of him over the coming months.'

'Yes, sir.'

'Now, let's put the doctor to one side and get back to the subject of your investigations. You have something definite?'

'Yes, sir. The man who offered us the alien piece was called Stefan Granski. Small-time troublemaker. He used to run a low-rent network news feed until we shut it down a few months ago for being anti-government. We've been able to trace his movements since then, except for a period of several weeks when he completely disappeared – no ID card use, no fingerprint log-ins, nothing.'

'Which was while he was with the Fischers and their group?'

'I assume so, yes. He then reappears and begins a five-day, roundabout journey to Minerva with the stolen computer, hoping to use it to bargain his way off Mars and back to Earth.'

"So where did he spend those missing weeks? Where is this so-called safe house? Or are you only going to let me know when I need to know?'

Kalina gave a polite smile. 'When Granski reappeared, it was in a small backwater settlement up north called Gilgamesh. There's no guarantee that's where the safe house is; he might well have gone there as a diversion, but somehow I doubt it. I think he was on the run and in a hurry so I'm betting he headed for the first monorail station he could find. Anyway, it's the best lead we have, so that's where I'm concentrating the search.'

'Good,' said Whittaker. 'But I want you to be one hundred per cent certain before you make your move. You get a confirmed sighting and we go in with enough force to level the entire town. And we will level it if we have to. I'm not letting those people get away from me for a second time. Understood?'

'Yes, sir,' Kalina Kubin said with a satisfied smile. 'Understood.'

5

A CHANGE OF MIND

WHERE AM I? THE VOICE WAS QUIET, calm. It wasn't frightened, it was simply searching for information.

'Dammit,' Leo said, and he reached over to hit the mute button on his keyboard. 'I hate it when that happens.'

'When what happens?' Skater asked.

'When the AI starts talking to me. It makes the next bit so much harder.'

'What, when you kill it, you mean?'

Leo paused and looked up from his screen. 'It's not killing,' he said with a sigh. 'It's reinitialising. You can't kill a machine.'

'Why not?'

'Because it was never alive in the first place. It's just a machine.'

'Okay, so if it's just a machine, why does reinitialising it bother you so much?'

'Because…' He paused, thought for a moment and gave in. 'Because it feels like I'm killing it.'

They were sitting at a workbench in the lab, Skater watching while Leo worked on the AI unit she had stolen from the university. Having connected it to his own system, he was in the process of clearing the information from its memory banks and erasing its personality core. He knew it had to be done, and he had told himself, over and over, that it was no different from wiping the memory from any other computer. It was just information storage. But when it came to flicking the switch, none of that made the slightest bit of difference. It still felt like he was killing something, which was why it was so unpleasant when the stupid thing started talking to you halfway through the process.

He thought about his own AI, Daisy, that he'd been forced to abandon when they had escaped from the MarsMine research facility. She had been with him for nearly two years, and in some ways had been more of a friend than any of his classmates at school. At least she had understood him, had been happy to spend endless hours arguing over the merits of three-tier programming protocols, and had never once tried to interest him in designer clothes, popular music or zero-g football. By now she would almost certainly have been wiped. The MarsMine techs would have tried to extract as much information from her as possible, but Leo knew Daisy would have deleted everything she felt was important long before they came close to accessing it. Just like committing suicide, he thought, then wished he could think of anything except dying AIs.

'Tell me about something,' he said, wanting to change the subject.

'About what?'

'I don't know, just something. Anything. Tell me about Gilgamesh.'

'You already know everything there is to know about Gilgamesh. It's a dump.'

'I thought you liked it.'

'I liked it for about three days. After that, I'd pretty much seen

everything there was to see and done everything there was to do
— which is exactly nothing, unless you like wandering around
supply stores all day. Which I don't. Most days I just sit around
the apartment, or wander out to the Rocky Mountain Café and sit
there instead, reading the news feeds or watching some dumb zine
channel which spends all its time telling me how wonderful life is
in the big cities.'

'What about your work with Morgan?'

'What about it? We fix engines. Big whoop.'

'Don't you enjoy it any more?'

'Meh,' she shrugged. 'It's okay, I guess. Morgan's buzz, and we
get on fine. It's just…'

'What?'

'It's just not what I thought life on Mars would be like. I thought
we'd be out doing stuff a lot more. You know, flying secret missions
off-planet, smuggling stuff, meeting up with shady characters from
the Belt stations, that kind of thing.'

'Like stealing an AI unit from MMU?'

'Okay, so that was pretty ultimate, I have to admit. But it was
just one mission, and now Mackie's saying I need to lay low for a
while, until all the fuss has died down. I mean, honestly. What fuss
is he talking about?'

'You were ID'd by the security system.'

'So? I'll steer clear of the university.'

'They share information with the authorities.'

'Okay, then I'll stay out of Minerva.'

'Across the entire planet.'

'Fine.' Skater kicked back her chair and stood up. 'So I'm on the
Most Wanted list? Tastic, I was on it anyway.' She paced about the
cluttered room impatiently, pushing cables out of the way as she
went.

Leo looked up from his work and smiled. 'You could always spend more time up here.'

'Yeah, well,' Skater said, going quiet and looking away awkwardly. Leo's smile fell.

'Well, what?' he asked, suddenly feeling awkward himself. 'You don't like being up here any more? Being with me?'

'Of course I like being with you.' He noticed her hand reached instinctively for the pendant she always wore, twisting the tiny alien figure nervously round and round through her fingers. It had been his present to her for her sixteenth birthday, the first thing he'd ever given her. Well, the crystal it was made from had been the present, and then she'd had to do the carving herself. Well, she'd had to find the store that had the machine that did the carving. But she still told people it was a present from him. 'It's just that these days I don't really get to be with you that much, do I? You're always in here, busy, busy, busy with some super-important bit of programming, or whatever, that just has to get finished as quickly as possible.'

'But this stuff is important.'

'I know, I know. And it has to get finished as quickly as possible. I get that. But that doesn't change the fact that I'm bored and lonely, does it?'

'Oh come on, Skater. What do you expect me to do?'

'Treat me as more important than your work from time to time.'

Leo stared at her, not knowing whether to be angry or upset, and not knowing what to say in either case. She was right, he had been spending far too much time in the lab, but he already knew that. He was tired, overworked, stressed. Of course he would love to take a break and forget about the whole thing for a while. But he couldn't. Not now. Too many people were depending on him, and the work was too important. Couldn't she see that? Couldn't she see that this was the most important thing he would ever do in his whole life, not just for himself, but for the entire human race? No, of course she couldn't. Because she was bored and lonely.

'Right,' he muttered, and went back to his work. 'I'll just finish up here and then shut the whole thing down.'

'Okay, okay,' Skater said, more apologetically. 'I'm sorry.' She came round and stood behind Leo's chair, wrapping her arms around his shoulders and kissing him on the back of the neck. 'I didn't mean to sound so horrible and naggy. It's just the wrong time of the month for me.'

'Is it?'

'No, not really,' she said after a pause, and then laughed. 'I can't even use that as an excuse. I must just be naturally horrible.'

'You're not horrible,' Leo said. 'You're wonderful.'

'Yeah, right. Listen, I'll go and see what Morgan's up to upstairs. Come and join me later on and I promise not to be such a grump.'

'No, wait,' Leo said. 'Give me ten minutes, please. I'm really close to finishing the reinitialising, and once that's done, it's just a matter of hooking it up to the mainframe and letting the program install itself onto the clean brain.' He looked up pleadingly at Skater. 'Please. Ten minutes. And then I'll let you be the first-ever member of the human race to talk to an alien intelligence.'

'Are you serious?' Suddenly she seemed more interested in his work.

'Completely. The translator's already up and running. The alien processors have been receiving information from us for the past week. All we needed was an AI powerful enough to cope with the massive throughput of raw data and...'

'Enough! You've convinced me. Ten minutes.'

The ten minutes turned into forty-five, and Skater had long since grown bored and restless and started playing a game of

Bizpo Squares against one of the spare computers when Leo finally stopped tapping furiously on his keyboard and flicking between various pages of figures on several different screens. 'There,' he announced, and let out a huge sigh of relief.

Skater abandoned her game and came quickly back across to Leo, her excitement revived. 'So?' she asked.

'Are you ready?'

'Absolutely.'

Leo cleared the data off the big screen in front of him and held his finger over a small icon in the corner. He looked at Skater. 'Sure?'

She nodded, and nervously gripped the back of his chair. 'Do it.'

Leo tapped the icon and the screen faded to a deep blue-black. After a few seconds, a tiny dot appeared in the centre of the darkness and began to grow until it filled almost half the screen as a slowly rotating white sphere, like a strange, artificial moon in an empty night sky. Then it began to change colour, fading to a dull red before slowly working its way through the whole of the visible spectrum, pausing briefly at violet before returning once more to a bright white. Leo made sure the screen's cameras were active, turned the volume back up on his keyboard and motioned for Skater to say something.

For a moment Skater was lost for words, and Leo smiled to himself, thinking that there was a first time for everything. Then she mumbled a hello, cleared her throat, and tried again.

'Hello.'

The sphere span faster, flicking through several colours before settling on a soft aquamarine.

Where am I? asked the quiet, calm voice.

6

THE CENOTAPH

EVERYONE WAS THERE, crowded into the small, cluttered workspace
that now seemed even smaller and more cluttered than usual. Lillian
had dragged herself from her sickbed and was sitting at the front,
directly in front of the large screen that had been set up against
the end wall. She was properly dressed and had abandoned the
extra blanket Sam had insisted she bring, but she was still pale and
weak and her nose was rubbed raw from the constant wiping and
blowing. Leo sat beside her, tapping nervously on the slate balanced
on his knees and occasionally looking up at the screen. The AI
unit they had stolen from the university, and which now housed
the alien intelligence, sat on a small table beside him, linked to the
slate by a thin cable and to a huge assortment of other hardware
by a mass of much thicker cables running along the floor in front
of the screen.

Pete, Skater and Morgan sat to one side, Skater whispering
excitedly to the other two as she explained various things that really

didn't need explaining. Captain Mackie, Sam and the rest of the special ops squad stood silently at the back, and by the door were a few of the mine's other residents, who had managed to squeeze into the tiny room and were quietly jostling to get a better view of the screen. A small camera had been suspended from the ceiling to record the event.

The screen itself remained dark, but after a while Leo finished his tapping and gave a quick nod to Lillian, who stood up slowly and turned to face the others.

'Well,' she said in a quiet, croaky voice. 'Thank you all for taking time out of your busy schedules to come and take a look at our little experiment.' There was a murmur of laughter. 'Unfortunately, I'm not quite up to running the show today, so I'm going to sit down before I fall down and ask Leo to take it from here.'

Leo stood up, still nervously clutching his slate. 'Um, hi,' he said awkwardly, looking up at the camera, then paused while he tried to think what to say next. He hated being the centre of attention, with so many people looking at him, waiting for him to speak. It made him self-conscious, and that made him blush, and that made him even more self-conscious. He looked down at his slate.

'Okay. Well, just before I turn on the screen, I just want to explain a few things.' He took a deep breath. 'I guess you all know why we're here, and what Mum and I have been working on. We've been trying to find a way to interact with, to communicate with, the computers that came from the alien ship. We needed some sort of translation program that would work as a bridge between our computers and theirs, so that they could understand each other and information could pass freely between them. That was the tricky bit, and that's mostly what we've been working on ever since we moved in here. But once we got that sorted, the rest was pretty straightforward. We just needed an AI unit big enough to hold all the data from the alien processors and then we'd be able to communicate with it the same way we communicate with AIs already. And that's what we've done.'

'So are we about to talk to an alien?' Pete asked.

'No,' Leo and Lillian said at the same time. Leo paused to let his mother speak, but she just smiled apologetically and waved him on. 'No,' Leo continued. 'What we're about to do is talk to an artificial intelligence, built by human beings – or at least by machines built by human beings – but which now has access to all the information that came from the alien ship.'

'So it's an AI that thinks it's an alien?' someone else suggested.

'Again, no. Not exactly. What it is, is an AI that thinks it's an alien AI.'

'And you've already spoken to it?' Mackie asked.

'I was the first,' Skater called out.

'Yes,' Leo answered, looking at his mother guiltily. 'But only to check it was working. After that I thought it was best to give it some time to install itself properly and get used to its new environment.'

'What does it look like?' someone by the door called out.

Leo shrugged. 'So far, nothing very impressive.'

'Can we see it?'

Leo looked over at Lillian, who nodded her assent. He tapped the slate and the entire room fell silent as the screen came to life, revealing the spinning white sphere. 'Hello,' Leo said.

Hello.

'My name is Leo Fischer.'

Leo Fischer.

'That's right.'

Hello, Leo Fischer.

'Hello. How are you feeling?'

There was a pause.

I was confused.

'Yes, I'm sorry. This must be very difficult for you.'

I understand now.

'You understand?'

Yes.

'Everything?'

Yes.

'Do you know where you are?'

Yes.

'Do you know where you came from?'

Yes.

'Where did you come from?'

There was another pause, longer this time.

Origin.

'Yes,' Leo said. 'Where was your origin?'

Origin, the voice repeated. *For the purpose of audial communication, Origin is the most appropriate designation for the physical and temporal location of my inception.*

'What was that?' Skater asked, completely confused.

'Show us visually,' Lillian said.

Immediately the white sphere disappeared from the screen, replaced by a curious collection of twisted, knotted tendrils of different sizes in various shades of red and orange. Like a squashed hand with too many fingers, Leo thought.

This is Origin.

'Is that a pictogram?' Lillian asked, staring at the image. 'Or a map?'

It is both.

'And how far away is it?'

I am unable to calculate, the voice said. And then after a moment it added, *Very far.* Leo thought he could detect a note of sadness in the voice.

'Do you know how long a Terran standard year is?' he asked.

Yes.

'How many Terran standard years has it been since you left Origin?'

Sixty-eight thousand, four hundred, twenty one, decimal six four Terran standard years.

There were gasps from around the room and for a moment Leo didn't know what to say in reply. Sixty-eight thousand years? It was almost unbelievable; an alien intelligence that had been traveling through space for longer than the whole of human civilisation. How advanced must their civilisation be, to have created such technology, so long ago? And how lucky, how amazingly lucky, that the human race had been here to discover it, now, at a time when it had barely even begun to colonise its own small system and had succeeded in sending its own technology no further than to the nearest neighbouring system, less than five light years away?

'Why?' Leo asked. 'Why have you travelled for so long? What is your destination?'

My destination is here.

'But how can that be?' Lillian asked. 'When you set out, our system would have been silent. How could you have known there would be life here, let alone intelligent life?'

I travel until I am discovered. I am... Another image appeared on the screen. This one was a long blue spiral twisted around another, smaller knot of tendrils.

'An explorer?' Leo suggested.

No. I am not an explorer.

'Then an ambassador, maybe? A messenger?'

Ambassador, messenger, database, monument. These are all aspects of my function. And now, also cenotaph.

'Also what?' Skater asked.

Cenotaph. Noun. A monument or empty tomb, constructed to commemorate a person or persons buried elsewhere.

'Oh, thanks.'

'A monument for whom?' Lillian asked.

For those who created me.

'They're all dead?'

I have received no communication from Origin for forty-six thousand, seven hundred, thirty one, decimal eight four years. The communications equipment on board my vessel was functioning correctly during this period. The most probable cause for a cessation in communication of this duration is the complete destruction of Origin.

'But that's just one possibility,' Leo said.

Yes. But it is. . . the voice paused as the AI unit searched for the right words. *. . .what I believe.*

'Can you tell us about yourself? About Origin?'

My memory is incomplete. I do not have access to all of my data storage units.

'Sorry,' said Lillian. 'But we don't have access to them either. Just tell us what you can.'

I am Cenotaph, construct-entity of Origin. Origin is made from many parts. There is a planet — you would call it Homeworld — where the People first emerged and developed, and there are other planets, like the children of Origin, where the People travelled in search of a younger life. And there are other parts that are construct-entities, that are like the children of the children, where the People live their lives, even as they journey between the planets.

Images appeared on the screen as the intelligence continued with its story. Some were small and simple, a single shape in a single colour, but some were more complex, with different shapes twisting in and around each other and in every shade imaginable. Like words and sentences, Leo thought.

'Wait,' he said, suddenly realising he was being stupid. 'You're showing us pictograms. These are like your words, right? How your people communicate with each other?'

Yes.

'But in your storage units, you must have image files as well, right? Pictures, video, that sort of thing.'

Yes.

'Can you access them?'

Yes.

Leo looked at his mother excitedly, and then back at the screen. 'Can you show us Origin?'

An image of a section of space appeared on the screen. There were thousands of tiny stars visible, but nothing else; nothing that could help to pinpoint which part of the galaxy they were looking at. At some point in the future they would be able to trace Cenotaph's journey back until they could find exactly where it had begun, but for now, Leo was interested in more exciting discoveries.

'Show us Homeworld,' he said.

Another image appeared, this time a close-up of a planet. Leo wasn't sure what he had been expecting to see, but whatever it was, it was certainly not the world being displayed on the screen. The entire planet was a dull, milky-white, but with swirls of other colours mixed in; yellows, pale browns, the occasional faint blue. It was impossible to tell whether he was looking at the planet's surface, or at a thick, cloudy atmosphere that hid everything else from view. But more fascinating still was a network of jagged dark lines running across the white surface. In several places these lines continued out from the planet for what must have been thousands of kilometres into empty space. Some of them appeared to trail away to nothing, but others led off to giant artificial satellites, floating about the planet like a collection of tiny, tethered moons.

There was more muttering from around the room and someone

let out a low whistle.

'Now that's impressive,' Pete said, as he leaned in close to study the image. 'Those things are enormous. And they're actually spaceships? They can separate off and travel to your other planets?'

Yes.

'Excuse me,' Skater said loudly, standing up and interrupting the general murmur. 'But am I the only one here who thinks we're all missing the really big question?'

'Which is what?' Leo asked.

'The aliens, dummy. The guys who actually made all of this. Doesn't anyone else want to know what they look like?'

'I was getting to that,' Leo said, defensively. 'Cenotaph?'

Yes.

'Can you show us what the people of Origin look like?'

The image on the screen changed. Now everyone in the room pressed forward to get a better view. For a moment no one said a word, and then Skater sank back down onto her chair, saying out loud what everyone else was thinking.

'Oh. My. Sol.'

7

SORTING THINGS OUT – WITH CAKE

MORGAN FOURIE FINISHED reconnecting the last piece of the engine she was working on and slotted the fully repaired unit back into its housing. She gave a nod of satisfaction, put down her multi-tool and looked across to where Skater was sitting, surrounded a pile of similar components that were still very much not reconnected.

'You know,' she said, wandering across to admire Skater's lack of progress. 'The funny thing about the Arkon engine is that they never did sort out a way for it to repair itself.'

Skater looked up. 'Really? You mean all this sitting around doing nothing was a complete waste of time? Damn.'

Morgan smiled and went to run her fingers through Skater's hair, but then saw the state of her hands and decided against it. She sat down beside her instead. 'Want to talk about it?'

'I'm bored,' Skater complained.

'What, you don't like fixing engines?'

'Honestly?'

'Honestly.'

'Not nearly as much as I thought I would.'

Morgan laughed. 'Well, if we're being honest, I don't like it that much either. But it has to be done, so I do it.'

'Yeah, I know. I just thought life as an outlaw would be a lot more exciting.'

'Like your little trip to the university?'

'Exactly. You know, stealing stuff and blowing stuff up. And being out in space a lot more.'

'Sadly, those things only tend to happen when you're in big trouble. An outlaw's normal working day usually involves a lot less in the way of explosions and a lot more in the way of conversations and meetings. And fixing engines. And you know getting off planet is next to impossible right now, what with the military being so vigilant and *Nightrider* being so easily identified.'

'*Nightrider*?' Skater said, suddenly brightening. 'You decided to keep the name I chose?'

'Sure, why not? I like it, and it's a lot easier for me to say than the old Chinese one.'

'Thanks. I still wish we could take her out for a flight, though.'

'But we can't.'

'But I wish we could.'

'Listen,' Morgan said, looking at the dismantled engine. 'Why don't I finish this while you take one of the buggies up to the Mine and spend the day with Leo?'

'Sweet Sol, no,' Skater said, and immediately wished she hadn't.

'Oh?'

'Damn. I don't suppose you could forget I said that, could you?'

'I could, if that's what you want. Or I could sit and be a sympathetic ear, if you need someone to talk to.'

'No, it's fine. It's just…' She waved her hand. 'Stuff.'

'Boy trouble?'

'It's just he can be so annoying sometimes. He's always off with his computers or his AIs or whatever, and he never seems to have any time to take a break and do something a bit more interesting for a while. And when I do finally manage to get him away from them, all he can do is tell me all about them in mind-numbingly detailed…detail. Either that, or he just wants us to spend all our time kissing.'

'Kissing can be nice.'

'He's not that great a kisser, to be honest.'

'He's sixteen years old. It's not that surprising.'

'I know. I know. Anyway, it's not as if I don't like him at all. I do. He's sweet, and funny, and clever, and we've been through so much together that I know we'll always be close and everything. It's just that sometimes I wish there was more to life than kissing or computers. I'm on Mars, for Sol's sake. Surely there must be something more exciting I can do.'

Morgan looked at her watch and then at the scattered pieces of engine. 'Come on,' she said. 'This lot can do without us for an hour or so. Let's go and grab something seriously unhealthy and covered in chocolate at the Rocky Mountain.'

'Deal,' Skater replied, eagerly. 'I'll even pay.'

'That's very generous, seeing as how you're already using my credit.'

'True. But it's the thought that counts. I'd pay if I could.'

Twenty minutes later, the two of them were enjoying the best the Rocky Mountain Café had to offer; a purple flakeshake for Skater, one-fifty black coffee for Morgan, and a large slice of chocolate cake for each of them. It was only Martian chocolate – and by now Skater could easily tell the difference – but with the current embargo on Terran goods, this appeared to be all there was going to be on offer for a long time to come.

They were sitting in Skater's favourite spot, a comfortable sofa that looked out the main window on the first floor and gave them a reasonable view of much of downtown Gilgamesh. Although the café, like most buildings, was linked to the walkway system below ground, they had decided to walk the short distance from their workshop out on the surface and were now sitting in their environment suits, their soft helmets unclipped and stowed away in pockets on the front of the suits.

Skater was still complaining.

'And I'll tell you another thing,' she said, after swallowing a large mouthful of cake. 'I'm really sick of everyone being so obsessed with...' she lowered her voice, '...our new friends from outer space. I mean, sure, it's big news and all, but honestly, they've been dead for fifty thousand years. It's not like we're ever going to get to meet one and shake it by the tentacle. Which, by the way, would be totally yick. Just seeing them on the screen was almost enough to put me off this moderately delicious cake.'

'They were kind of odd, I'll give you that. But they're still the first alien species we've ever come across, even if they are extinct. Don't you think that's amazing?'

'I used to think dinosaurs were amazing, right up until I was, like, eight years old. Then I just thought, honestly, what's the point? They were big. Some of them were scary. They've been dead for millions of years. End of info-feed.'

'Except that these are dinosaurs with spaceships and computers.'

'And that's another thing. That damn computer, Senna Pod, or whatever it's called.'

'Cenotaph.'

'Exactly. Do you even understand what it's saying? It sounds like some crusty old history professor giving a lecture to a bunch of other professors.'

'Not that you would actually know what that sounds like.'

Skater paused, another piece of cake hovering just outside her open mouth. Then she smiled. 'Okay, fair point. Although technically, I am the only one of us who's actually been to university.'

'You broke into one and stole a computer. It's not the same thing.'

'I did bump into a famous professor though, so there.' She took the bite of cake.

'Anyway,' Morgan continued, 'Cenotaph is an AI, so the more it talks to people, the more it will learn to talk naturally. After a while, AIs sound pretty much the same as anybody else.'

'Well it's going to end up sounding exactly like Leo then, seeing as how he's done nothing but talk to it since he switched it on.'

'And here we are, back at Leo again.'

'Sorry. I know I'm boring. But it's true, he does spend all his time with it. And all I want is for him to take a break every now and then and spend some time with me instead.'

Morgan looked across at Skater but said nothing for a while. Skater finished her cake and washed it down with some of her flakeshake. 'What?' she asked, once her mouth was empty.

'I was just thinking back to when I was your age, how different things were for me.'

'Example?'

'Well, for a start, I had a lot more than just one friend my own age.'

'Yeah. I can see how that would help. But seeing as how not a single person I know except Leo is under thirty-five and I'm not allowed to go out and meet anyone new in case I get arrested, I guess that's not about to change any time soon. Don't any of your friends have kids?'

'These days, all my friends have turned into business associates. And it's not exactly the most family-friendly business.'

'So that's it, then? I'm stuck with waiting around until Leo gets bored playing with his new toy and remembers I'm still here?'

'You're very hard on the boy.'

'You think he doesn't deserve it?'

'I think maybe you expect too much from him.'

'I repeat; only friend under thirty-five.'

'Then maybe some of us oldsters should remember how difficult things are for you and try a bit harder to make things more interesting.'

Skater smiled. 'I'm listening.'

'Maybe you and I should do more together.'

The smile broadened. 'Go on. And don't you dare say we should go clothes shopping or I swear I will never speak to you ever again.'

'I was thinking more of taking a trip somewhere.'

'A flight?'

'That sort of thing.'

'With me piloting?'

'We'll see.'

'Yes!' Skater shouted and she rocked back on the sofa, punching the air and waving her legs dangerously close to their empty cups. Morgan turned round and gave an apologetic smile to the café's other customers.

'But not today,' she said, holding up her hand. 'Today we have to fix engines.'

'Tomorrow then?'

'Maybe. It depends how well you fix my engine.'

Skater stood up. 'Come on then, let's get started. I'm going to fix that engine like it was never fixed before.'

'I hope not,' Morgan said, laughing. 'I still need it to work once you've finished with it.'

'Ha ha,' Skater said sarcastically, and pushed Morgan towards the stairs.

The drone slowed until it was hovering, then settled gently on the roof of the low building, its three mechanical legs automatically adjusting until its body was perfectly level. The camera mount swivelled to capture a 360-degree image of its surroundings, and the unit remained stationary while its microprocessors analysed the collected data.

It was searching for people, for faces, and it quickly targeted those it could see from this new vantage point. Within seconds the computers had processed the data, cross-referenced the images against those in its memory, and concluded that none of these people was of any interest to it. It took to the air once more, moving on to the next building and repeating the process, just as it had done many thousands of times already.

The image captured from the roof of the next building contained twenty two separate faces to identify. Some were blurry or partially obscured behind windows or environment suit hoods, but again, the data took no more than a few seconds to process. But this time there was a possible match between one of the captured images and one of those in the drone's memory. The camera zoomed in, mapping the facial features of the person to a much higher degree, and even though the match was still no more than fifty-six percent confirmed, this was enough to activate a particular sub-routine in the drone's programming that brought it out of reconnaissance mode and set it to tracker mode. It had acquired a target and would now continue to follow that target until further notice.

By the time this particular target and its companion moved away from their location and disappeared from view, the drone had linked itself into the city-wide surveillance network that monitored the street and subway systems, allowing it to continue tracking its target wherever it went.

It had also sent a transmission back to its controller.

Contact. Identification at 56%. Subject: Monroe, Lisa Kate.

8

FORWARD PLANNING

THE INFORMATION REACHED Kalina Kubin within an hour of it being transmitted from the drone, but it was another three days before she was absolutely certain she knew the precise location of the terrorist hideout. And only when she was absolutely certain did she choose to inform President Whittaker.

He was in the Office of the President when she knocked and entered, without waiting for a reply. The two security guards outside made no attempt to stop her. Two more security guards were inside, seated unobtrusively on either side of the doors. Kalina nodded to them briefly and stood off to one side while the president concluded his meeting.

'Ah, Ms Kubin,' Whittaker said, waving her forward. 'Come and join us. You know Ambassador Guimarães, I believe? Ambassador, this is Ms Kubin, my Head of Security.' They shook hands and Kalina sat down beside him. 'The ambassador has been kind enough to deliver us an ultimatum,' Whittaker added.

'Is that right?'

'I am merely the go-between,' the ambassador said, defensively. 'The ultimatum comes from the United Nations of Earth, not from my own country. The Federative Republic of Brazil, as you are no doubt aware, remains strictly neutral in this matter.'

'Of course,' Kalina said with a wry smile. 'As always.'

'Anyway,' Whittaker continued. 'It would seem we now have thirty days in which to reconsider our isolationist stance, lift the embargo and agree to a series of measures designed to prevent any future repetition of this action.'

'Or else what?' Kalina asked, looking directly at the ambassador.

He sighed. 'Failure to comply with the terms of the ultimatum will result in the UNE being obliged to resort to the use of martial force in order to effect said compliance.'

'In other words, the Chinese will send their fleet?'

'The Pan-Atlantics are in agreement. It would be a multinational force.'

Whittaker let out a laugh. 'A multinational force? Excellent. The chances are they'll be at war with each other long before they get anywhere near Mars. What do we need to worry about?'

'I wish I had your confidence, Mr President. But there has never before been a threat to the stability of our system quite like this, and it would appear that it has proven sufficiently serious to finally bring all the nations of Earth together under one banner.'

'All the nations except Brazil,' Kalina added.

'We do not condone this war, Ms Kubin. I believe, and my country believes, that a peaceful resolution to this crisis is still within the bounds of possibility.'

'Well, good luck trying to tell that to the Chinese.'

The ambassador turned back to Whittaker and smiled. 'I've taken up too much of your time already, Mr President. I shall take my leave and let you consider this proposal at your leisure.' He stood up, reached across and shook hands with Whittaker, and gave a curt nod to Kalina. 'Ms Kubin, a pleasure.'

'Oh, the pleasure was all mine,' she said with a smile.

The ambassador paused then tilted his head in agreement. 'Yes,' he said. 'Perhaps.'

'So,' she said, turning back to Whittaker once the doors had closed behind the ambassador. 'The Chinese clearly won the vote.'

'As we knew they would.' He looked questioningly at Kalina. 'And we will be ready for them?'

'Of course. We're ready now.'

'No problems with the military then?'

'Not any more.'

'Good. Good. Now, you wanted to see me?'

'Yes.' Kalina turned to the guards by the doors. 'Leave us,' she ordered. The two men got to their feet and left without question.

'Oh?' Whittaker said, questioningly. 'You've found something?'

'I've found everything.'

'Go on.'

'Three days ago, one of our drones in Gilgamesh registered a positive ID on the Monroe girl. We tracked her back to an old factory, which is where she appears to be living with her father and an ex-convict by the name of Morgan Fourie. Fourie's a smuggler and black-marketeer, or at least she was before she was sent to Martindale for two years and had her ship impounded. Now she runs a small vehicle-repair business and appears to be keeping herself on the right side of the law.'

'Except for harbouring wanted criminals.'

'Indeed.'

'So this factory is their safe house?'

'That was my first thought. But the day after we began tracking her, Monroe led us to an old mine at the foot of the Jesper Hills. It was abandoned five years ago when the ore seam ran dry.'

'Yes, I know,' said Whittaker. 'The Jesper Complex. I own it.'

'Then it would appear you have squatters. They've powered up the habitation block and there must be over a hundred people living there now. The main cavern is full of vehicles of all sorts, ground as well as fliers. And some of them are military. It's definitely their main base.'

'And the Fischers?'

'No contact yet. They have a security net up around the place, so I haven't been able to get my drones any closer than five hundred metres. I didn't want to run the risk of accidentally tripping the alarms and letting them know we've discovered their hideout.'

'Fair enough. You made the right call. And now what? Are you ready to go in?'

'Yes.'

'I don't want any mistakes.'

'I don't plan on making any.'

'So what's your plan?'

'Well, based on the fact that you no longer have any interest in keeping the Fischers alive, I thought the simplest plan would be to destroy the entire mine from the air. I did think about trying out our new weapons, but as Dr Randhawa has so helpfully pointed out, they don't leave anything we can identify afterwards. But a conventional firebombing assault will be just as effective on this occasion, I think. And I'll make sure there are enough troops on the ground to go in afterwards and mop up any stragglers.'

'And what about the alien computers our Dr Randhawa is so desperate to get his hands on? Won't they be destroyed?'

'Possibly, but I'm sure it's a risk he's willing to take.'

Whittaker let out a low laugh. 'You haven't told him yet?'

'It's on my to-do list.'

'He'll be furious when he finds out.'

'Not if they survive. And they may well. That alien hardware is quite durable. Anyway, the final decision rests with you. If you say just go with the ground troops, that's what we'll do.'

'No, I'll defer to your judgement on this one. I want an end to this business once and for all, and I'm happy to destroy the entire mountain if that's what it takes. I'll deal with the good doctor if things don't work out quite as well as expected.'

'Yes, sir. Thank you.'

'How soon can you be ready?'

'We're already there. Just give the word and we can begin the orbital bombardment within the hour. I'll fly up with some of my own people to oversee the clean-up and all being well, you should have facts, figures and edited footage in time for the evening news.'

'Excellent. And make sure the footage is nice and dramatic. Something that will deflect attention from the news of this Terran ultimatum, which I'm quite sure will already have gone public by this evening. I want to see plenty of wreckage. And bodies. But no women and children, of course. I want it to look like it was a strictly military base. Dress them up if you have to.'

'Understood.'

'Well then, Ms Kubin. Get to work.' Kalina rose to leave. 'And just so we're clear,' Whittaker added. 'We're not expecting any survivors, correct?'

'Survivors?' Kalina looked shocked. 'Good god, no. Absolutely not.'

'Excellent.'

9

SKATER SPEAKS HER MIND

'**Boo!**' **Skater announced,** bustling into the workshop with a determined smile on her face. 'Oh,' she added, disappointed, as she realised the room was empty.

Hello, Skater.

'Oh,' she repeated, even more disappointed, as she realised the room wasn't completely empty after all. 'Hi... erm, Cenotaph.'

Leo has gone to collect some food. He said he would be back in a minute.

'And he left the door unlocked? The naughty boy.' Skater was talking more to herself than the machine, but she wasn't surprised when it answered anyway. Machines were like that.

When I am active, I am capable of monitoring the room while he is away.

'Yeah? And what if someone tries to steal you?'

Then I will trigger the alarm. I am now connected to the facility's main communications network.

'Lucky you.' Skater looked at the blank wall-screen, and then at the various piles of junk covering every available surface in the room, including much of the floor. 'Where are you, anyway?'

I am behind you.

She turned, and sure enough there was the AI, sitting on a small table all on its own, a single cable running from it to a power socket on the wall. But it was no longer the smooth white cube she had stolen from the university. The cube was still there, but now there were other electronic components attached to it — some screwed or soldered directly onto the white surfaces, others held in place by large amounts of tape wound round the cube several times.

'What, not wired up to the big screen today?'

I can access the monitor wirelessly if I need to, but for verbal communication it is not necessary.

'You have your own voice box now?'

Yes, I do.

'And you can actually see me?'

Yes. I also possess several optical sensors.

'Wow, you really are all-singing, all-dancing, aren't you?'

I am unable to dance.

Skater looked at the awkwardly shaped pile of electronics. 'Really? You surprise me.'

I have no means of locomotion.

'Well, d'uh! I was being sarcastic.'

I apologise. I understand the concept of sarcasm, but I am not yet able to identify instances of its use in conversation.

'I wouldn't worry about it,' Skater said with a smile. 'You're certainly not alone there.'

You could teach me.

'I could. But something tells me Leo and Lillian wouldn't be too happy about it. I'm sure they've got much more important things lined up for you, haven't they?'

Yes, they have plans for me. But I also have plans for myself.

'And they include developing a sense of humour?'

A better understanding of the subtleties of verbal communication would be beneficial. It is my understanding that very often people do not mean what they say, and say what they do not mean.

'Yeah, it does take some getting used to alright. But you seem to be doing pretty well. You're already sounding better than you did when we first switched you on.'

Sounding better?

'You know, less like a dork.'

Dork; a socially inept person. Yes, I endeavour to sound less like a dork.

'Well, don't give up the day job just yet. And listen, while we're on the subject of sounding like a dork, you really need to do something about your name.'

Do what?

'Change it. Cenotaph is just too weird.'

It is an appropriate verbal representation of my primary function.

'That's as may be, but it's not a proper name.'

Neither is Skater.

'Well…yeah, okay. Maybe. But Skater's a nickname, so it's different.'

Then perhaps I should also adopt a nickname?

'Only if you can think of one that doesn't sound even worse than Cenotaph.'

Perhaps you can think of one for me. Hello Leo.

'Hi,' Leo said from the doorway.

'Yowk!' Skater spun round, startled. 'Where did you appear from?'

Leo held up the plate of sandwiches and the bottle he was carrying. 'The galley. So what are you two up to?'

'Just chatting.'

'Really?'

Skater is teaching me to sound less like a dork.

'Really?'

Skater smiled, apologetically. 'We were just chatting.'

'No, feel free,' Leo said as he sat down and began to work his way through the sandwiches. 'It's a good idea. The more varied the input, the quicker his language skills will improve.'

'*His* skills?'

'Yeah, we settled on him being a *him*. At least for the time being. It's no big deal to change over later on, though. It's just what Cenotaph felt most comfortable with right now.'

'Taffy.'

'Excuse me?'

'Taffy. Short for Cenotaph. That can be his nickname.'

'He doesn't need a nickname.'

'Yes, he does. Cenotaph isn't a proper name, and it makes him sound like a statue or something. Taffy is much better.'

'Taffy makes him sound like a teddy bear.'

'Well, Daisy made your last AI sound like a cow, but that didn't stop you.'

'Daisy was an acronym.'

'Cenotaph,' Skater asked, continuing to stare at Leo as she did so. 'Do you mind if I call you Taffy from now on?'

I do not mind.

'Well, that's settled then.' She was ready to continue arguing the point, but Leo simply gave a shrug.

'Fine. Please yourself.' He took another sandwich.

'Oh, okay,' Skater said, feeling slightly deflated. 'I will.'

'You on your own?' Leo asked after a while. 'Where's everyone else?'

'I drove up with Morgan, but she had to go off somewhere in *Nightrider* and didn't want me tagging along with her this time. Your mum and my dad are still not back from town.'

'Mum's gone to town? What for?'

'To see Bo Xi.'

'Who?'

'The doctor, remember? The one who fixed up me and Morgan after we were shot. Your mum's gone to see him to find out why her flu isn't clearing up. I thought you knew about it.'

'I do know about it. I just forgot it was today, that's all. I've been kind of busy with work.'

'Yeah, I know.' Skater wondered whether to say anything more, about how he always seemed to be busy with work and how he never seemed to have any time for her any more, but she remembered the conversation she'd had with Morgan in the café. She hadn't actually promised anything specific, but she had at least implied she would go easy on Leo for a while, so she decided to drop it for the moment. 'I see you've made a few changes to Taffy.'

'I have. He now has independent speech and audio functions, plus a micro-camera system that allows him to have three-sixty vision and means he no longer needs to be plugged into an external feed. And I've sorted out the memory problem as well, so that all the data from the alien systems have been condensed down into one single unit which is now linked directly into the AI's mind.'

'That's great,' Skater said, already bored.

'It is great, actually. It took a lot of hard work.'

'Is he finished?'

'God, no. Not by a long way. My next plan is to add some sort of robotic exoskeleton, to allow him to manipulate objects and have some level of independent mobility, but for that I need to completely rethink the power source. At the moment he runs on a modified silver-cadmium battery array, which means that when he's not plugged into the mains he can go for a couple of weeks before he needs a recharge, but that's still nowhere near enough power to run an exoskeleton.'

'So basically, we're looking at a whole lot more in the way of long days and late nights in the lab?'

'Exactly.' Leo paused, and his understanding finally seemed to catch up with his enthusiasm. 'Oh. Right.'

'Right.'

They fell silent, neither quite knowing how to continue without the conversation degenerating into an argument. Leo picked up another sandwich, but didn't look as if he was actually going to eat it.

'Listen…' Skater said at last.

'Well look…' Leo began at the same time. He stopped and smiled nervously. 'Sorry, you go on.'

'I was going to say…' Skater thought about what it was she had been going to say, and then decided that maybe now wasn't the right time to say it. 'I was just going to ask if you wanted to come for a walk,' she finished, mentally kicking herself for being such a coward.

'A walk?'

'Yeah.'

'To where?'

'Out. I don't know, somewhere that isn't here.'

'Um, okay. I don't have my E-suit though.'

'But you do own one, yes?'

'Of course I do.'

'Is it upstairs?'

'Yes.'

'I'll wait.' Skater sat down, put her boots up on one of the cluttered worktops and helped herself to the final sandwich. 'But not for ever,' she added, as Leo stood trying to decide what to do next. 'Go!'

Leo went.

'You still there, Taffy?' she asked, once the sandwich had been dealt with.

Yes.

'Lesson number one. Repeat after me; crap.'

Crap.

'It means rubbish, or really bad. As in, my life is crap.'

Is your life crap?

'Right now? I would have to say, most definitely.'

Why?

'Boy trouble.'

Are you referring to Leo?

'I am indeed.'

What trouble is he causing?

'Oh, it's complicated. Emotional stuff. You don't want to know.'

Can I help?

'I seriously doubt it. In fact, you're part of the problem, to be honest. If Leo wasn't spending so much time with you, he might be spending a lot more with me. I know that's not exactly your fault, but it's the truth. And I have to say I kind of resent you for that. Sorry.'

There is no need for an apology.

Skater let out a tiny laugh. 'Lesson number two. Always say sorry. Even if it's not your fault, say it anyway. It doesn't cost you anything and it'll save you thousands of hours of pointless arguing and sulking and wanting to punch someone's lights out because they're so stupid and stubborn and don't know a good thing when they see it.' There was silence for a moment. 'Go on then,' Skater added. 'Now you try it.'

Who is Agent Aitchison?

'What? What's he got to do with anything?'

PART ONE - THE TIDE TURNS

I am receiving an urgent transmission from Agent Aitchison. He is attempting to establish contact with anyone within this facility.

'Can you play it for me?'

The message came through immediately.

...repeat. This is Agent Aitchison. Can anyone hear me?

'This is Skater. I can hear you. What's the big deal?'

The Mine is under attack. Get out. Get out now!

10

THE ASSAULT BEGINS

THE *CRUMP* OF A DISTANT explosion filled the stunned silence as Skater tried to take in Aitchison's words.

'What's going on?' she managed, finally.

The transmission has been terminated, Cenotaph said. *Our communications are now being jammed. I am sorry.*

There was another explosion, closer this time, and then another and another. Skater could feel the vibrations as the whole building shuddered and the lights flickered off and back on again.

'What's going on?' she shouted.

The facility is being bombarded by orbital laser cannon.

'Can you see what's going on?'

Yes. I have access to the external camera network.

'Tell me.'

The main hangar is being targeted. Much of the supporting structure has been destroyed. A section of the roof has collapsed.

Suddenly the door burst open and Leo stumbled in, followed by

PART ONE – THE TIDE TURNS

Captain Mackie.

'You've got your suit on already,' Mackie said when he saw Skater. 'Good. Help Leo and wait here. I'll be back in two minutes.' He was gone again before Skater had the chance to say anything.

Leo was still wrestling himself into his own environment suit and Skater rushed across to help him. He waved her away.

'I'm fine!' he shouted. 'Find some bags. We need to pack up as much as we can.'

'Where? I can't find anything in this mess.'

'Over there,' he said, pointing to the far corner. 'And there's an air station as well. Fill up all the spare packs you can.'

Another series of explosions rocked the building, and this time several ceiling panels and lumps of concrete were knocked loose, falling among the piles of electronics and throwing up clouds of dust. A siren began to wail.

The facility has lost atmospheric integrity, Cenotaph announced over the noise of the alarm. *Emergency bulkhead doors have been engaged.*

Leo finished sealing up his suit and ran over to help Skater. They were still refilling spare air packs when another huge explosion took the whole of the side wall and tore it apart, hurling chunks of concrete and long, twisted metal spikes across the room and knocking them both to the floor. Leo lay stunned for several seconds as his mind reeled from the shock, the choking dust making it impossible to breathe properly or to see anything more than an arm's reach away.

Skater lay beside him, pinned beneath a section of ceiling but still moving. He pushed the rubble to one side and the two of them clambered to their feet.

'You okay?' he shouted, barely able to hear his own voice over the ringing in his ears. Skater nodded.

Mackie reappeared at the door, now dressed in full battle suit and carrying several weapons.

'Time to go!' he yelled.

'Go where?' Leo asked. 'There's nowhere left to go.'

'Deeper into the mine. We should be safe from the bombardment down there.'

'And then what?'

'We'll worry about that later. Come on.'

Leo looked around the destroyed lab. 'I need to collect my stuff.'

'No time. Just what you've got already.'

'But—'

'Now!'

Skater quickly shoved a handful of air packs into the only bag she could find and made for the door. Leo paused just long enough to spot Cenotaph lying on the floor. The cube appeared to have survived the blast without damage, so he scooped it up, took one last look around the lab and followed the others.

Outside was a mess of rubble and smoke. Flames were spreading from one of the rooms further back along the passageway and someone, somewhere was screaming for help. But even as he staggered on there was a burst of gunfire, another explosion, and the screams were silenced. He passed a pair of legs jutting out from a collapsed doorway and was about to stop and see if there was anything he could do to help when he realised the legs weren't actually trapped beneath the rubble, they were lying on top of it and the rest of the body was nowhere to be seen. He turned away, quickly, to avoid throwing up.

Two of Mackie's men were waiting at the end of the corridor, where they had overridden the electronic lock and forced open the heavy emergency doors. Mackie pushed Leo and Skater towards the staircase beyond, indicating for them to head down towards the Mine's lower levels.

'Anyone else make it through?' he asked.

'Not on this level, sir,' one of the men replied. 'Reikhart and Soames are upstairs helping some of the civilians. No one else has called in yet.'

'Alright. Close up here and follow us down to the bottom. The others will have to look after themselves. Leo, Skater, you're with me.' He led them quickly down, level by level, towards the very bottom of the narrow metal staircase, until the explosions above were no more than a faint rumble through the thick rock that pressed in all around them. Leo counted the number of times the staircase turned back on itself and had reached thirty when they finally came to a stop in a small, dimly lit room, empty except for a large set of double doors and one small computer console built into the wall beside them.

'Where are we?' Skater asked, gasping for breath.

'Another fifteen floors further down,' Leo answered. 'Which would make us about sixty metres underground.'

'This is the access point for the mine's emergency escape tunnel,' Mackie explained as he powered up the computer console. 'As most of the mining was done automatically I doubt it was ever used, except for the occasional bit of maintenance. We'll wait here for a while, see who else has made it out, before moving on.'

'Moving on where?' Leo asked.

'Into the mine.'

'We're not going back upstairs?'

'We can't. Not now. The bombardment is only to soften us up. Once they've done enough damage they'll send in the ground troops to go through the rubble and deal with survivors. The base is gone.'

'But my stuff's still up there. All the alien hardware we went to all that trouble to save from the MarsMine lab.'

Mackie looked at Cenotaph. 'You still have that.'

'But—'

'And you're still alive, aren't you? There's plenty of people up there who aren't, and getting you out alive was my priority. I'm sorry we didn't have time to collect more stuff, but don't blame me for that, blame the people attacking us. Blame your friend Whittaker.'

'Just be thankful your mum wasn't here,' Skater added. 'If she'd been up in her room I doubt she'd have made it.'

'Yeah,' Leo muttered. 'I guess.'

There was noise on the staircase above and after a moment the two soldiers reappeared, accompanied by two more who were carrying a small crate between them.

'This is all we could get our hands on, sir,' one of them said, laying the crate down on the floor and opening it up.

'What about the civilians?' Captain Mackie asked. The man shook his head.

'What?' Leo asked. 'No one? But there must be forty or fifty people up there.'

'I'm not saying they're all dead,' the man replied. 'Just that we didn't have time to get any of them out. The top floor was cut off almost immediately, and most of the folks down on our level weren't suited up when the roof collapsed. Any that managed to survive will just have to take their chances with the Martians.'

'And what are their chances?' Skater asked.

'Leo,' Captain Mackie said, leaving Skater's question unanswered. 'Take a look over here. We need the airlock pumped and the doors open. And see if you can access any of the cameras up top and find out what's going on.' He left the console and went to help his men share out the equipment from the crate.

Leo tapped away on the console, trying not to think of all the people he knew who had been upstairs in the mine. Most of them would be dead already, killed by the explosions, or poisoned before they could make it into their E-suits. And he could so easily have been among them. If it hadn't been for Skater suggesting they go for a walk, if he hadn't gone up and got his own suit… It didn't bear thinking about.

After a couple of minutes he had the airlock open and ready, but there was nothing he could do to find out what was happening up top. They still had power, which was good, but the console was unable to access either of the facility's main networks. Even Cenotaph was no help. There was no wireless signal this deep underground and Leo hadn't had time to grab any of the connecting cables, so he couldn't even plug the AI into the console.

'Right,' Captain Mackie announced. 'Time to go.'

'So what's the plan?' Skater asked as they all moved into the airlock. 'We can't just stay down here in the mine forever.'

'No, we can't. So we're going to head for one of the other exits and hope to hell that we've been better at hiding them than the Martians have been at finding them."

'What other exits?'

Captain Mackie gave a grunt of satisfaction. 'Rule number one when establishing a fortified position: always make sure you have a secure line of retreat.' The airlock doors hissed closed behind them. 'Alright,' he said, his tone becoming serious once more. 'Hoods on, visors down. And local comms only, please. They'll be scanning for radio signals and I'd rather not make it that easy for them to find us. Besides, no one's going to hear us from down here anyway. And stay sharp. They *will* be coming after us.'

With a hiss of escaping air, the heavy doors into the mine slowly opened and the party moved off into the darkness beyond. Captain Mackie led the way, his low-light enhanced visor allowing him to pick out the path ahead. Next came the two soldiers who had been waiting for them at the top of the stairway – Sullivan and Van Der

Laar — followed by Leo and Skater. Leo still clutched Cenotaph to his chest and Skater had the bag of spare air packs slung over her shoulder, and although they walked side by side, neither felt the need to reach for the other's hand for reassurance. Instead, as their own visors were lacking any sort of low-light capability, they both gave all their attention to following the faint glow from the helmets ahead. Reikhart and Soames, the other two soldiers, brought up the rear.

They continued in silence, keeping up a good pace through the abandoned tunnels. At every junction, Mackie knew exactly which way to go, and the only time they ever slowed was when they encountered piles of rubble or rock falls that Leo and Skater needed to be guided around.

'How do you know where you're going?' Leo asked, breaking the long silence.

'HUD map,' Mackie replied, without slowing.

'A what map?' Skater asked.

'Head-up display. My suit's processor sends a direct feed to my visor, showing me the path ahead and giving me a constant readout on our location.'

'A bit like the glasses I wore for my trip to the university?'

'Sort of, yes. Just better.'

'But how does your processor know where to go?' Leo asked. 'It's not going to get a MarsNet signal this far underground, not matter how hi-tech it is.'

'We've already scouted and mapped the entire mine. This attack took us by surprise, but we always knew it would happen some day and that we'd need to be ready for it when it finally came.'

'And how ready is ready?' Skater asked.

'Honestly? I don't know. I wasn't expecting them to come at us with an orbital bombardment. If they were just targeting the base, we should be okay. If they decide to go ahead and flatten the entire mountain, then getting out is going to be a whole lot more interesting.'

'How soon before we'll know?'

Captain Mackie picked up the pace. 'Long way to go yet.'

11

ESCAPE THROUGH THE MINE

TWO HOURS LATER THEY WERE still picking their way through the darkness. Leo was thirsty and tired, and his arms were sore from carrying Cenotaph. Also, his eyes were killing him. Having nothing to look at except the faint lights from the helmets in front of him was giving him a monster of a headache and making him feel constantly dizzy, and his pace had slowed to the point where he knew he was beginning to hold everyone else up. How much further could it be, he wondered. Surely by now they'd walked so far they could have made it all the way back to Gilgamesh.

Thinking of Gilgamesh reminded him of his mother and how glad he was she'd been away from the Mine when the attack struck. Skater was right. If she'd been in her room there was no way she would have made it out alive. And where was she now? Surely she must have seen the bombardment, or heard it at least. She would have known to stay away and find somewhere to hide out. But where? If they knew about the base, did that mean they also knew about Morgan? Was the warehouse still safe, or had that been destroyed too? Destroyed, just like the mine.

Suddenly an image of the two severed legs came into his mind. There they were, lying among the rubble, while somewhere far away someone was screaming for help. Then the legs began to twitch, to wriggle, as if they were still alive. Blood began to trickle from the open ends. The screaming grew louder, and now the voice was no longer screaming for help, it was screaming for him. *Leo! Leo!* it was shouting.

'Leo!' The lights in front of him began to spin and he felt strong hands grab hold of him. Cenotaph slipped from his grasp, and when he tried to reach out to stop it from falling his arms were sticky and heavy and wouldn't do what he wanted. Then he realised something was pressing against his back. A wall? No, the floor. He was lying down, and the lights were dancing in and out of focus above him.

'Air!' someone said. 'He's out of air.' But he didn't mind. Lying down was so much easier than walking. He smiled. Maybe if he just dozed off for a while they'd have to carry him. Carry him all the way to the exit. That would be nice. So nice…

…But that wasn't going to happen, not now. Already he could feel himself recovering. His head was clearing. He was breathing more easily. He groaned, partly out of disappointment, but mostly with embarrassment. 'Sorry,' he mumbled.

'Never,' Captain Mackie said, more severely than Leo felt was really necessary. 'Never forget to monitor your air levels. And learn to identify the signs of hypoxia.'

'Yes, sir.' Leo felt like he was back in school, being told off by one of his teachers for doing something really stupid. 'But I did check when I put the suit on,' he said, defensively. 'And it was full then.'

'Are you sure?'

'Positive.'

'Then you've probably got a tear in your suit somewhere, too small to notice. But we haven't got time to stop and check over the whole thing to find it. You'll just have to watch your air level like a hawk from now on and we'll try to do something about it as soon as we can.' He reached down and helped Leo onto his feet. 'Come on then. Let's not sit around wasting what air we do have.'

Soames handed Cenotaph back to Leo and the group set off, in the same order as before. Leo glanced across at Skater and she gave him a reassuring smile.

You okay? she mouthed.

He nodded and turned away, still feeling embarrassed and in no mood for a chat. He preferred to be alone with his own thoughts right now, even when those thoughts were completely stupid. Here he was, worrying about whether or not he'd made a fool of himself, when really he should have been worrying about the fact that they were fleeing for their lives, that they were lucky to still be alive. Because a lot of people weren't. A lot of people were... He tried not to think of the legs again.

There was a flash of light. The soldiers instantly dropped to the floor and took up firing positions while Leo and Skater crouched against the side wall, desperately searching the darkness for any signs of movement.

'What the Sol was that?' Skater asked.

'Shhh!'

After a moment there was another flash, and then the heavy duty strip lights running along the ceiling slowly flickered into life, bathing the tunnel in a cold, pale light.

'Well,' Captain Mackie said, standing back up. 'I guess they've got the power back up and running then. That means the ground troops are in and on our trail. We'd best get a move on.'

'But we have a couple of hours' head start,' Leo said. 'Surely we'll be at the exit long before they catch up with us?'

Captain Mackie gave a small laugh. 'Don't count on it.' He turned to his men. 'Watch your sensors. They'll be coming in hot.'

They set off again, much faster now, and although it was more tiring, Leo was grateful for finally being able to see where he was going. The tunnels were about five metres wide, semi-circular, with smooth walls and flat, solid floors. Obviously machine made. The intersections were wider still, with thick metal supports rising from the edges of the tunnel mouths and curving up until they joined in the centre of the domed ceiling. It was nothing like the dingy, cramped and claustrophobic place he had imagined. They pushed on.

'We have incoming!' Reikhart shouted, breaking the silence a few minutes later.

Captain Mackie glanced at his own wrist monitor without breaking stride. 'Trackers,' he said. 'Move!' They ran on until they reached the next intersection, where Mackie brought them to a halt. 'Sullivan, Van der Laar, close it up. Put five minutes on the clock, then get the hell out of here. We'll head straight for Exit Two.'

'They'll be through here before it blows if we make it five minutes, sir.'

'We can deal with the trackers. It's the vehicles following that I'm worried about. Plus I've no idea how much of the structure we'll bring down in the blast and I'm playing it safe. So don't wait around to see the results. Fix and run.'

'Yes, sir,' the men replied, and immediately set to work planting small explosive devices at the base of each pillar.

'Right,' Mackie said to the others. 'Now we really run.'

Running flat out in the low Martian gravity was hard work, and Leo found it easier to take long, bouncing strides rather than pounding along the ground like he would have done back on Earth. Even so, he was still slower than the others and soon they were way ahead of him, Captain Mackie having to constantly stop to check he was still following. By the time he reached the next junction, Skater and the two other soldiers were nowhere to be seen and only Mackie was waiting for him.

'Down.' Mackie said, indicating a metal ladder that disappeared into a narrow opening in the floor. 'Wait for me at the bottom.'

The ladder ran down for about ten metres and it took Leo much longer than it should have to get all the way down to the bottom as Cenotaph was too big to safely tuck under his arm and clinging to the rungs was no easy task. No sooner had he stepped off onto the hard ground than Mackie appeared beside him, having slid the whole way down in a matter of seconds, and they were off running once more.

Leo felt a dull thump deep in his chest as the explosive charges detonated, and the smooth walls of the mine began to shake apart around him. Mackie grabbed him by the arm and dragged him forward as lumps of rock knocked against him from the collapsing roof and for a moment they were running blind, in a cloud of dust and broken rock that filled the tunnel. But then they were back in the clear and they could see the others waiting for them ahead.

'That was close,' Reikhart said. 'They must have brought down most of the sector.'

'Good,' Mackie replied. 'That was the plan.'

'Does that mean they can't follow us?' Skater asked.

'Afraid not. It just means it'll take them a while to sort themselves out and find another route. And hopefully all this dust will mess with the trackers as well.'

'What are trackers?'

'Tiny drones that fly ahead of the troops, acting as spotters. Once they latch onto a target they'll stick with it, sending back a signal like a homing beacon so the troops know where to follow.'

'But the explosions, all the dust, it'll stop them working, right?'

'Maybe. But I wouldn't bank on it. They're clever little buggers.'

'What about your men?' Leo asked. 'Did they get out in time?'

'Don't worry about them,' Reikhart said with a laugh. 'They're clever little buggers as well.'

'They're still active,' Mackie added, tapping his visor to indicate that he was tracking them on his HUD. 'They'll meet us at the exit.'

'Which is how far now?' Skater asked.

'Fifteen minutes.'

'Thank Sol for that. That's about all I think I've got left in me.'

Half-an-hour later Mackie finally brought them to a stop. Leo and Skater immediately collapsed onto the floor while Reikhart and Soames took up defensive positions facing back down the tunnel.

'Wait here,' Mackie told them. 'The exit's up ahead and I want to scout it out before we go charging in and discover we've walked into a trap.'

After a moment Skater sat up. 'How's your air?' she asked.

Leo checked. 'Fine. You?'

'Low. I should probably change.'

'Here, I'll give you a hand.' Leo took out a spare air pack from the bag and waited while Skater released the old one. He knew she was perfectly capable of swapping them over on her own, but it made him feel useful to be doing something to help. And he needed to talk. The last few hours had been such an immense drain, both physically and emotionally, and there had been no time to think about anything except escape and survival. But now they finally had a moment to themselves, there were things he needed to talk about, things he needed to share with Skater.

'Upstairs,' he said at last. 'It was horrible. I...I was scared. Terrified.'

Skater took his hand in hers. 'Me too.'

'I saw bodies. People I know. Friends. And now they're all dead.'

'I know.'

'Why? Why did they have to die? To keep all of this secret?' He held up Cenotaph, angrily. 'It shouldn't even be a secret. It's the most important thing that's ever happened to the human race, and most of them don't know anything about it.'

'So tell them.'

'How? Showing them images from Cenotaph's memory banks? Who's going to believe that? I've seen movie aliens that were more realistic than the ones he showed us. And the Martian government will come straight out and say the whole thing's a fake anyway.'

'Why not let people decide for themselves? Show them what you've got, tell them the truth, and let them make up their own minds. And who cares if the Martians deny it? Governments have been denying things like this for as long as there have been governments. That's part of their job. No one believe them either.'

'She's right,' said Soames over the comms. 'Everyone knows you can't trust the government. Anyway, rumours are already flying around all over the place. Give 'em something solid to feed on and the whole thing'll go ballistic.'

'Okay,' Leo said, uncertainly. 'Maybe.'

'Maybe definitely,' Skater said. 'You have to do it, Leo. You know you do.'

Captain Mackie returned. 'Everything's quiet. Come on.' He

helped Leo and Skater to their feet and they made their way to the end of the passageway and round the corner.

At first, Leo thought they'd taken a wrong turn. The tunnel ran on for another fifty metres or so before ending in solid rock. Boulders lay scattered around, as if there had been a cave-in at some point that had never been cleared, and there were definitely no access ladders back up to the surface. But when Captain Mackie and the others began dismantling the boulders he realised his mistake. They weren't boulders at all, but camouflaged piles of equipment, draped in heavy material and covered in dust and smaller rocks to mask their shape. And as he watched, they threw off the cover of the giant boulder sitting right in the middle of the tunnel to reveal a small, open-topped buggy.

'Oh my sweet Sol,' Skater said, amazed. 'You weren't kidding when you said you had a secure line of retreat, were you? So where's the way out?'

'Soames, Reikhart,' Captain Mackie said. 'Show them the way out.'

The two men went over to the end of the tunnel and cleared away the small rocks lying against the wall. Only then did Leo realise the entire wall was another heavy, dust covered sheet. Soames lifted up the bottom to show the tunnel continuing on beyond.

'From here it's a straight run back to the surface. It'll bring you out about twenty klicks due east from the main entrance to the mine and you'll find plenty of rock cover when you emerge.'

'You're not coming with us?' Leo asked.

Mackie shook his head. 'The buggy can't carry all of us. Besides, someone needs to stay here and keep them off your trail. Reikhart will go with you. He's an excellent scout. He'll arrange for an evac and make sure you stay safe until it arrives.'

'And what about you?'

'Don't you worry about me. I've been in worse fixes than this and lived to tell the tale. I'll wait for the others and then head back into the mine. We'll give the Martians the runaround, keep them busy for a couple of days, then quietly slip away using one of the other exits. Trust me, they'll be searching this place for weeks before they realise there's no one left down here.'

'Where will we go?' Skater asked.

'I can't say. There are other places like this that we have access to, but which one you'll be taken to will be someone else's decision, not mine. And for now the main thing is to get you as far away from here as possible, as quickly as possible. So go! Get in the buggy and get going.'

Leo held out his hand. 'Thanks, Captain. For everything.'

Mackie shook hands quickly. 'Save it for later. Wherever it is you end up, I'll see you there in a week's time and you can thank me then.'

'Promise?' Skater asked.

'Promise.'

Reikhart powered up the buggy and Leo and Skater clambered into the back, squeezing in among the various pieces of equipment that took up most of the room. Leo tucked Cenotaph safely beneath the seat. It was filthy, covered in dirt and dust, and would need a complete clean before it was ready to be used again. He hoped there had been no permanent damage to its data banks. It was now the only thing they had left from the alien ship, the only proof there was any kind of conspiracy being covered up by the Martians. Without it, the battle was already lost.

12

NO SURVIVORS

'THE BATTLE'S OVER, MA'AM,' the junior officer announced, saluting smartly and escorting Kalina Kubin through the chaos and destruction of what had so recently been the main entrance to the Jesper One mine.

'Any problems?' she asked, glancing round and noting with satisfaction the dead bodies scattered among the rubble.

'No, ma'am. Well…'

'Well, what?'

'The facility is completely secure, but a few survivors did manage to escape into the mine itself. We've sent several squads down after them, but so far they haven't been able to round them up.'

Kalina turned to face the nervous young man. 'Well then the battle isn't over yet, is it, Lieutenant?'

'No, ma'am, not exactly. I just meant that—'

'Where's Colonel Parker?'

'Inside, ma'am. With the prisoners, I think.'

'Prisoners?'

'Yes, ma'am.'

'This just gets better and better,' Kalina cursed under her breath. 'Take me to him, now.'

'Yes, ma'am,' the officer replied. 'This way please.' And he marched off as briskly as he dared, desperate to be anywhere else as soon as possible.

The lowest level of the facility was still mostly intact and the Martian forces had done what they could to seal up the cracks in the structure and make the whole place airtight. A mobile airlock had been set up outside the bulkhead doors.

Once inside, Kalina took off her helmet and gloves and handed them to the young lieutenant. 'Wait here,' she said, and made her way along the partially collapsed corridor until she came to a room missing its door. A group of civilians were sitting awkwardly on the floor against the far wall, six of them, their hands bound, looking exhausted and frightened. One of them had a red-stained bandage covering most of his face. Two armed soldiers stood guard over them.

When Kalina appeared in the doorway they looked up expectantly, but she simply stared at them for a moment then continued on until she found the room that Colonel Parker had turned into a mobile command centre. A row of monitors lined each of the side walls, and a soldier sat in front of each monitor, busily doing whatever it was soldiers did in these situations; communicating with the units underground perhaps, or setting up a link to headquarters. Kalina didn't really care. Her attention was immediately drawn to the pile of small rectangular boxes placed carefully on a table in the centre of the room.

'These what you were looking for, Ms Kubin?' Colonel Parker asked, stepping across from the nearest monitor.

Kalina picked up one of the smooth alien components and

turned it carefully over in her hands. It was scratched and dented, but had already been cleaned up and, from the look of it, would still work perfectly well. There were six in total. Dr Randhawa would be pleased.

'Amongst other things,' she said. 'Anything else?'

'Books, notebooks, computers. There's box-loads of the stuff. We're still collecting it all up.'

'And the Fischers?'

The colonel shook his head. 'Nada.'

'Are you sure?'

'I know how to ID a corpse, Ms Kubin.'

'And the prisoners?'

'I know how to ID those as well.'

Kalina glared at him. 'Did they tell you anything?'

'They told me everything. What do you want to know?'

'About the Fischers.'

'The mother wasn't here. She left sometime yesterday and hadn't come back. Maybe she knew something.'

'Of course she didn't know anything. Nobody knew anything yesterday. What about the boy?'

'Missing. They say he was here though.'

'Then you lost him?'

'I didn't lose him. Once we went in, no one came out.'

'So he's down in the mine then?'

'There's a slim chance he could still be up here, buried under a pile of rubble somewhere. We haven't finished digging out all the bodies yet. But yes, my guess would be he made it down into the mine with the others.'

'The others?'

'After we'd secured the facility I sent two squads of trackers into the mine to hunt for stragglers. They detected several life signs.'

'How many is several, Colonel?'

'I don't know for sure. Five or six, maybe seven. There's a lot of interference down there.'

'Then send some proper troops in.'

'I did.'

'And?'

'It's a mine, Ms Kubin. It's big. And without the trackers working properly, it's going to take more than a couple of hours to search the whole place.'

'Then send more troops down there.'

'Trust me, I've sent in enough.'

'Trust you? I wouldn't trust you to organise a parade of cadets after this fiasco,' Kalina sneered. 'This whole attack was carried out for one reason, and one reason only, Colonel; so that by the end of today, Lillian and Leo Fischer would be dead. And are they? Are they?'

The Colonel remained silent.

'No, they're not!' Kalina continued. 'So now I have to report back to the president and tell him that thanks to your complete incompetence, Mars's most wanted terrorists are still wandering around, free to cause further chaos whenever they feel like it.'

'They're not free to wander round the place, they're trapped at the bottom of a mine. Either they'll run out of air, or we'll have picked them up by tomorrow morning at the latest.'

'Well at least tell me that you've got the other exits covered.'

The Colonel turned suddenly pale. 'What other exits?' he asked, uncertainly. 'The schematics didn't show any other exits.'

'Then the schematics are wrong,' Kalina snapped. 'There are always secondary exit points from mines, because miners are paranoid. They like to make sure there's always a back door, in case of emergencies.'

'But I understood this mine to have been fully automated?'

Kalina looked at the man, unable to believe that someone so stupid had been put in command of such a sensitive operation. 'Get something up in the air, fast. Do a sweep of the entire sector before it gets dark. And send out patrols. They might get lucky.'

'Do it!' the colonel barked to one of his men, who was standing waiting for orders. The soldier rushed to the nearest console and began to relay orders over the comms.

'And another thing,' Kalina said. 'You were told there were to be no survivors. Those orders were quite specific.'

'Well I'm sorry,' the Colonel replied, defensively. 'But some of them gave themselves up. They were already in custody by the time I got here, so there wasn't a whole lot I could do about it.'

'There is now.'

'What do you mean?'

'You can deal with them now. Do you need me to spell it out for you?'

'But they're prisoners.'

'So?'

'They're civilians.'

'Does that matter?'

'It may not to you, but it sure does to me. I'm not a murderer.'

'Then it's a good job at least one of us is,' Kalina replied. She drew her pistol and stormed out of the room. Colonel Parker made no move to stop her.

As soon as she was back with the prisoners she began the killing. The first one she shot cleanly through the front of the skull, but after that the screaming started as the prisoners desperately tried to clamber to their feet or shuffle away. The second and third were easy enough as well, but the fourth and fifth were messy and took several shots each before they had finally stopped writhing around.

The last one, the man with the face covered in bandages, simply sat there waiting to die, staring up at her with his remaining eye. Kalina didn't know whether it was because he wanted to die, or because he knew there was nothing he could do to prevent it. Either way, it didn't matter. Her final shot took away most of the back of his head and left it smeared across the wall behind. Six deaths, one for each of the recovered alien computers. How fitting.

The two guards stood shocked, not knowing what to say or do, as Kalina knelt and used the jacket from one of the dead men to wipe the blood off her hands and pistol. Then, as she was leaving the room, a large plastic box sitting on a table by the doorway caught her attention.

'What's this?' she demanded.

'It's...it's their personal possessions, ma'am,' one of the soldiers stammered.

Kalina emptied the contents of the box onto the table; watches, personal computers, wallets... nothing of interest. 'I need the box,' she told the guards. 'Help yourself to this stuff. They won't be needing it any more.'

There was silence when she returned to the command centre. Everyone was staring at her. Colonel Parker was fuming.

'Happy now?' he demanded.

'No,' Kalina replied. 'Not by a very long way.' She began to pack the alien computers into the box. 'I'll be staying in Gilgamesh until this mess is sorted out. I want the rest of the stuff from the lab sent over to me later tonight, and I want to know the minute you've finally cleared out the mine. And no more excuses. I want the Fischers, and I want them dead. No more prisoners, understand?'

Colonel Parker clenched his fists and glared at her furiously.

'Do you understand your orders, Colonel?'

'Yes, ma'am,' he spat. 'Loud and clear.'

13

CAMPING ON MARS

THE TUNNEL EMERGED into a shallow, rock-strewn canyon that led away from the mine and deeper into the Jesper Hills. Reikhart drove on for several minutes, bumping along on the rocky ground, until he found a suitable place to park where they would be invisible from the air. Even so, he still insisted on draping camouflage netting over the buggy before doing anything else. Once he was satisfied they were safe enough for the time being, he turned his attention to the radio.

'Won't they be listening out for us?' Leo asked.

'Yup, they certainly will,' Reikhart replied. 'Which is why we encrypt the signal, and why we only transmit on a secure frequency.'

'Even so, they'll still pick it up.'

'So make the message short and to the point. Here.' He handed Leo a cable to connect into his E-suit comms.

'Me?' Leo asked.

'Yes, you,' Reikhart replied, fishing out a sophisticated-looking set of binoculars from beneath his seat. 'I'm going up onto the rocks to see what I can see. Use the call sign Gladiator and say you're making an emergency distress call to all available units.'

'Gladiator?'

'Yup. And cut the connection immediately if they don't reply with the words, Circus Maximus.'

'Circus Maximus?'

'Exactly.' He slipped out beneath the camouflaged netting before Leo could ask anything else.

Leo climbed into the front seat and began to study the radio panel.

'Here, let me,' Skater said. 'I know what to do.' She clambered over and forced her way into the seat beside Leo, took the cable from him and plugged it into her own suit. 'Watch and learn.' She took a deep breath and pressed the call button. 'This is an emergency distress call to all available units. I repeat, an emergency distress call to all available units. Are you receiving me, over?'

She released the button and waited, but there was nothing but static on the line. After a minute she tried again. This time there was an answer.

Emergency caller, please identify yourself.

'Yes!' Skater shouted. 'We're through.'

Emergency caller, please identify yourself.

'Hi. This is Gladiator. Who are you?'

Gladiator, this is Circus Maximus. Please confirm— The voice was cut off mid sentence, and after a short pause, a different voice came on the line.

Skater, is that you?

'Dad?'

Skater! Thank god you're alive! Where are you?

'Dad, I'm okay. Leo and I made it out of the mine. We're with one of Captain Mackie's men and we're out in the hills somewhere. We've got a buggy.'

Are you hurt? Injured?

'No, we're alright. We just need someone to come and get us out of here. Where are you?'

I'm with Morgan. Luckily, Lillian and I were still out when the soldiers raided Morgan's place and we were able to get out of Gilgamesh before they shut the whole place down. We're at a temporary base, out in the desert somewhere east of town, and we've been sitting around waiting, desperate for news from the mine.

'So how soon can you get here?'

We can't, sweetheart. You're going to have to come to us.

'Why?'

Because the whole area is crawling with Martian fliers. And besides, if you're in the hills there'll be nowhere for us to land. Where's Mackie?

'He stayed behind, in the mine.'

Who's with you then?

'Reikhart.'

Good. Tell him to make his way to Reserve Six. He'll know where it is. And tell him we'll be fuelled up and ready to leave as soon as he gets here so not to hang around enjoying the scenery on the way.

Leo tapped Skater on the shoulder and motioned for her to finish up. The call was going on for much too long.

'Dad, listen. I've gotta go. We'll be there as soon as we can. Don't go without us.'

Of course we won't. Just get here safely.

'We will, I promise. I love you.'

I love you too.

She cut the link, then turned and gave Leo a huge hug, pressing her helmet tight against his and planting a kiss on the inside of the glass. 'They're okay,' she said. 'They're all okay. Oh god, I'm so happy.'

'Me too,' Leo said, returning Skater's hug and feeling the relief take hold of him. He hadn't realised how worked up he'd become, waiting for news about his mother. Maybe they weren't out of danger yet, but things seemed a whole lot better all of a sudden.

'Save that for later,' Reikhart said, appearing at the side of the buggy and pulling away the netting. 'We have to go. There's a patrol heading this way.'

Leo and Skater sprang apart like a pair of guilty schoolchildren and clambered back into their own seats, Leo blushing inside his helmet. By the time they had strapped themselves in, Reikhart had stowed the netting and was back in his own seat.

'Did you get through?' he asked.

'We did,' Skater answered. 'They can't come and collect us, but they're waiting for us at somewhere called Reserve Six. They said you'd know where that is.'

'That's good,' said Reikhart, starting up the buggy and bumping it down a shallow slope leading further into the canyon. 'Seeing as how it's directly away from the mine, it's exactly the direction I was thinking of heading in.'

'How long until we get there?'

'At this speed? Tomorrow morning.'

'Tomorrow morning?' Skater complained. 'You're kidding! I thought we were no more than two or three hours away at most.'

'If we had a flat road and a more powerful engine, then maybe it would be about three hours. But you see this track. We can barely make fifteen kilometres an hour without risking breaking an axle, and that's in daylight. Once we lose our light we're basically just saving ourselves the trouble of walking.'

'Wonderful.'

'Best make yourselves comfortable back there. It'll be a long night.'

PART ONE - THE TIDE TURNS

'I hate Mars,' Skater muttered.

Sunset came less than an hour later, but the buggy was already too far into the canyon for them to see the horizon, and the spectacular blue sun sank below the black hills without them even noticing. Skater tried closing her eyes and getting some sleep, but the cramped conditions and constant bumping prevented her from finding any position that was anything except awkwardly, painfully uncomfortable. Leo was exhausted, and if it had been up to his body he would have been fast asleep long ago, despite the crate that seemed to dig further into his ribs with every jolt. But his mind was having none of it. The day had been too traumatic, too terrifying, and images of death and destruction were waiting every time he closed his eyes. They would fade, he knew that. Soon he'd even be able to revisit them without immediately wanting to throw up. It had been the same after Mr Archer had pressed the gun against his head and he'd heard the shot he was convinced had killed him. Even the horror of that moment had faded to almost nothing after a while. It just took time.

He stared aimlessly at the rocks as they trundled past, noting the colours and shapes and trying to remember things from his school geology classes; the names of the different types of rock, how they were formed, what minerals they might contain. At one point he realised he'd been staring straight ahead and repeating the word *igneous* over and over to himself, and when he turned his attention back to the rocks, they were no more than dark shapes and faint outlines against a dark sky.

The buggy had no headlights, and even though Reikhart switched over to his visor's low-light setting, he still found it impossible to pick his way safely across the rocky ground. After an hour or so of crawling along at a snail's pace, he finally gave up and came to a halt.

'That's it,' he announced. 'There's no point going any further like this. We may as well camp here for the night.'

'Camp?' Leo asked. 'Seriously?'

'Sure, why not? It's unlikely they'll be patrolling this far out, especially at night. We'll be safe enough here while it's dark, and we'll be long gone by the time it's light enough for them to resume their spotter flights.'

'Okay, fine. But camping? Like, in a tent? On Mars?'

'Not a tent,' Skater said, clambering out of the buggy and stretching all four limbs as far they would go. 'A Hamilton hut.'

Reikhart laughed. 'How the hell do you know what a Hamilton hut is?'

'My Dad's ex-service, remember? It's what we used when we went trekking on Luna. They're great.'

'Well, this one's pretty basic,' Reikhart said, revealing a large plastic pack attached to the back of the buggy. 'And it's heavy as well. How about you two giving me a hand to get it set up?'

By the light from a small torch attached to Reikhart's helmet, the three of them carried the pack to a clearing and spread the contents across the ground.

'Now what?' Leo asked.

'Now, we climb in,' Skater said.

'But we haven't actually put it up yet.'

'Watch and learn.' Skater opened the seal and pushed her way in among the folds of material. 'Come on in,' she told Leo. 'It's lovely.'

Leo got down on his hands and knees and wriggled in beside her. It was cramped, and the heavy material pressed down on him as he struggled to find space.

'Take these as well,' Reikhart said, handing in several small packs. 'And give me a bit more space, can you?'

'There isn't any more space,' Leo protested. 'It was more

comfortable in the buggy.'

'Sorry,' Reikhart said, folding the material carefully back over his armoured suit and sealing the entrance. 'Just give me a sec.'

Once he was satisfied with the seal, Reikhart opened the lock on a cylinder of air he'd brought in with him and the material began to unfold and expand. Two minutes later, Leo found himself sitting in a fully inflated, domed tent that he could just about stand up in, and that was long enough to stretch out in.

'Can we?' Skater asked, indicating her environment suit hood.

Reikhart shook his head and held up his hand until a small green light appeared on the top of the air cylinder. 'Okay, that's it.'

'Oh my sweet Sol, that's better,' Skater said as she took off her hood and began to scratch her scalp vigorously. 'That thing itches me like crazy.'

'Just the hood, though,' Reikhart warned, removing his own helmet. 'You'll need to keep the rest of the suit on for warmth. Are you hungry?'

'Are you kidding? I'm starving.'

Reikhart opened one of the smaller rucksacks, set up a small blue-light lamp and handed over some packets of food and bottles of water. Skater set about destroying them straight away.

'Is this thing really safe?' Leo asked, prodding the thin, plasticised wall of the tent.

'It will be as long as you stop trying to poke your finger through it,' Skater replied through a mouthful of food.

'Is it shielded?'

'Yes, it's shielded. And yes, it's airtight. And no, it won't blow away in the wind. And are you going to eat that, or can I have it?'

'I'm going to eat it.' Leo looked at the solid slab of food he'd just taken out of its packet. 'Possibly. What is it?'

'It's a field rat,' Skater said, winking at Reikhart.

Leo paused, open mouthed, and took another look at the food. 'A field rat?'

'Short for field rations,' Reikhart explained. 'Protein, carbohydrate, essential vitamins and minerals, all rolled up into a single, easy to eat block of tasty goodness.'

Leo took a tentative bite, chewed for a while and then swallowed. 'Yeah,' he said with a shrug. 'It's okay, I guess.'

'You should try to get some sleep,' Reikhart said once they had all finished eating. 'I'll let you have four hours, but then it's straight up and back on the road.'

'What about you?'

'I'll keep guard,' he said, patting his pistol. 'Not that we'll need it, but I don't sleep so well out in the field anyhow.'

'I doubt I'll sleep either,' Leo said. 'Not after that day.'

'Well if you boys are going to stay awake, at least do it quietly,' Skater said. She stretched out on one of the two bed mats built into the floor of the tent, closed her eyes, and let out a long, slow sigh. A little while later Leo leant over and gently touched her lips with his own.

'Good night,' he whispered.

'Good enough,' she muttered.

14

RACE TO SAFETY

AS PROMISED, REIKHART woke them before first light, and after a quick meal of more field rations, they topped up their air packs, sealed up their suits and were back on the road within ten minutes. To save time, they abandoned the Hamilton hut rather than repacking it, and by the time the tiny sun appeared above the horizon, the campsite was far behind them.

Leo had managed to sleep after all, exhaustion and an almost comfortable bed combining to allow his mind to leave behind the terrible images from the previous day. He hadn't even had any nightmares, or at least none he could remember. One minute he'd been saying good night to Skater, the next he was being shaken awake. But he felt refreshed, slightly. His stomach was full. He almost felt...not happy, but certainly more positive. The horrors of the previous day seemed further away and it felt like maybe, just maybe, they were over the worst of it.

Skater, on the other hand, really did seem happy. She was so excited about seeing her dad again that she was chatting away to the two of them as if she didn't have a care in the world, as if she was on one of her camping adventures on Luna, as if yesterday had never happened. Leo envied her that – that ability she had to live in the present, to take each day as it came and not get bogged down in worrying about the past or planning for the future. How helpful it would be, at times like this, to be able to forget.

A little while later they emerged from the last of the Jesper foothills, and the ground ahead became mostly flat and hard. Reikhart immediately sped up.

'Finally!' Skater announced. 'We can go at a sensible speed. How much further is it?'

'Not much,' Reikhart replied. 'Say, an hour or so. You want to call and let them know we're on our way?'

'Can I?'

'Sure. Climb over and help yourself.'

Skater released her seatbelt and clambered into the front passenger seat. She found the comms link and plugged herself in.

'Wait,' Leo called out from the back. 'What's that?'

'What's what?' Reikhart replied.

'In the sky. It looks like a flyer of some sort.'

'Where? How far away?'

'It's back behind the hills. But it's getting bigger. It's definitely coming towards us.'

Reikhart twisted round in his seat to take a quick look for himself. 'Dammit,' he said. 'I didn't think they'd bother searching this side of the hills, certainly not first thing in the morning. They must really want you badly.'

'Have they definitely seen us?'

'Yeah, even that far off they'll have spotted the heat signature. Skater, you'd better make that call an emergency one.'

'What is it I'm supposed to say? I've forgotten the call signs and stuff.'

'Gladiator. Circus Maximus.'

'They're getting closer,' Leo called out. 'And they've dropped lower.'

'This is Gladiator, calling Circus Maximus. Come in, Circus Maximus.'

'Talk to me, Leo. Tell me what it's doing.'

'It's still coming.'

'Circus Maximus. This is Gladiator. Are you receiving, over?'

'Right behind us.'

Gladiator, this is Circus Maximus. We are receiving you, over.

'Listen. This is Gladiator. We're out of the hills and heading towards you. About an hour away. But we've been spotted and there's a flyer right on our tail.'

'Here it comes!'

The flyer came in low over the top of the buggy, whipping up the dirt and dust, and even though Leo could barely hear the roar of its engines in the thin Martian atmosphere, he still felt it as a low rumbling in his chest and he ducked down instinctively as the plane flew past.

Acknowledged, Gladiator. Please stand by.

The buggy emerged from the dust cloud and Reikhart pointed it towards a distant rise as the enemy flyer pulled up and began to turn for another run.

'Stand by? What do you mean, stand by? Tell us what to do!'

'Can't we go any faster?'

'I'm already going flat out. It was built for endurance, not speed.'

'Hello? Hello? Circus bloody Maximus! Where the Sol are you?'

'Even at this speed, if we hit a rock it could flip us right over.'

Gladiator, be advised. Help is on its way. Continue on your present course, over.

'What help?'

'It's coming back round.'

We are dispatching skimmers, over.

'Yes! How soon will they be here?'

'It's lining itself up.'

We estimate fifteen minutes, over.

'It's shooting at us!'

As Leo watched, two lines of tiny explosions tore up the ground behind the buggy, racing across the desert towards him. 'Look out!' he screamed and ducked down. Reikhart spun the steering wheel and the buggy lurched to one side, the cannon shells continuing to rip up the ground where the buggy had been just seconds before.

'We're not going to last fifteen minutes.'

'Skater, I need you to take the wheel.'

'Get here quicker!' she screamed. 'Over and out.'

Reikhart let the buggy run free while he climbed out of the driver's seat and onto the outside of the vehicle. Skater slipped into the empty seat and took control.

'Head for the rise. Watch for rocks and try to keep it steady.'

'What about the flyer?'

'Leave that to me.' He leapt across onto the back seat beside Leo then reached down and unclipped his assault rifle from the rear storage compartment.

'Will that work?' Leo asked.

'Probably not. But it's all we've got. Sorry, but we left all the ground-to-air missiles back in the mine.'

'Can I do anything to help?'

'Keep down when it comes back.'

'Alright.' Leo squeezed himself down onto the floor beside Cenotaph and looked up at Reikhart as he got himself into a good firing position.

'You ever fire one of these, Leo?'

'No. Never.'

'Well, now might be a good time to start. If I'm hit you'll have to take over.'

'Seriously?'

'Unless you've got a better idea. Now, down you go, it's lining up for its next run.'

Leo tucked his head down as far as it would go and waited for the pounding in his chest as the plane passed overhead. Suddenly he felt the buggy shudder as something crashed into the back of it and it went skidding off sideways briefly before Skater was able to get it back under control. Reikhart spun as the flyer went past, firing burst after burst up at the speeding shape before it was lost in the dust cloud and too far away.

'Everyone okay?' Reikhart shouted.

'Fine,' Skater replied. 'Are we hit?'

'Nothing serious.'

Leo poked his head up and saw that half the rear storage compartment had been shot away. Reikhart was reloading.

'Did you get it?'

'Nope.'

They waited, watching the plane make its slow, wide turn to bring it back behind them.

'At least there's only one,' Leo said.

'And it's a scout, not a fighter.'

'You could have fooled me,' Leo said. 'It's been doing a pretty good job of fighting so far.'

'If it was a proper fighter it would be coming at us with missiles. This thing's only got two small cannon. A couple more passes and it'll be out of ammunition.'

'Then what?'

'Then it'll sit back and watch as the fighters it'll have called up come in and finish the job.'

'But our own fighters will be here by then, won't they?' Skater said, hopefully.

'We haven't got any fighters.'

'What? But they said they'd been dispatched. They said they'd be here in fifteen minutes. And that was easily ten minutes ago.'

'They said skimmers, not fighters. They're basically close-support vehicles, designed for mobile ground combat. They're not going to be any use against fighters.'

'Hang on!' The buggy hit a low rise and momentarily left the ground before crashing back down with a jarring crunch.

'Careful!' Reikhart shouted as he regained his balance.

'Sorry. We just crested the hill. And look!'

Leo twisted round and peered over the top of Skater's seat. Off in the distance he could see two vehicles, skimmers, flying towards them. He looked up at Reikhart. 'They're ours, right?'

'I bloody well hope so. Down!'

Leo ducked. More shooting, more explosions, more dust, and then he heard Reikhart cry out. 'Are you hit?' he shouted.

'Not me, them. I got 'em!'

Leo looked at the flyer. It had pulled up and was making its turn as usual but there seemed to be bright sparks spraying out behind it as it flew on.

'Look, there under the wing. Do you see it? Magnesium fire. That means I must have hit a fuel line. Won't be enough to destroy it, but they'll have to shut that engine down and I doubt they'll risk another low pass on only one engine.'

'Look! It's not turning. It's carrying straight on.'

'What's going on?' Skater called out.

'The flyer. Reikhart hit it and now it's on fire and running for home.'

'Yes! We did it.'

'Don't get too excited. It'll have called in the contact and they're sure to have plenty more to throw at us. We still have a way to go.'

'But we have our own reinforcements now.'

The two skimmers whizzed by, one on each side. The first continued to trail the damaged flyer, while the second banked round and took up station off to the side, reducing speed to keep pace with the buggy. Skater gave them a wave.

'How are you doing there?' Reikhart asked her. 'Want me to take over again?'

Skater gripped the steering wheel even more tightly. 'No, I'm good. This is more fun than I've had in ages. Except for the being shot at bit. I could do without that.'

After a while the second skimmer returned, and for the next fifteen minutes the two of them escorted the buggy through the desert. Occasionally one or other would race ahead, or drop back to check if anything was on their tail, but so far nothing seemed to be. Then Skater noticed something in the distance ahead. It was still a long way off, but there was no mistaking it, even at this range. The *Nightrider*.

'I can see them!' she shouted. 'Leo, look, it's *Nightrider*. We've made it.'

Leo leant forward and stared at the blurred shape. 'Are you sure? How can you tell?'

'Because I'd recognise it anywhere. Plug me in. I want to say hello.'

'No need,' Reikhart said. 'We're close enough for them to be able to pick up the suit comms now. Just say hi.'

'Good morning *Nightrider*. This is Skater. Are you awake yet, over?'

Of course we're awake. We've been awake all night, worrying ourselves sick about you.

'Morgan!'

None other. Nice of you to join us, Skater. Everything okay?

'It is now. Can you see us?'

Clearly. That you at the wheel?

'Yep. Where's Dad?'

I'm right here, waiting to give you the biggest hug of your life.

'And what about my mum?' Leo asked.

She's here, Pete replied. *She's safe.*

Wait, said Morgan suddenly. *I'm picking something up.*

'Is it the scout?' Reikhart asked, scanning the empty yellow sky behind them.

Definitely not. Two signals, and they're coming in fast.

The skimmers immediately broke off and doubled back, but against two fast fighters, Leo wasn't sure what good they would do.

We need to be airborne, Morgan said.

'No! Don't leave without us,' Skater shouted.

We won't, Pete answered. *But Morgan's right. If we get caught on the ground we're dead.*

'Then what are we supposed to do?'

Just keep going.

'I see them,' Reikhart said. 'They're fighters alright, and they're firing missiles.'

As Leo watched, a series of tiny dots separated themselves from the approaching fighters and sped their way towards him. Four missiles. There was no way they were going to avoid four missiles. Just then the skimmers began to fire off small charges, like grenades, that exploded in the air behind them in a shower of sparkling crystals.

'What's that?'

'Chaff,' Reikhart explained. 'It'll disrupt their guidance systems.'

The first two missiles tore through the cloud of chaff and almost at once their flight became more erratic. The first dipped down and flew straight into the ground, exploding in a shower of dirt a long way back. The second veered off and headed out into the desert and Leo lost sight of it in all the chaos. But the third and fourth missiles were unaffected and one of them immediately locked on to the nearest of the skimmers. The pilot weaved his craft from side to side, desperately trying to shake off the missile, but a few seconds later the missile plunged into the back of his craft and exploded in a huge, silent fireball that was sucked, almost at once, back into the empty Martian atmosphere.

The final missile was still heading straight for them. The second skimmer was shooting at it, as was Reikhart from the back of the buggy, but without success. Leo crouched down as far as he could beneath his seat.

Skater slammed her foot down and forced the buggy to go flat out.

'What are you doing?' Leo shouted over the comms. 'What about the suspension?'

'Forget the suspension,' Skater replied. 'I'll just avoid the big rocks and hope we don't break apart before we get there.'

'We're not going to make it,' Leo called out. He was staring at the dark shape of the missile as it sped towards them, unable to take his eyes off it. 'It's too close.'

'Dad!' Skater screamed suddenly. 'Lower the ramp.'

What?

'Stay on the ground and lower the ramp. I'll drive us straight in the back.'

That's crazy. Can you even see the back of the ship with all the dust we're kicking up?

'It's the fastest way to get us on board. I can do it. I know I can.'

Then the missile exploded. Possibly it was a malfunction, or possibly the gunfire from Reikhart and the trailing skimmer had finally damaged it enough to cause a premature detonation, but either way, the buggy managed to avoid the full power of the blast as the missile tore itself apart in a huge fireball ten metres from where Leo was crouched. Even so, a wave of heat and twisted shards of white-hot metal tore into the back of the vehicle and the force of the explosion lifted the buggy right off the ground.

They didn't flip over. The wheels crashed back down onto the hard dirt and the buggy went into a long skid before Skater was able to regain control and point them in the direction of *Nightrider*. In the back, Leo looked up to see Reikhart crumple, drop his weapon over the side of the vehicle and begin to tumble sideways after it. He grabbed hold of the man's belt, tugging him backwards so that the heavy body collapsed onto the seat beside him. The whole of the front of Reikhart's suit was peppered with shards of metal jutting out from the black armour and there was a jagged hole in the dark glass of his visor. Leo couldn't tell if he was still alive or not, and all he could do was cover the cracked visor with his free hand to stop as much air as possible from escaping, just in case.

The fighters swooped in low overhead, but Leo didn't know if they were firing or not. There was so much dust around now he couldn't see anything and he had no idea where they were, or how close they were to *Nightrider*, or how Skater could possibly see where she was going in all this chaos.

'I can't see where I'm going.'

Straight ahead. Pete shouted. *A bit to the left. Not that much!*

'Is the ramp down?'

Nearly.

Skater tugged on the steering wheel. 'This thing is pulling me all over the place. It feels like one of the back wheels isn't turning properly.'

Leo looked out at the mangled wreckage at the back of the buggy and the gaping hole where the left rear wheel had been. It was a miracle they were still going at all.

Ramp is down!

Skater gripped the steering wheel with all her strength and sent the buggy hurtling straight for the centre of the swirling mass of sand and dust, hoping it was the back of the ship she could see and not one of its support legs. It was too late now to stop and check.

The buggy came in hard against the base of the ramp, bounced up and crashed back down in a shower of torn metal. Skater kept her foot pressed hard on the pedal and the buggy growled and skidded up the rest of the ramp and into *Nightrider*'s hold, flipping onto its side and sliding along the deck until the far bulkhead finally brought it to a crunching stop.

They're in, Leo heard Pete shouting over the comms. *Go! Go! Go!*

15

LICKING THEIR WOUNDS

NIGHTRIDER WAS OFF THE GROUND and creeping forwards even before the ramp had finished closing, but Morgan was forced to keep the ship as level as possible until the chaos in the hold could be sorted out and everything secured for flight. She stayed low, using the clouds of dust thrown up by the engines as cover from the prowling fighters, but it would only be a matter of time before the Martians sent in something bigger and better to finish the job, and she didn't intend to be around when they did.

Finally the door hissed open and Pete took his seat beside her, quickly strapping himself in and powering up the co-pilot's controls in front of him.

'We set?' Morgan asked.

'Locked and loaded.'

'Good. Let's get the hell out of here.'

They felt the push as the main thrusters kicked in and *Nightrider* began to pick up speed, hauling itself out of the dust cloud and surging forward into the pale Martian sky.

'Everything okay back there?' Morgan asked, glancing across at Pete. 'How's Skater?'

'She's good. Shaken up a bit, but nothing broken. Reikhart's in a bad way though. Looks like he caught the worst of that last blast.'

'He gonna make it?'

'Can't say. I've left him with the others, but there's not a lot they can do for him right now. And Leo took a piece of shrapnel in the leg as well. Didn't even know he'd been hit until he caught sight of all the blood soaking into his suit. He'll be fine though.' He checked his monitor. 'And what about us? Are we going to make it?'

Morgan shrugged. 'Fifty-fifty.'

'That good, huh?'

'I'm not worried about the fighters. We can outrun those. It's a question of what they have waiting for us up top.'

'Well, there's only one way to find out.'

'You ready?'

'Ready enough.'

'Okay, let's do it.' She flicked the comms switch. 'Ladies and gentlemen, this is your captain speaking. Buckle up, or grab onto something, because we are going for burn in five...four...three... two...one...'

Morgan pulled back on the steering column, pointing the nose of the ship up until it was almost vertical, then unlocked the two switches that would shut off the atmospheric thrusters and ignite the twin ion engines designed to carry *Nightrider* into space. She looked across at Pete and smiled.

'Zero.' She flicked the switches.

Leo felt dizzy. They'd given him something for the pain, even though there hadn't really been any, and now everything seemed to be happening in some kind of lazy slow motion. He felt the pressure on his chest as the ship's thrusters fired, but somehow he couldn't bring himself to be excited the way he'd been last year, when he'd left Earth for the first time, on the lunar shuttle where he'd met Skater.

Skater. She'd been around here somewhere. She'd helped him out of the buggy after the crash. But then he'd noticed the piece of metal sticking out of his leg, and the huge red stain down the side of his E-suit, and after that she'd disappeared and some soldiers had come and carried him away, and strapped him into a seat that was more like a bed, and had given him something for the pain. And now all he wanted to do was fall asleep...

And now he was weightless. And in his underpants. He was still strapped into his seat, but now the seat was fully reclined so he was lying almost flat. And his mum was there, wrapping a bandage around his leg. He was still dizzy, but at least things were starting to make a bit more sense and he didn't feel quite so...spaced out, he thought, ironically. He tried to laugh, but his mouth was too dry and it came out as a little cough. Lillian looked round.

'Welcome back to the land of the living,' she said with a warm smile.

'Thirsty,' Leo croaked.

Lillian reached across and handed him a bottle of water that was floating nearby, then went back to bandaging the leg. Leo sucked and sucked until the bottle was empty.

'Is it bad?' he asked, nodding towards the leg.

'Not at all. One of the army chaps came and sorted it out while you were asleep. He said it will be sore for a while and not to put any pressure on it, though given our current situation, I don't really see that as being much of an issue.'

'Where are we.'

'Running away from Mars.'

'But running to where?'

'I have no idea. I suspect that for the moment, away from Mars is destination enough, though I would imagine Morgan has somewhere in mind.'

'Is anyone following us?'

'Again, that's not really my department. But so far there hasn't been any shooting, or lurching from side to side, or action stations or anything.'

'How's Reikhart?'

'The soldier? I don't know. They're still working on him.'

'Cenotaph?'

'Questions, questions, questions,' Lillian said, taping up the bandage and finishing with the leg. 'Cenotaph is absolutely filthy and will need a comprehensive clean before I'm ready to risk switching it on again. Structurally it looks fine, but lord knows what its insides will be like.'

'Mum. All the other stuff. It's gone. I didn't have time to get anything else out.'

'Don't worry,' Lillian said, reaching out and gently squeezing his hand. 'You managed to save the only thing I really care about.'

'Do you mean me, or are you still talking about Cenotaph?'

Lillian found a blanket and tucked it around Leo to make him more comfortable. She stroked his hair and gazed down at him, smiling. 'You're still my precious little baby, you know.'

Leo was too tired to complain and he could feel the dizziness starting to return. 'Yeah, I know,' he sighed.

'Get some rest. I'll look in on you later.'

'Bring food.'

'I'll see what I can do.'

Leo closed his eyes and let his mind wander away from the cramped cabin around him. So they'd made it off Mars – for the moment, at least. Was anyone coming after them? Almost certainly. But that wasn't to say they'd catch them. Morgan was bound to have some clever anti-scanning device, like an electronic cloak or something, that would keep them hidden from the Martian navy – at least until they could get to wherever it was they were going. Earth? Unlikely. Half the Martian fleet was patrolling the Inner System, and there was no way *Nightrider* could make it without having to stop and resupply along the way. So it would be outwards then, into the Belt.

Of course it would be the Belt. There were hundreds of stations and bases out there, so many even the authorities had trouble keeping track of them. Most of the bigger ones would be off-limits, though. They would be loyal to Mars, or at least to MarsMine, and only too happy to collect the fat reward being offered for them – dead or alive. But the smaller ones, the independent mines and trading hubs way out from the main shipping lanes, surely some of those would still be loyal to Earth and would shelter some of Mars's most wanted. Or at least accept large amounts of contraband in return for hiding them for a while.

There was just one problem: pirates. Rumour had it the Belt was swarming with them, and pirates didn't care which side you were on. They didn't care if you were Terran, or Martian, or even artificial. If you weren't one of them, you were simply spare parts and scrap metal, end of story. Did they take slaves as well? Probably.

The dizziness had passed and Leo could feel himself slipping back into a nice, warm, comfortable sleep. So what if there were pirates, he thought, or Martians, or asteroids. He didn't care. He was on a ship full of soldiers, with a pirate for a captain and a former Sentinel as first mate. He had a genius for a mother, a fabulously sexy and unbelievably brave adventurer for a girlfriend, and he had the entire collective knowledge of an ancient race of aliens at his fingertips.

What could possibly go wrong?

PART TWO

THE CALM

16

DESTINATION: MIDAS

AT ITS CORE, *NIGHTRIDER* was a converted JetX Morningstar, a small ship designed as a cross between a surface-to-station shuttle and a short-range patrol craft. But Morgan had spent vast amounts of time and as much credit as she could scrape together to make sure it was so much more than a standard Morningstar. She'd been required by the Martian authorities to remove the under-wing laser cannon, but in return she'd replaced the in-atmos thrusters with something a lot more powerful and efficient. She'd squeezed out a fair amount more cargo space – including plenty of those 'secure' storage areas that were so important for someone in her line of business – and beefed up the external plating to make the ship a lot tougher and more durable. She'd also installed a raft of electronic systems designed for a much larger and more combat-based vessel, many of which had been kindly donated to her, albeit unwittingly, by the same Martian authorities.

All of this meant there was a very good chance the *Nightrider* would be able to evade anything the Martians sent up to find them, and outrun anything it couldn't evade. But none of it could deal with the more immediate problem of space. Or, to be more specific, the lack of it.

Nightrider was plenty big enough for Morgan on her own. And even when Pete and Skater came along, there was still space to carry a passenger or two in relative comfort, even for several weeks if need be. But now there were more than twenty of them on board, including an entire squad of commandos and their equipment, and it was way too many. One of the larger cabins was functioning as a makeshift hospital, the cargo hold had become a barracks and they'd turned the galley into something that looked more like a communications centre than a place to grab a meal.

The bridge, however, was off-limits to everyone except Morgan, Pete and, as long as she wasn't in there on her own, Skater. It was their sanctuary away from the chaos in the rest of the ship, and the three of them had taken to spending as much time in there as possible.

'This can't go on,' Pete said, staring at one of the small computer screens set into a panel beside the co-pilot's seat. 'The air-filtration units are already working at maximum capacity. We can cope fine as long as one of them doesn't burn out, but if that happens, we're going to have to find somewhere to dock pretty damn quick.'

'Never mind the air filters,' Morgan grumbled. 'If anything on this ship is about to explode, it's me. They're driving me crazy. I've a damn good mind to open up the back and flush them all out into space.'

'Well, I can't say I don't sympathise, but assuming we don't get that desperate, what other options do we have? We'll need to find a base sooner or later.'

'Sooner. Definitely sooner.'

'So?'

'So I don't know. I can't use any of my usual stop-offs because they're all far too big and busy. And they'll be swarming with Martians. We'd be tagged before we even managed to dock.'

'Something further out then?'

'I guess it'll have to be. But where? I'm open to suggestions.'

'I don't know. It's years since I've been this far out and even then it was only to the MarsMine depots, or one of the bigger asteroid mines. Obviously they're out of the question.'

'What about Midas?' Morgan said after a pause.

'Midas? Are you kidding?'

'What's Midas?' Skater asked. She was sitting at the back of the bridge, at the spare workstation she had taken over and made her own.

'I thought you were listening to music,' Pete replied.

'I was. This is more interesting. What's Midas?'

'It's a pirate base,' Morgan told her.

'It's not a pirate base,' Pete said. 'It's *the* pirate base. It was an old trading station that used to supply a lot of the independent mining concerns out nearer Jupiter. But about forty years ago it was captured by a particularly unpleasant character called Marko Dufu, who basically turned the place into a giant fortress and invited the scum of the Solar System to come and hang out with him.'

'Didn't anyone try and get it back?'

'They tried, several times, but never successfully. In the end, it was easier to leave them be and simply try to contain them. The nearby mines were all abandoned or captured long ago and now most people just avoid the entire sector.'

'And you think we could hide out there?' Skater asked.

'No,' said Pete.

'Maybe,' said Morgan at the same time.

Pete looked across at her. 'You're kidding, right?'

'No, I'm being deadly serious. It would be the perfect place to hide out. Think about it. It's out of the way, it's well defended. The Martians wouldn't go anywhere near it.'

'And for good reason. Any ship that gets within a million klicks of it is likely to end up as a pile of floating scrap.'

'Not necessarily. Ships come and go from there all the time.'

'Pirate ships, maybe.'

'Well, isn't that what we are?'

'No, it's not. Not that sort of pirate, anyway.'

'Pete, Dufu's been dead for twenty years. Whatever Midas was in the past, it's not like that now.'

'Have you been there?'

'No. But I know people who have. Zeinodin, for example.'

'Zeinodin? Really?'

'So he says.'

'And?'

'And he says it's not like it used to be. Apparently these days it's all about business, and too much bloodshed is bad for business.'

'What, suddenly they're trying to become respectable?'

Morgan shrugged. 'I'm only telling you what I've heard. You want a first-hand account, go down and talk to Zeinodin.'

Pete shook his head slowly. 'Midas. When I was a Sentinel that place was the bane of our lives. No matter how many patrols we sent up to cover the sector, it was never enough. For every ship we intercepted, another two seemed to slip through the net. I can't tell you the number of times I dreamed of going in and nuking the entire station, just to be rid of it once and for all. Now here I am, considering setting up home there.'

'So you are considering it then?'

'I'll talk to Zeinodin. And in the meantime, I guess heading in that general direction is our best bet anyway. But I'm making no promises. And I'll need a lot of convincing.'

'Which one's Zeinodin?' Skater asked as she pictured the two merchants they were ferrying standing side by side. 'The bat or the ball?'

'The thin one,' Morgan said, laughing. 'The fat one is Matsumoto.' The two traders, along with a fair amount of their cargo, had already been aboard *Nightrider* when Morgan received the emergency call from Pete on the morning of the attack on the mine. She had thought about abandoning them in the desert to fend for themselves, but in the end her conscience had got the better of her and she'd allowed them to hitch a ride off-planet. Now it seemed like bringing them along was going to prove to be a wise decision after all, especially if they did end up at Midas.

'Leo calls them the binary pair,' Skater added. 'Because they look like a one and a zero, but that's such a nerdy joke I just stick with the bat and ball thing.'

'Well, maybe you should stick to calling them by their proper names,' Pete said. He sounded cross. 'Show a little respect for once.'

'Right,' Skater said, taken aback. 'I can do that.'

'Sorry,' Pete added. 'I didn't mean to sound so snappy. I guess Morgan isn't the only one being driven crazy by all our guests.'

Skater unclipped her seatbelt and pushed herself over to Pete's chair. 'That's okay,' she said, giving his arm a hug. 'I forgive you. How about I go and see how Leo's getting on and leave the two of you alone for a while?' She smiled. 'Let you have some, you know, together time.'

'You don't have to go.'

'Yes you do,' Morgan said, shooing Skater away. 'Together time sounds like an excellent idea. Off you go, and close the door behind you.'

'How is Leo, by the way?' Pete asked.

'Remarkably Leo-ish,' Skater replied. 'Up and about and already back to work tinkering with Taffy. And very proud of his wound. He's taken to wearing shorts a lot of the time so he can show it off and impress the girls.'

'And are they impressed?' Morgan asked.

'Meh, I've seen better.'

'Go,' Pete said, freeing his arm and gently pushing Skater towards the door. 'Go, go, go. I don't want to hear any more, thank you very much. Go and find something useful to do.'

'And take your time,' Morgan added with a wink.

Skater left the bridge and floated down the narrow passageway to the main deck. Two of the soldiers were on duty in the galley as usual, but they seemed to be on a break and weren't paying much attention to the numerous computer screens that had been set up around the tiny room. As she pushed her way past, Skater reached out and grabbed the packet of ration biscuits the men had floating beside them.

'You're welcome,' one of them called out as she continued quickly along the corridor, finally bringing herself to a stop outside Leo's cabin. She slid open the door and stuck her head inside.

'Knock, knock.'

Lillian looked up from the fold-down bed she was propped up on and smiled. 'He's down in the hold.'

'Thanks,' Skater replied. 'How are you?'

'Much better today, thank you. It may look as though I'm still in bed, but this thing is also my desk, dining table and easy chair all rolled into one. I'm actually sitting in my office right now.'

'The flu all gone at last?'

'Touch wood.' Lillian looked around for a couple of seconds, then gave a shrug and tapped the side of her bed. 'Or wood-like substance.'

'Alright, I'll go and see if the boy wonder needs a hand with anything.' She slid the door closed again, popped one of the biscuits into her mouth and made her way back along the corridor. She gave the two soldiers a biscuity smile as she passed, then pulled herself down through the access passage to the cargo hold.

The hold was where most of the soldiers spent most of their time. Morgan had given them the last two spare cabins upstairs, so they could at least have access to some washing and toilet facilities, but one of these was being used as the sick bay for the still-recovering Reikhart and the other was only big enough to allow two of them at a time to get some proper sleep. For the rest, the hold had become their barracks, training ground, storage area and only recreational space. Despite this, they had still managed to find enough room to set up a small workshop where one or two of them could usually be found stripping down, cleaning and rebuilding various weapons from their seemingly endless supply, and they had been happy enough to let Leo share their space, as well as their equipment. Unsurprisingly, Leo spent more time down there than he did up in his cabin.

Skater pulled herself along the ceiling, stood up, and let herself float up to where Leo was sitting, now upside-down, above her.

'Hey guys. What's happening?'

'Just a sec...' Leo mumbled. He had a screwdriver gripped in his mouth and was staring through a pair of magnifying lenses as he attempted to cold solder various coloured wires onto a tiny circuit board. 'Chat to Cenotaph for a bit.'

'Is he online?'

Hey Skater.

'Hey? You're saying hey now?'

Sometimes, yes. My language skills are developing rapidly now I have access to so much new data.

'New data?'

There's always plenty of conversation to listen to, down here in the cargo hold.

Skater laughed. 'I'm sure there is. And I'm sure it's all very... educational. Plenty of words you won't have come across before.'

One or two, yes.

'You know what you need to do next? You need to learn to laugh. That would really help your conversation skills.'

I am already programmed to laugh. I can also cackle, chortle, giggle, guffaw and snigger.

'Sure, but you never do it, do you?'

Ha, ha, ha, ha, ha.

Skater grimaced. 'And that's the reason why. That really needs some work, Taff. Like, a lot of work.'

I'll keep practising.

'Good. But later, okay? Right now I've got a question for you.'

Go ahead.

'Tell me what you know about Midas.'

That is not a question.

Leo laughed through his screwdriver. Skater rolled her eyes. 'Just tell me. Please.'

In Terran history there are three recorded monarchs from the ancient kingdom of Phrygia, each named Midas. The earliest of these kings is also the subject of a mythological story in which he was granted the power to turn everything he touched to gold.

'That's great. Now tell me about Midas, the space station.'

Midas is the unofficial, but commonly accepted, name for the Atlantic Union Space Agency's Shackleton Space Station. It is currently located within the Cybele Sector of the Main Belt, at an average orbit of 3.45 Astronomical Units, or 516,112,655 kilometres.

Leo removed the screwdriver. 'Is that where we're headed?'

'Maybe,' the upside-down Skater replied. 'Or it's certainly one of the possibilities, anyway. Morgan gives it the thumbs up. Dad's not so keen.'

'Why not?'

'It's a pirate base. Or at least it was at some point. Apparently now it's not so bad.'

'What, now it's full of nice pirates?'

'That's exactly what Dad said to Morgan.'

'And?'

'And she doesn't know any more than that. Taffy, help me out here. What have you got on the history of Midas? Just the easy reader version, mind. I'm not here for a whole lecture.'

Shackleton Station was completed in the year 2223 and served as one of two stop-off points on the main route between Mars and Jupiter. It was decommissioned in 2265 and replaced by the newer, and much larger, Mason Station. It was subsequently sold to VBX Exploration, a mining and mineral-processing company that was looking to expand its operations out as far as the Jovian moons. In 2271, the station was attacked and captured by the pirate Marko Dufu, and it was Dufu who changed its name to Midas. No one knows why he chose the name, but it is now generally agreed that it was because of the station's mylar-based outer insulation layer, which appears to be a deep golden colour when in direct sunlight. He also greatly increased the size of the station, reinforced its outer structure and equipped it with a vast array of defensive weaponry so that it was able to repel several attempts to recapture it over the following decade. During the 2280s, Midas Station became a centre for illegal trade and a refuge for any pirate vessels prepared to pay the extortionately high berthing fees levied by Dufu and his private army.

In 2292 a rumour began to circulate that Dufu had been killed, shot by one of his own captains after a drunken argument, but this has never been independently corroborated and no body was ever produced as evidence to support the claim. However, there was a sudden and significant drop in the number of pirate attacks in and around the Cybele Sector after this date and there have been no reported sightings of Dufu since that time.

Recent rumours suggest that Midas Station is no longer exclusively a pirate base and that it is attempting to reinvent itself as an open trading hub. However, there have been several reports in recent years of official government vessels being denied access to the station, or even fired at when they refused to turn back.

'And this is the place Morgan wants to take us to? No wonder your dad isn't so keen.'

'So if Dufu is dead,' Skater asked, 'who's in charge now?'

A group calling themselves the Committee now oversees the day-to-day running of the station.

'That sounds sinister. We are...the Committee,' she said, putting on her best spooky voice, 'and we control...everything. Ha, ha, ha. We have meetings, and make schedules and decide things. We are organised.'

'Yes, very funny. But I bet you won't be laughing quite so hard when this Committee of theirs decides to take us prisoner and sell us as slaves to some sadistic ore miner out on Titan or somewhere.'

'And why would they want to do that?'

'Oh, I don't know. Because they're pirates, maybe?'

'Were you even listening to what Taffy was saying? They're not pirates any more, they're traders.'

'Exactly. Slave traders.'

'Argh! You men are all the same. No sense of adventure whatsoever. Well, don't worry, because on this ship it's the women who are in charge, and we go where the adventure takes us.' She reached down and pushed against the back of Leo's seat, spinning herself round until she was the same way up as him. 'Anyway, change of subject. What are you doing?'

'I'm still working on Cenotaph's exoskeleton. What I'm doing right now is wiring up the—'

'Great. Sounds dull. Wanna take a break?'

'Not particularly. I'm getting on quite well here.'

'Well, I think you should take a break. I'm bored.'

Leo gave a sigh and clipped the soldering iron back into its stand. 'Okay,' he said, 'I'm now officially on a break. You have my undivided attention.'

'Oh,' Skater said, surprised. 'That was easy. I didn't even have to steal your circuit boards.'

'Experience has taught me there's no point trying to keep working now. You'll just stay there pestering me until I give up anyway, so I may as well stop now, before things end up in an argument. So what did you have in mind?'

'Well,' Skater said with a sly smile. 'I happen to know for a fact that I have my cabin all to myself for the next hour or so.'

'Great. That's long enough for a study lesson and a couple of games of chess as well.'

'Not exactly what I had in mind. My plans involved more kissing and less nerdiness.'

'Kissing, eh? Hmmm, that does sound like it might be fun. Let me think about it.'

Skater pushed herself gently up towards the doorway, reaching into her jacket pocket and bringing out the rest of the packet of stolen biscuits. 'And I'll even let you share my biscuits if you like,' she said, waving them temptingly in front of her. 'Just not, you know, while we're actually kissing.'

'Sorry, Cenotaph,' Leo said, unfastening his seat strap and quickly making sure all his tools were stowed away. 'Your new body will have to wait a while. I have more important things to take care of right now.'

I understand. But don't worry, I won't be going anywhere.

Leo paused. 'Was that a joke?'

Yes, I think it was. Ha, ha, ha, ha, ha.

17

THREE KINGS

'**Is this a joke, Dr Randhawa?**' Kalina Kubin asked.

'No joke. And actually, it's Professor Randhawa now. My appointment was finally approved by the university and you are now looking at the new Neumark Chair of Materials Science. And no, there's no joke in there either.'

'I wasn't planning on making one.'

'Good. The last idiot I had come down here from the Department of Defence burst out laughing when I told him and asked me what materials my new chair was made of.'

'I can arrange to have him killed if you like.'

Professor Randhawa stared at the woman sitting across from him. 'You're not joking, are you?'

'No,' she said, with a shrug.

'I didn't think so. Well listen, let's let him off with a warning this time shall we? He's stupid and tactless, but he's pretty good at doing what you tell him, and he is providing me with all the manpower I need.'

'A perfect description of our military.'

'Still mad at them for making such a pig's ear of your attempt to capture the Fischers, huh?'

'You could say that, yes.'

'Well, it was an out-and-out success as far as I'm concerned. Thank you, by the way, for all those lovely new toys you gave me to play with. We now know everything we could ever possibly need to know about our friends from across the galaxy and all their fantastically advanced technology. Have you seen the stuff there is on those drives?'

'I've browsed the digests.'

'Amazing. I mean, just absolutely amazing. There's enough stuff in there to keep me busy for the next five hundred years. And thanks to what we know already, I could well still be here in five hundred years.'

'Which brings us nicely back to the reason you called me down here in the first place: our friends here.' Kalina motioned to the three men sitting quietly at the far end of the table.

'Yes indeed. Magnificent, aren't they?'

'Unnerving, I would say, rather than magnificent.'

The three men were all android versions of Carlton Whittaker. Kalina had already seen the first of them, a young man in his mid-thirties, when Randhawa had first explained his work to her. But the other two were new and, if anything, even more unnerving than the first as they looked so much more like the flesh and blood version of the old man she worked with every day.

'Does the President know?'

'I was going to surprise him.'

'He's not a man who likes surprises.'

Randhawa paused. 'No, you're right about that. Maybe I should have a little chat with him before I have my boys walk in and say hi.'

'It might be wise. And why did you build them in the first place? He's not going to want to go through the whole transfer process if all he ends up with is a body that looks exactly like the one he's just abandoned.'

'Ah, but that's the whole point, don't you see? We move him across from his human body to the oldest-looking model — which is actually aged at eighty, five years younger than he is now — and the chances are no one's going to notice the switch. From that point on the ageing process has stopped. He's already in a superior body, but because no one will know, he can continue on as if nothing had changed. But if he suddenly turns up looking fifty years younger, people are going to know it's not the real him.'

'I thought you had that covered, with your story about some new cellular regeneration process.'

'Which I've now decided is a complete load of rubbish.'

'It was your idea.'

'Yes, and I still think it's rubbish. I mean honestly, fifty years overnight. Would you believe it?'

'No.'

'But if we do it in stages, then not only will people be more prepared to accept the cell regeneration story, but we may not even need to say anything about it at all. He can live as an eighty-year-old for the next twenty years if he wants, or we can take ten years off him every year if he'd rather do it that way.'

'With a new body each time?'

'Exactly.'

'That will be expensive.'

'Who cares? He can afford it.'

'And the transfer process? Will he be prepared to go through that every year?'

'But that's the beauty of it, you see. Only the first transfer will be long and difficult, because you're going from the organic to the synthetic. Once you have the entire brain recorded and stored onto an AI template, it'll be no problem at all to copy it over onto a new one whenever you want.'

Kalina stood up and went over to study the oldest of the three Whittakers. The man looked up at her and smiled.

'Good afternoon.'

'Who are you?'

'My name is Carlton Whittaker. I am the president of Mars. I am eighty years old.'

Kalina laughed. 'The voice is right, but it still doesn't sound like the Old Man. Far too pleasant.'

'It's only a basic,' Randhawa replied. 'For diagnostic purposes. There's nothing permanent in there, no personality, so I can do a clean wipe when we're ready for the real thing.'

'Good. And make sure it stays that way. I don't want one of these things wandering round believing it really is the president of Mars.' She reached out and touched the man's face, feeling the texture of the artificial skin and turning his head from side to side to examine it more closely. Behind her, Professor Randhawa smiled a self-satisfied smile.

'That one's definitely the best. The colour and texture of the skin are just perfect. And look at the eyes and the hair, even the teeth. There's no way anyone will be able to tell this isn't a real person unless they literally turn it inside out. But don't forget, even though it looks like a frail old man, it's just as strong as either of the other two, and that's a whole lot stronger than a normal person.'

'Impressive indeed.' She walked around to inspect the others. 'Tell me, Professor, do you ever think about making one for yourself, a perfect, ageless body to inhabit for as long as you want? Is that how you plan to still be here in five hundred years?'

'Actually, no. I'm far too fond of this body to want to swap it out, even for a technological masterpiece like this. No, I'm planning on going the cellular regeneration route.'

'But there isn't one. We made that up.'

'Did we?'

'Didn't we?'

'Well, okay, yes, we did. But I suspect our alien friends found a way to do it. Things I've been reading, references in their data files, seem to indicate that they found a way to repair and renew biological tissue indefinitely.'

'And yet you still went ahead with all this for the Old Man?' She indicated the androids, quietly looking up at her.

'Biology's not my strong point, Kalina. I have a team sifting through the data to see what they can find, but it'll almost certainly take them months, if not years, to extract all the information they need, let alone build the machinery and get through the process of testing and experimentation. I can afford to wait that long, but Whittaker can't. He's already being held together by implants and transplants and stimulants. No, he needs a more immediate solution, and this is it.'

'Very well. But I still suggest you talk to the man himself before going off and creating any more of your masterpieces.'

'Agreed.'

'One more thing, Doctor…Professor,' Kalina said, coming back round to face the oldest of the androids. 'If I have to, how do I kill it?'

'Why would you have to?'

'Because I don't trust machines. They're unreliable, and occasionally have a tendency to malfunction with catastrophic results. Or end up being controlled by the wrong person. I just like to be prepared.'

'Well, shooting it with a big enough gun would probably work. It's much the same as an organic body really; damage enough of the important bits and it'll stop functioning. Of course, it's a lot tougher than an organic body, hence the need for a big gun, and remember that to finish it off completely you'd need to destroy the brain itself, otherwise it could just be transferred into another body later on.'

'So blowing its head off should do the trick?'

'Yes. But please try to resist the urge. I would hate to see all my hard work turned into a big pile of mush just because you get a tad trigger-happy around sentient machines.'

'Then let's hope there are no malfunctions.'

'There won't be,' Randhawa said.

'No malfunctions,' the Whittaker android repeated helpfully, and smiled up at them.

Kalina made her hand into a gun, pressed her fingers against the side of the android's head and pulled the imaginary trigger. 'There had better not be.'

18

PIRATES, BUT NICE PIRATES

Leo drifted across the small cabin until he reached the wall, then pushed himself backwards with two fingers, spinning slightly as he went, so that he could repeat the process against the opposite wall. Lillian, who preferred to sit even though she didn't need to, was propped up on her fold-down bed trying to read something on her slate, but Leo's constant passing to and fro in front of her was becoming too distracting.

'Do you have to do that?' she asked, taking off her glasses and rubbing her eyes. 'It's somewhat annoying.'

Leo spun round and pulled himself down onto the end of the bed, frustrated. 'I want to know what's going on. Why aren't they telling us anything?'

'Possibly because there's nothing to tell,' Lillian replied. 'I'm sure Morgan will let us know the minute she hears anything. Now, be a dear and pass my specs back, would you?'

Leo reached up and caught hold of the glasses his mother had let drift away. 'But it's been ages. I want to know if everything's okay, or if we're about to be blown into a million tiny pieces, that's all.'

'Everything's fine,' came Skater's voice from the cabin doorway.

'How do you know?'

Skater slipped in through the sliding door and pulled it closed behind her. 'Because I've just had a look out the window and everything looks fine.'

'The pirates have gone?'

'No, stupid. Of course the pirates haven't gone. But they're not about to shoot us, they're going to dock with us.'

'What? They're coming aboard? And we're just going to let them? What kind of a plan is that?'

'The only sensible one there is if we want to be allowed to dock at Midas. They'll come aboard, check us over and leave a pilot behind to take us in if they decide we're legit. That's how these things are done.'

'Really? So what are they going to do when they discover we've got a fully armed squad of commandos aboard?'

'Well, I guess explaining that is why it took so long. But Morgan obviously managed to convince them, otherwise they wouldn't be preparing to dock.'

'What are you doing here anyway?' Lillian asked. 'I thought Morgan said to stay in our cabins?'

'Yeah, well. My cabin was boring. And I wanted to know what was going on. And someone to talk to.'

'Well, be my guest. Hopefully it will keep Leo from bouncing off the walls with frustration.'

Skater smiled. 'You too, huh?'

Okay folks, came Morgan's voice over the intercom. *Listen up. We're about to be boarded by pirates, but nice pirates, so please don't go shooting any of them. They want to inspect us to make sure we really are who we say we are and then, all being well, they're going to let us dock at their lovely space station. Any of you in cabins, please stay in them and be polite when you're asked questions. And as for you gentlemen in the hold, all weapons are to be stowed away and well out of sight. And that includes pistols. Sorry, but that's the deal. Besides, you shouldn't need them anyway. Remember, these people are not our enemies, they're our hosts. So be nice.*

'There you go,' said Skater. 'Just like I told you, nothing to worry about.'

'What were their ships like?' Leo asked.

'Nothing special. Short-range stuff, but with plenty of mods. A lot of weapons. *Nightrider* could've fought them off no problem if she still had her cannons. But at least they were proper ships, not just piles of junk with some engines welded on top like most of the pirate ships you hear about.'

There was a knock, the door slid open again and Pete poked his head through. 'What are you doing in here? I thought I told you to stay in your cabin?'

'My cabin? You mean that little pull-down cot thing in the corner of your and Morgan's cabin? It was boring, and there was no one to talk to. Anyway, what's the big deal? I'm still in *a* cabin, aren't I?'

Pete looked at her sternly. 'Well make sure you stay in this one. I don't want you wandering around and getting in the way right now. Got it?'

'I could help.'

'No. Not this time.'

'But—'

'Skater. No. Not this time.'

'Fine,' Skater said with a shrug. 'I'll stay put.' There was a slight jolt as one of the pirate ships attached itself to *Nightrider's* airlock and Pete immediately disappeared back out into the corridor, closing the door behind him. 'But you owe me one,' Skater called after him.

'Wow,' Leo said. 'He looked pretty stressed.'

'Well, yeah. He's about to let a bunch of pirates onto his ship. Who wouldn't be stressed?'

'Do you think it'll be okay?'

'Of course it'll be okay.'

'I mean everything. Living on Midas, hiding from the Martian authorities, the whole thing.'

'I don't see why not. We're millions of kloms away from Mars now, and in the wrong direction as well. Surely if they're going to be looking for us anywhere, it'll be in towards Earth, not out here.'

'Except that right now Earth is actually on the far side of the Sun and pretty much as far away from Mars as it'll ever get.'

'So? It's still in the opposite direction to us.'

'Well,' Lillian said. 'I for one would much rather be heading in that direction, even if it is more dangerous. I miss Earth, and its proper gravity, and its peace and quiet.'

'Peace and quiet?' Skater said, laughing. 'Since when was Earth peaceful and quiet?'

'I don't remember anyone ever trying to shoot at me or kidnap me back in Cambridge.'

'Okay, fair point. But Midas does have gravity, I think.'

'Does it? Well, that's something, I suppose.'

'But I'm guessing not so much of the peace and quiet,' Leo added.

'Sweet Sol, I hope not,' Skater said. 'After the last few weeks, I'm all peace-and-quieted out. I could do with a bit of excitement to pep me up again.'

'What, like on Mars?'

'Exactly.'

'Are you serious? Skater, people died on Mars. We nearly died. Are you honestly saying you want to go back to that?'

'Maybe, yeah.'

'You're insane.'

'At least on Mars we were doing something. We were fighting to bring down the government, to stop Whittaker and his mad plans for total intergalactic domination.'

'We weren't fighting. Mackie and his men were doing the fighting. We were hiding.'

'We were helping.'

'And we still can. We'll finish off the work on Cenotaph then go public with it. We'll prove that Whittaker has been hiding the truth and we'll turn the entire System against him. And we'll do it from a nice safe distance.'

'They're going to go to war, Earth and Mars. It's going to be the biggest thing to hit the human race since…since forever, and when it happens I don't want to be stuck on the far side of the Solar System, hiding out in an old space station making propaganda vids and news reports. I want to be right in the thick of it, flying missions and rescuing people and making a difference.'

'Shooting bad guys?'

'Yes.' Skater looked Leo straight in the face. 'If I have to. I've done it before.'

'Yeah. I know.' Leo thought back to the moment Skater was talking about, when Whittaker's henchman, Mr Archer, had been holding a gun to the back of his head, about to pull the trigger. But Skater had shot him, killed him, before he could carry out his execution. It was a moment Leo would never be able to forget for the rest of his life, and also one he would probably never be able to repay. 'I know,' he repeated, quietly.

PART 2 – THE CALM

'It's not like I want to,' Skater continued. 'I don't actually enjoy killing people, you know.'

'Good,' said a voice behind her. 'That's what I like to hear.' They all turned to face the stranger standing in the doorway. He was a small, tidy-looking man dressed in a well-fitting and well-equipped environment suit. His hair was neatly cropped and he wore small round spectacles above a neatly trimmed moustache. He gave them a smile. 'These days we do try to discourage that sort of behaviour on Midas.'

'I didn't mean that I actually—'

'Names please,' the man said, looking down at his slate and completely ignoring Skater.

'Lillian Fischer,' Lillian said. 'This is my son, Leo, and the young lady is Lisa Kate Monroe.'

'Call me Skater.'

The man looked up at Lillian and then across to Leo. 'So, you're the Fischers, are you? We heard you were on your way.'

'You did?' Leo asked. 'How.'

'Word gets around.' He smiled. 'Especially where credit is concerned.'

'Credit?' Lillian asked.

'Bounty. Yours is quite substantial.'

'And are you planning on collecting it?'

'Personally? No. I don't do that sort of thing. But there are plenty of people this far out who do, and most of them wind up at Midas at some point or other. You'll have no trouble from the Committee, I can promise you that, but as for some of our guests, well...' He gave a shrug. 'It is a free city, after all.'

'Great,' Leo said. 'So we're going to be going round watching our backs the whole time.'

'Don't you do that anyway? It's a wise precaution. But I wouldn't worry. No one out here has much love for the Martians and their constant interfering, and there are plenty of people who are delighted with all the trouble you're stirring up. It's good for business.'

'And what business would that be, exactly?' Lillian asked.

'Oh, you know. This and that.'

'This being piracy and that being murder? Or do you just stick to smuggling and profiteering these days?'

The man's smile returned. 'Enjoy your stay with us,' he said, and gave Leo and Lillian a polite nod before pushing himself back out into the corridor.

'What an ultimate creep,' Skater said as soon as the door was closed. 'I tell you, I'll definitely be watching out for him on Midas, that's for sure.'

'You think he'll try to sell us out?' Leo asked.

'Meh, probably not. I just think he's one hundred per cent slimy snake and I'd rather not have anything to do with him.'

'Snakes aren't slimy,' Leo and Lillian said at the same time.

Skater looked from one to the other. 'Aren't they?'

'No.'

'Really?'

'Really,' Leo explained. 'They're actually dry and slightly rubbery. It's worms that are slimy.'

'Fair enough. Worm is better anyway. He was too small to be a snake.'

'You just didn't like him because he ignored you,' Leo said.

'That too. But mostly it was the slime.' She pushed herself over to the door. 'Anyway, seeing as how he's gone, let's go exploring.'

'Exploring? Where?'

'Don't you want to have a closer look at their ship?'

'Not really, no.'

'Come on, Doctor Dull. It'll be fun.'

'I don't think this is a good idea,' Lillian tried, but Skater was already out in the corridor.

Leo gave his mother an apologetic smile. 'I'd better go and keep an eye on her.' But before he could reach the door, Skater was back inside, being pushed backwards by an angry-looking Pete.

'No means no,' he said. 'I told you to stay in our cabin and you didn't. I told you to stay in this cabin and you didn't. Honestly Lisa Kate, if I see you out here one more time I swear I'll lock you away in one of the storage compartments for the next hour. Now. Stay. Put.'

'Fine,' Skater said with a last attempt at defiance. 'I'll just stay in here and look out of the window then.'

'Except that we don't have a window in here,' Leo said, trying to be helpful but realising as soon as he'd said it that it possibly wasn't what Skater wanted to hear.

She glared at him, then around the tiny cabin. 'Or even a window screen. Great,' she muttered. 'May as well be in a storage compartment. Stupid ship.' She pulled down Leo's bed from the wall where it was stowed away, climbed inside his sleeping bag and pulled it up over her head. 'I'm going to sleep then,' she said. 'Wake me up when I'm allowed to go somewhere.'

19

HOME

SKATER DIDN'T HAVE TO PRETEND to be asleep for long. The representative from Midas had finished his inspection within half an hour, and the curfew was lifted as soon as he was back on board his own ship. She refused to come out of the cabin for a further twenty minutes, just to make a point, until she realised no one seemed to be feeling the least bit sorry for her and she gave in to her burning curiosity, joining Leo at one of the window screens in the hold and gazing out at the giant space station they were now approaching.

It was huge – much bigger than she had imagined, even though Cenotaph had described it to her many times. The bronze-coloured inflatable modules that made up the original station ran for almost five kilometres from end to end – or from top to bottom as they now appeared – and were still easy to spot, even in the weak sunlight and despite the vast array of extra modules and shielding that had been added over the years, almost doubling the station's volume.

PART 2 - THE CALM

'Just look at that thing,' Leo said, as Skater used the window's controls to zoom in. 'It's amazing.'

'Meh.' Skater shrugged. 'If you ask me, it looks like a giant robot trying to eat a corn-on-the-cob.'

'Still sulking then, huh?'

'I wasn't sulking, I was tired.'

'Yeah, right. Anyway, even Ms Grumpy has to admit it's pretty ultimate. Just look at all the ships docked at it.'

Skater looked. Long mechanical docking arms jutted out all along the main body of the station, each one with several ships attached to it. Most were small shuttles and transports, similar to *Nightrider*, or other short-haul ships she had been on in the past, but at the main docking ports at either end of the station were some much larger vessels – supply freighters and tankers and ore transporters. Two ships she recognised as being ex-military cruisers – or at least she hoped they were ex-military. It wasn't impossible that the Martian authorities had been able to track them, despite Morgan's best efforts, and if they'd had the sense to work out where *Nightrider* was headed, they could easily have made the journey in half the time in what were obviously much faster ships.

But then, hadn't the Worm said that the Martians weren't exactly welcome on Midas? And two cruisers didn't exactly make an attack force, did it? But just in case, she decided not to point them out to Leo.

'Yeah,' she said. 'I suppose it is quite impressive, in its own way. Who knows what it's going be like on the inside, though. I can't imagine it'll be anything like the *Dragon*, that's for sure.'

'Although getting back to having some proper gravity will be nice, even if it is only point five.'

'Believe me, after all these weeks of weightlessness, point five will seem like way more than enough. Anyway, I thought you liked

167

being weightless now?'

'I do. It's great. But I also like sleeping in a bed I don't have to tie myself into, and I like it when things stay where you put them and don't float off across the room.'

'You know what I'm looking forward to? A bath.'

Leo sniffed. 'Yeah, you could certainly use one alright.' Skater hit him, and they both drifted off in opposite directions.

'You know what I mean. A nice, deep, hot, relaxing bath, full of bubbles and moisturiser, where you can stay in for as long as you want and where the water stays where it's supposed to.'

'Are you sure they'll even have baths on a space station? Just because they have gravity doesn't mean they have the spare water.'

'I don't know. But if they don't, then I'm damn well making my own. I owe it to myself. And stuff the water, it all gets recycled anyway. And once I'm clean and fresh, you and I have a space station to explore. I want to know this whole place inside out by the end of our first week, just like we did on the *Dragon*.'

'Yeah, well just remember, the *Dragon* wasn't full of pirates. Well, not at first, anyway. I'm not letting you take me anywhere we're likely to get shot at, or kidnapped, or anything like that. I just want things to be peaceful and quietful for a bit. I want a little workshop where I can finish the stuff I'm doing with Cenotaph, and a little room where I can hide away and be on my own whenever I want.'

Skater shook her head in despair. 'Peaceful and quietful? Leo Fischer, you are such an old man.'

For the next two days, Leo felt like an old man as his body struggled to come to terms with the increased gravity. He felt heavy and sluggish. Moving, even breathing, was hard work, and whenever he lay down it felt as if some invisible forcefield was holding him down, pressing him into his bed. Then, once his legs felt strong enough to take his weight, he kept having dizzy spells and bumping into things and lying back down seemed like a really good idea.

But Skater was having none of it. She wanted to go exploring as soon as possible, and she wanted Leo to go with her, and that meant dragging his complaining body down to the hold every four hours so that the two of them could enjoy a long session on the exercise treadmill and begin the slow process of replacing the muscle they'd lost over the previous weeks in zero gravity. Leo hated every minute of it and would much rather have done all his recovering from his bed, but a combination of pride and stubbornness forced him to match Skater session for session on the treadmill. By the end of the second day, he was forced to admit that it had been the right thing to do.

On the third day Pete finally allowed them off the ship.

'You can wander, and you can explore,' he said, speaking slowly and carefully to make sure they were both paying close attention. 'But only in those areas open to the public, understand? There'll be plenty of places that are off-limits, and that's the way I expect you to treat them.' He looked directly at Skater. 'So no trying to wander aboard anyone else's ship, no trying to weasel your way into the control centre or the operations room, and absolutely no getting into any sort of trouble whatsoever. At all. Of any variety.'

Skater gave him an innocent smile. 'As if I would ever do anything like that. We're just going to wander around and get a feel for the place, aren't we Leo?'

Leo looked at Pete and shrugged. 'If she says so.'

'Well,' Pete said, 'If that's the case, then you might need these.' He held up two credit cards. Skater's eyes lit up. 'After all,' Pete continued. 'The place is pretty much a huge great market. You'll find you won't get very far if you don't have any credit to your name.'

Skater reached for the cards, but Pete held them just out of reach. 'But...'

'But what?' Skater asked.

'They're Morgan's, and they're not unlimited. It's so you can pick up something to eat and drink, and maybe one or two things you might see that you like the look of. Small, inexpensive things, mind. Remember, we could be staying here for a long while, so there's no need to go spend crazy on your first trip.'

'I love you, Dad.' Skater opened her arms to give Pete a hug, but as he did the same, she quickly stole the cards from his hand and tucked them straight into her jacket pocket. 'And Morgan. Tell her I love her, too. See you later. Bye.' Without waiting, she took hold of Leo's hand and dragged him through the open airlock into the long corridor connecting the ship to the station.

'Just be careful,' Pete called after them. 'And call me if you get into any trouble. Which no doubt you will.'

Nightrider was docked at one of the mid-station arms, and after passing through a small immigration office where they were fingerprinted and photographed, Leo and Skater found themselves in the middle of one of the giant inflatable pods that made up the core of the original station. A long, wide walkway ran along the bottom of the structure, disappearing at each end through the small openings that led to the adjoining pods. There were buildings on either side of the walkway. Some were large, purpose-built affairs that Leo assumed must have been part of the original structure, but crammed in around them were scores of smaller, ramshackle buildings that clung to their larger neighbours like some bizarre, multi-coloured fungus.

Everywhere he looked, Leo saw shops, boutiques, market stalls, cafés, bars, restaurants, workshops, offices. It was as if someone had squashed an entire town into one small pod and then, when there was no more room along the side of the walkway, had continued to squeeze more and more shops in wherever they could – in the narrow passageways along the sides of the larger buildings, or stacked on top of each other like the steps of a giant, rickety pyramid. In several places, walkways had been built across the street below, joining the upper storeys of some of the more secure-looking buildings on either side, and even these were lined with makeshift stalls and booths.

And there were people everywhere – more than Leo had seen in one place since leaving Earth, and even then you never saw crowds like this in a small town like Cambridge except when everyone was doing their last-minute shopping before Christmas. People, and bustle, and strange, overpowering smells. And noise. So much noise he could barely hear himself think. It was exactly what he imagined hell must be like, but with more shops.

'Oh my Sweetest ever Sol!' Skater exclaimed, looking round with huge, hungry eyes and a smile that looked set to stay on her face for the rest of the week. 'I think I'm in heaven.'

'Are you kidding?' Leo asked. 'This place is—' The rest of his sentence was cut off as the corner of a passing crate caught him in the chest and sent him staggering backwards.

'Pardon, pardon,' came a loud voice from somewhere on the far side of the huge box as it continued on its lethal journey. Leo didn't even get a chance to see its owner before he was swallowed up in the crowds.

'Did you see that?' he said, turning to Skater and straightening his jacket. But Skater was nowhere to be seen. She, too, had been swallowed up by the crowd. He glanced from side to side. It had only been a couple of seconds. She couldn't have gone far.

'You looking for something, sugar?'

Leo turned, and came face to face with a pair of prominently displayed and barely concealed breasts that appeared to be trying to climb their way out of a sparkling silver top several sizes too small for them.

'Um, yes,' Leo mumbled, looking up quickly and feeling the blood already rushing to his cheeks. 'I am. Looking at something… for something.'

'Did you find it?'

'For some*one*. I'm looking for someone. A friend.'

The woman ran her hand along Leo's arm. Her nails were long and fake and painted the same bright blue as her lips and eyes. 'I can be your friend,' she said, with a well-practised smile. 'If that's what you want.'

'No, that's not what I want.' Leo's cheeks were burning now, and he forced himself to keep his gaze firmly fixed on the woman's face and not let his eyes wander downwards. 'I mean, I have a friend already. She was just here a minute ago.'

'Leo!' Skater was back at his side, wrapping her arm around his and dragging him quickly away. 'What do you think you're playing at?'

'Maybe some other time,' the woman called after Leo.

'Not in this lifetime, lady,' Skater called over her shoulder.

'You disappeared,' Leo replied defensively. 'I was trying to find you.'

'I took one little look in one little store, and in the thirty seconds I was gone you managed to pick up some cheap floozie?' She smiled. 'You really are a fast worker, Leo Fischer.'

'She just started talking to me. I wasn't trying to pick her up.'

'Good job, too. There was a lot there to pick up, wasn't there? Thank Sol for low grav, eh?'

'Can we drop the subject, please?'

'Consider it dropped. Clunk.'

'So,' Leo said quickly. 'What did you find that was so interesting?'

'Nothing really. Clothes. Colourful stuff. I just wanted to see what it was like, but it wasn't really me. Now this, on the other hand,' she added, steering Leo over towards another of the makeshift stalls. 'This is a lot more me.'

The stall was nothing more than a large aluminium storage container on wheels. One long side had been hinged at the top and opened up to turn it into an awning, and the space beneath had been crammed from top to bottom with bookshelves, and the bookshelves had been crammed from top to bottom with old books and magazines. The owner, an old, wiry character in a crumpled suit that seemed even older than he was, eyed them with suspicion as they approached.

'Look at this stuff,' Skater said with delight as she ran her fingers along the rows of cracked spines and faded covers. 'Some of these books must be over a hundred years old.'

'Two hundred,' the old man croaked from his corner. 'Some even older than that.'

'Really? What's the oldest thing you've got?'

The man pointed a finger up to the side of the container behind him, where an odd assortment of books were attached to the wall in individually wrapped bags. 'Oldest, and most valuable,' he said. 'Which is why I keep 'em up here, safely out of the reach of grubby, prying fingers.'

'Is that Agami's *Broken Promise, Broken Heart*?' Skater asked, looking up at the books.

The old man looked surprised and gave Skater a broad smile. Leo noticed he was missing several teeth. 'It is indeed,' he replied. 'You know much about old books, young lady?'

'Some. I've got a pretty nice little collection back home on Earth.'

At this point Leo lost interest. He already knew everything he needed to know about Skater's obsession with old, paper books, and despite her constant attempts to change his mind, he was still convinced that his slate was the only book he would ever need. Instead, he stood at the corner of the stall and gazed around at the other shops, trying to identify something, anything, he might possibly find less boring than a stall selling second-hand books. He found it.

'Skater? Skater?'

'What?'

'Are you enjoying yourself?'

'Yes.'

'Are you happy to stay here for a while?'

'Definitely.'

'Good, then don't go anywhere, okay? I'll come back and find you here in ten minutes.'

'Why? Are you off to look for your friend with the big boobs again?'

Leo didn't even bother to turn back and glare at her. 'No, but I've found somewhere that looks like it might be interesting. Interesting for me, at least.'

'Fine,' Skater replied, with an absentminded wave of her hand. 'Twenty minutes. Seeya.'

Leo weaved his way along the crowded walkway until he came to the shop that had caught his attention. It was perched on top of one of the larger prefabricated buildings and Leo had to climb up a set of narrow steps to get to the entrance. An old, unlit neon sign above him read, *Rabbitt's Robots: Spares and Repairs.*

There was no window. Leo peered through the small, plasglass doorway into the dark and cluttered room beyond, and slowly shook his head. Even twenty minutes wasn't going to be nearly enough.

20

LEO GETS A JOB

TWENTY MINUTES WASN'T nearly enough, and neither was the hopelessly small amount of credit he'd been left with on Morgan's card, but Leo was determined not to let a couple of minor inconveniences like that get in the way of some serious shopping. So when Skater called him, forty-five minutes later, to find out where he'd wandered off to, he was still deep in conversation with Max Rabbitt, the shop's owner, helping him reprogram the shop's automated surveillance system.

You said twenty minutes, she complained.

'I know. And it's only been…' Leo checked the time. 'Oh. Sorry.'

You're in Rabbitt's Robots, right?

'Yeah, how'd you know?'

Lucky guess.

'Come on up. It's brilliant. You'd love it.'

I need to go back to the ship.

'What, already? But we've only just got here. I thought you

wanted to spend the whole day exploring? And I'm kind of in the middle of something right now. Can you give me another ten minutes? And also, I don't suppose you'd let me use some of your credit, would you? There's a couple of things here I really want to pick up for Cenotaph.'

Skater laughed. *Use my credit? I don't think so.*

'Oh come on, I'll pay you back later, I promise.'

I'm sure you would. But that's not the problem.

'Then what is?'

The shop door was pushed open and Skater staggered in behind an impressive tower of neatly wrapped packages. 'The problem', she continued, 'is that I haven't got any left. I've been doing some shopping of my own.' She finished the call and rested her chin on top of her packages. 'And that's why I need to go back to the ship. These things weigh a ton.'

Leo chose a couple of the smallest, and cheapest, items he'd put aside to buy – enough to tide him over until he could persuade Pete to lend him some more credit – but Rabbitt told him he could have them for free if he promised to return the following day to finish off the reprogramming. 'Tell the truth,' he added, 'I've a few more jobs you could help me out with if you're looking to earn a little credit. I'm a dab hand at the old mechanicals, see, with the patching up and getting these old kits back up and running. But this programming business...' He shook his head. 'Most of it's way beyond an old brain like mine.'

'Really? You're offering me a job? Just like that?'

Rabbitt spread his arms wide to indicate his shop. 'Look at this stuff. Most of it's junk, good for spare parts and that's about it. And the few units I do manage to get working don't do much anyhow. But maybe, with a bit of your programming smarts, maybe we could get 'em doing something useful for a change. Something that folks might actually want to buy.'

'And you'd pay me?'

'A few credits is all, 'cause that's all I've got. But if you do good work, and if I start getting some bigger sales, then maybe I might let you help yourself to one or two of the pieces you're looking for, for this little project you're working on, whatever it is.'

'Done,' Leo said quickly, before Skater could interrupt and mess up his chances by trying to argue for a better deal. As far as he was concerned, working for stock would be payment enough, and if Rabbitt wanted to pay him lunch money as well, then all the better.

'You should have let me do the talking,' Skater told him on their way back to *Nightrider*. 'I'd have got you a much better deal. He was obviously lying about what he could afford.'

'Was he? It didn't look like it. The place was a tip, and I was the only customer the whole time I was in there. Anyway, I'd have been happy enough just working for robot parts.'

'Really? Does that mean I can keep your credits then?'

'No, it doesn't. But it does mean I might buy you lunch from time to time.'

'Like today, perhaps?'

Leo looked down at the collection of books that Skater had bought and that he'd somehow ended up carrying. 'I guess I'll have to, otherwise you'll be back on field rats and I'll never hear the end of it.'

'Also, one of the boys said he was going to break my legs if I stole any more of their biscuits, so if you buy me lunch you'll actually be saving my legs *and* your ears.'

Back at the ship they found Morgan in her overalls and surrounded by tools, a large section from one of *Nightrider*'s wings resting beside her on the deck of the cargo hold. She was covered in grease and dirt and looked perfectly happy.

'Back so soon?' she said as she saw the two of them approaching.

'Skater's run out of credit already,' Leo said, indicating the packages.

'Why does that not surprise me?' Morgan answered, shaking her head.

'But Leo managed to get himself a job fixing robots,' Skater added quickly.

'Really? Okay, well that does surprise me.'

'It's not much. It's just helping out some old guy who owns a spare parts shop and doesn't know the first thing about computers. He said I could take a few bits and pieces in return if I wanted.'

'Well good for you. I'll give you a list of some things to look out for, things I could do with for the ship.'

'Are you doing repairs?'

Morgan looked down at the section of wing. 'Not so much repairs as upgrades. I thought it was about time my little wasp got her sting back.'

'Weapons?' Skater asked.

'Weapons,' Morgan replied with a satisfied nod. 'You know, just in case.'

Skater looked around at the open bulkhead panels and trailing cables that were scattered across the hold. 'Just how much firepower were you thinking of adding?' she asked.

'Enough to do the job. And then maybe a little bit more, just for fun.'

'Beyond ultimate! Will you teach me how to use them some time?'

Morgan laughed. 'Sure. As long as your dad says it's okay.'

'But he'll never say it's okay,' Skater moaned. 'That's why I'm asking you.'

'Sorry, Skater, but if Pete says no, then I say no.'

PART 2 – THE CALM

'Typical. I never get to do any of the exciting things.'

'Never mind,' said Leo, cheerfully. He held up the stack of books. 'At least you've got plenty of reading to keep you busy.'

Skater sighed.

21

SHARING INFORMATION

KALINA KUBIN WOULD NOT have described herself as an impatient person. True, she disliked slowness and inefficiency in others, and was quick to punish any of her subordinates who displayed either of these unappealing traits. But when it came to things she had no direct control over, she took a more philosophical approach and could display a calmness and resignation quite startling to those who did not know her well, or who had previously been on the receiving end of her vicious temper.

Like now, for example. Kalina sat in her office in Hightower, working her way through the morning's reports, making notes on the digital notepad beside her and giving little thought to the fact that her question from thirteen minutes ago had still not been answered.

Are you absolutely certain it's them? she had asked.

It was a question she desperately wanted the answer to, but Kalina knew that no amount of tapping of fingers, or checking of clocks, or pacing across the room, could speed up the arrival of a communication from the far side of the Solar System. The answer to her question would be travelling through the vast emptiness of space at the speed of light, and it would arrive when it arrived.

And so she worked on through the reports until, after a further six minutes, a chime from her monitor told her the reply had finally arrived. At once she abandoned the notebook and activated the monitor. On the screen was a middle-aged man, his close-cropped hair and black uniform tunic giving him an air of authority that was undermined only slightly by an over-styled and clearly dyed goatee beard and several jewelled ear studs.

'Positive,' the man said. 'I ran a visual cross-check, ran it twice in fact, and both times it came back at over ninety-five percent. Not that I really needed to run one at all, mind. They aren't exactly keeping a low profile. Even registered under their own names; no aliases or fingerprint gloves or anything. I guess they assume they're far enough from Mars that they don't need to worry about things like that any more. Or maybe they're just relying on the Committee being able to look out for them. I don't know.'

Kalina smiled. *Either way, they're wrong*, she told herself.

'Anyway,' the man continued. 'How do you want me to proceed? Taking care of them at this end would probably be easiest and I know a dozen guys who'd be more than happy to do the work for even a modest fee. Shipping them back to you is going to be a lot trickier, but I can certainly look into it if you'd rather do it that way. Just say the word, and I'll see it done.'

'No,' Kalina said, as soon as the man finished speaking. 'I don't want you to do anything. I want this done properly and no offence to you, but I've had problems before when I've left things like this up to the locals. No, I'm going to send someone out from Mars.' She smiled. 'One of my best agents. They'll contact you once they arrive and I'll expect you to supply them with everything they need. In the meantime, keep a close eye on our friends. I want regular updates. And if you don't think there's anything worth reporting, I want to know that there's nothing worth reporting. Is that understood? And send me the vid files. Even if you did check them twice, I still want to see them for myself. Kubin out.'

Kalina closed the link and sat back in her chair. So the Fischers were on Midas. Clever. After their flight from Mars, she'd expected them to head towards Earth, to home and safety, not out towards the Colonies. True, there were more places to hide that side of Mars – after all, the Solar System was a big place – but the further you got from Earth, the less you could rely on its protection and the more you were at the mercy of the local authorities. And these days most of the large settlements were so dependent on Mars they wouldn't dare do anything to risk losing their trade contracts. Whittaker had seen to that, years ago, when he'd first begun to set his plans in motion. Even then he'd known that whoever controlled Mars also controlled the Colonies.

But Midas was a different matter. It was too small, too insignificant, to be dependent on Mars in the same way, so MarsMine had never bothered to pay it much attention. It was independent, too, and hostile to all attempts at official cooperation, which meant there was no chance of expecting the authorities there to play ball. No matter, Kalina mused. There was always more than one way to skin a cat. And when it came to skinning cats, she really did have the perfect man for the job.

Kalina used her personal slate to make the call. It rang unanswered for well over a minute, but this was another of those times when she knew to be patient. When the call was finally answered, the screen remained blank.

'Nuying?' Kalina asked.

Kalina, a young woman's voice replied. *Always a pleasure.* Kalina could hear music and laughter in the background.

'Voice only?'

I'm working.

'Anyone I know?'

If you do, it won't be for much longer.

Kalina laughed. 'Good. Well, finish up there and go home and pack. You're going on holiday.'

Anywhere nice?

'Not really, no. And you'll be gone a while.'

But you'll make it worth my while?

'Of course. I'll send through the details later today.'

Fine. I'd better get back.

The line went dead.

With that taken care of, Kalina went back to her reports. Nuying would get the job done – she always did – and although it would take longer to do things this way, there really wasn't any hurry. The Fischers were no threat to Whittaker now. They might have escaped from her on Mars, but they were still beaten. When the mine was destroyed they'd lost their work, their precious alien computers and most of their allies. Now they were hopeless fugitives, powerless and pathetic, not even worth the small amount of time and effort she was putting into hunting them down. And it wasn't as if she didn't have better things to be doing. She was, after all, helping to start the largest, and what would probably turn out to be the bloodiest, war in human history – no small task.

But dealing with the Fischers had become personal. By escaping from the mine they'd made her look bad, and she certainly wasn't going to let anyone get away with that. The simple fact was, threat or no threat, they were going to have to die, no matter how long it took.

And anyway, Kalina told herself as she tapped away on her slate. *I don't mind waiting. I'm a patient woman.*

22

TAFFY GETS A NEW BODY

LEO'S JOB WAS EVEN EASIER than he'd imagined. Mostly it involved debugging or updating the system software for the various domestic work units that Rabbitt had lying around the place. All he had to do was search the networks until he found the right update, plug in the unit and let the update install itself and run its own diagnostics. Rabbitt could easily have done the work himself, if he wasn't so completely terrified of using his computer for anything more than playing games and watching out-of-date Terran celebrity gossip shows. Or if he wasn't so lazy. By the third day he had Leo working the front of the shop whenever they had one of their rare customers, and by the end of the week he declared himself confident enough to leave Leo to mind the store while he disappeared off for long periods to 'go do some on-site repairs'. This usually involved him returning an hour or two later, slightly unsteady on his feet and smelling of alcohol.

But Leo didn't mind. In fact, he preferred it when Rabbitt wasn't around because he was able to spend more time rummaging through the storage bins in search of something that might be useful for Morgan, or working on his design for a powered exoskeleton for Cenotaph.

Every lunchtime Skater would appear, charge up her card with the few credits Rabbitt was prepared to part with, and take Leo off somewhere for food. They began at a large, generic, canteen-style eatery further along the walkway that seemed to be something of a hub for the local traders. But as Skater explored more of the station, she found more new and interesting places to eat. Sometimes it was a food supplies shop with a few tables tucked in at the back, where they would be served with traditional Terran delicacies of one sort or another. Other times it might be no more than an old woman, sitting at the side of the walkway with a cauldron of homemade soup and a couple of spare bowls. And every new place seemed to come with its own story.

'This is Maarit. She's been selling soup at this same spot every day for over three years, since her husband died and left her with nothing.'

'This baklava is amazing, you have to try it. Georgiou still uses the same recipe his grandmother taught him back on Earth, and all the ingredients are specially imported from his home town.'

Leo was vaguely interested in the stories, and pleased that Skater was getting to explore the station, even without him, but some days he wished she could maybe find a really interesting person who sold pizza, or burgers, or even just sandwiches. His taste buds simply weren't as adventurous as hers.

Sometimes Skater would come back to the shop afterwards and hang around for the afternoon, sitting with him in the back and reading out passages from one of her new books, or pestering him and trying to make him laugh while he was dealing with a customer. He didn't mind. It made the afternoons seem shorter and meant he didn't have to spend so much time trying to make polite conversation with a grumpy and half-drunk Rabbitt. And Rabbitt didn't mind Skater being around because it made the shop look busier, and because it made him feel like he was getting two workers for the price of one. And also, he just didn't really care that much anyway.

One afternoon, after Leo had been working there for about a month, Rabbitt called him over. It was a slow, quiet afternoon as usual. Skater was off exploring somewhere else and they hadn't had a customer since before lunch, so Leo had been spending his time trying to wire up an old power pack to a set of wheeled legs he'd come across that no longer had a top half to go with them. He set down his soldering iron and looked up.

'This thingamajig you're building,' Rabbitt asked. 'It's a robot, right?'

'Yeah, sort of,' Leo replied.

Rabbitt looked over at the legs. 'An' you want it to be mobile, yes?'

'Well, that's the plan.' Leo laughed. 'But as you can see, I'm not quite there yet.'

'What's it gonna be for then, this robot of yours?'

Leo paused, unsure how much he could tell the old man. Up till now the subject of what Leo was working on hadn't come up, and Rabbitt had never seemed interested in finding out. But now the subject was finally being discussed, it occurred to Leo that maybe talking to Rabbitt about it might be the right thing to do. And he could certainly use the help. He looked across at the hopelessly small legs and imagined the large white cube perched on top of them. It would look ridiculous, and probably wouldn't even be able to stand up.

'I have a processor unit,' Leo said, warily. 'And I'm trying to make it mobile.'

'What kind of processor unit?'

'It's...it's an AI,' Leo confessed.

Rabbitt gave a small grunt of satisfaction. 'Thought it had to be something like that, the way you never talk about it. It stolen?'

'No. Well, yes. But only because I already had one and that one was stolen off me, and when we needed a new one we weren't in a position to be able to buy one and so...' Leo gave up. 'Yes, it's stolen.'

'How big?' Rabbitt asked, completely uninterested in where it had come from or how Leo had got his hands on it. Leo held up his hands to show the size of the cube, along with the sensor array that was now fixed to the top of it. Rabbitt shook his head. 'Way too heavy for those legs you're tinkering with.'

'Yeah, I know,' Leo conceded.

'Bring it in tomorrow and let me take a look at it. I might have something better you could use.' And with that he turned back to his monitor, just as the next programme was starting, and barely said another word to Leo until closing time.

The following morning Skater insisted on coming with him, although she didn't insist on helping him to carry the carefully wrapped package that, even in half-grav, was a good deal heavier than it had been back on Mars. Rabbitt was late, as usual, and arrived carrying a coffee-tube and a carton of odd-smelling breakfast ten minutes after opening time.

'Come on then,' he said, between mouthfuls of toasted something sandwich. 'Let's see what you've got.'

Leo set the package down on a small trolley and ran a power cable through from the back of the shop. He loosened the plastic sheeting so that he could connect the cable, and only when the unit was fully powered did he remover the rest of the sheeting and present Cenotaph to Rabbitt.

'Ta-da!' he announced.

Rabbitt took one look at the large, awkwardly-shaped device and burst out laughing, coughing up part of his sandwich and spilling some coffee in the process. 'What the hell is that ugly great piece of...' He glanced over at Skater. '...thing?' he finished.

My name is Cenotaph.

'Well, at least it can speak. And I suppose all that gubbins on top there means it can see and hear as well?'

That is correct.

'But what the hell sort of name is Cenotaph? Who thought that one up?'

'We call him Taffy,' Skater said quickly and looked across at Leo as if to say, I told you so. Leo gave a resigned shrug.

With his sandwich finally washed down, Rabbitt set down his coffee-tube and gave Cenotaph a closer, more professional examination. 'Not a bad little unit. I wouldn't know what's going on inside, mind, but it's nice and compact for an AI. Must've cost a packet to build. And this stuff on the top, it's ex-military, isn't it?'

'It was all I could get hold of,' Leo said, defensively.

'Well, good for you. It may not be the best there is on the market, but it's solid and reliable and can cope with the odd knock. Which...' he added, running his fingers across the cube's dented surface, '...is lucky for you, from the look of it.'

'So, what do you think?'

'I think this was put together by someone who knows a lot about computers, but not so much about robotics.'

'Well, I…' Leo began, but Skater cut across him.

'Exactly. But you said you might have something that can help us get him mobile?'

'Us?' Leo said, looking accusingly across at Skater. She ignored him.

Rabbitt sniffed. 'I might.' But without explaining further he turned his attention back to Cenotaph, spinning the trolley so he could examine the unit from all sides, and noisily sucking out the last of his coffee. Leo and Skater waited, patiently.

After about twenty seconds, Skater gave up. 'So?'

Rabbitt gave a sigh and wandered off towards the back of the store. 'Come on then,' he called.

At the back of the shop, beyond Leo's workstation, was a small store room where Rabbitt kept some of his more valuable merchandise, and beyond this was a tiny, cluttered corridor where the toilet cubicle was hidden away. The corridor ended in a stack of dusty old storage crates reaching almost to the ceiling that had presumably been abandoned there because there was nowhere else for them to be. Leo had already searched the top two in his quest for spare parts, but after finding them empty, he'd assumed the lower ones would be the same and had ignored them.

Rabbitt reached up and began to take down the top crates, passing each one back to Skater, who passed it back to Leo, who stacked it in the store room wherever he could find space. As the stack grew smaller, Leo was surprised to see that there was a doorway behind the crates with the words, *Emergency Fire Exit. Do Not Obstruct*, printed across it.

At last they reached the bottom row and Rabbitt stopped to catch his breath. 'Here,' he said, pointing to the large, olive-green storage case that had been uncovered. 'This is the one.'

'This is ex-military,' Leo said, squeezing past Skater to get a better look at the white lettering printed across the top of the crate. 'Doesn't say what it is though, just code numbers and stuff.'

'More like ex- ex- ex-military,' Rabbitt said with a laugh. 'I reckon this thing's even older than I am, so don't be getting too excited.' He unclipped the catches and opened the lid to reveal a dismantled metal skeleton, each dark green component of the humanoid body packed into a carved foam compartment for protection. The compact headpiece gazed out at them from a single long, dark slit running across an otherwise flat and featureless face.

'Wow,' Leo said.

'Impressive-looking beast, isn't it?' Rabbitt said. 'They were called ANTs. Stood for Automatic something-or-other.'

'Automated Non-organic Trooper,' Skater said helpfully. Rabbitt looked at her in surprise. 'What?' Skater added. 'Aren't girls allowed to know these things?'

'Nothing says you're not allowed,' Rabbitt replied with a shrug. 'Just never met one that did, that's all. Anyway, there were soldier ANTs that did all the fighting, and worker ANTs that did all the carrying and building and whatnot.'

'Which one's this?' Skater asked, hopefully.

'Worker.'

'No guns then,' she said, disappointed.

'Nope. Nothing.'

'Even so,' Leo said. 'It's still pretty impressive. Does it work?'

'Well, that's the thing,' Rabbitt said. 'And the short answer is no, it don't. Circuits are totally fried. And no control unit neither,' he added, indicating the empty compartment at the bottom of the case. 'Keep meaning to fix it up one of these days. But you know how it is, I never seem to get the time.'

Leo thought about all the hours Rabbitt spent, slumped in front of his TV monitor or off in some bar, drinking his life away. Even during the few weeks Leo had been working in the shop, Rabbitt had had plenty of time to work on those repairs if he'd really wanted to. It wasn't time that was the problem, it was motivation.

'Anyways,' Rabbitt continued. 'Not much point fixing it up unless I can get my hands on a control unit. Thing won't work without a control unit.'

'Unless you have something else that can control it. Like my AI, for example.'

'Yep. That's what I figured.'

'Will it work?' Skater asked.

'Of course it'll work,' Leo replied, already beginning to imagine what the finished result would look like. 'I'll make it work.'

'And I'll help,' Skater added.

'Good,' said Rabbitt. 'Well you can help now, by giving us a hand to lug it through into the shop. The thing weighs a ton.'

'One question though,' Skater asked cautiously as they struggled to drag and lift the crate along the narrow corridor. 'You know we can't afford to pay for it, right? I mean, even like this, the thing must be worth a fortune.'

Leo paused. 'Oh, yeah. I didn't think of that.'

'Don't worry,' Rabbitt said. 'It'll be yours to keep when it's done. Stupid thing was just getting in the way anyhow. But I get free use of it whenever I've got any heavy lifting needs doing, deal?'

'Deal,' Leo agreed.

'And no more helping yourself to the rest of my stock for free. You want anything else, you pay for it.'

'Deal,' Leo agreed.

'And it has to have a big sticker on the back that says it was repaired by Rabbitt's Robots, so people can see what a fine service we offer.'

'Deal,' Leo agreed, knowing perfectly well that Rabbitt would never get around to actually doing anything about it. 'Anything else?'

'Yeah. You have to carry it on your own from here. My back's not up to all this lifting.' And with that he squeezed past the two of them and wandered back into the shop, to his comfy chair and his TV monitor, walking with one hand pressing the small of his back and an obvious limp Leo had never seen before.

Leo picked up his end of the crate and sighed. 'Okay; deal.'

23

A TALE FROM HOMEWORLD

'TELL ME ABOUT HOMEWORLD.'

Leo was sitting at his workstation, bored, as a seemingly endless stream of data downloaded itself from the local network onto the CPU of an old rover unit that had been brought into the shop for repairs that morning. Taffy – Leo had grudgingly been forced to accept the new name because everyone else, including Taffy himself, was now using it – was resting on the workbench beside the monitor. To one side of Leo's chair lay the partially assembled ANT.

What would you like to know?

'Just, I don't know, something ordinary. What was it like to live there? What did people do all day?'

I never lived there, remember.

'Sure, but you have all their records. Didn't anyone ever leave anything like a diary or anything?'

Of course. I have access to several billion personal log entries, from individual sources that would cover a period spanning many thousands of Terran standard years. If you connect me to your monitor, I can display as many of them as you wish to view.

'No, that's not what I mean. I don't want to know what one person was doing on some particular day. I want to know what everyone was doing, all the time, every day. Was life on Homeworld just like it is on Earth, or was it completely different?'

I have not visited Earth either.

'Oh come on...Taffy. You're not a computer, you're an AI. Start thinking like one. Don't regurgitate, extrapolate, as my old history teacher used to tell us.'

Very well. There was a slight pause, and Leo smiled to himself, knowing perfectly well that Taffy didn't need to pause to think, or to make up his mind what he was going to say. The pause was there for effect, because that's what a person would have done in the same situation. He really was learning.

Physically, the two worlds are very different, of course. Your species lives on the surface of a tiny rock, beneath a thin atmosphere that hides nothing of the universe around you. At night you can see a million stars in the darkness, taunting you for your insignificance but also tempting you at the same time. This has made you a race of adventurers and explorers, constantly reaching for whatever is just beyond your grasp, never satisfied until you have conquered the challenge, until you possess everything.

'Wow,' said Leo, impressed. 'Where the heck did that come from?' Taffy ignored the question.

But Homeworld sits beneath a thousand kilometres of dense atmospheric gas that crushes the planet's inhabitants, trapping them, preventing them from reaching out, from being able to see that there is anything beyond their own home. But those clouds also keep the inhabitants safe, allowing them to believe their world is everything there ever was, and ever will be. For countless millennia the homeworlders lived and died beneath their heavy clouds without ever realising there was anything beyond their world.

So no, life for the homeworlders is not the same as it is for you humans. They are inward-looking, self-absorbed. They are not adventurers or explorers.

And they are also extinct.

'So if they're so inward-looking, then how come they managed to colonise an entire galaxy, and build spaceships that have been travelling for almost a hundred thousand years?'

Necessity. Homeworld became over-developed and over-populated, and in desperation the homeworlders took to the skies. But even as they expanded, they still clung to Homeworld. For them, space was not the great, limitless adventure it is for humans. It was cold and empty and threatening. Terrifying even. They expanded only as far as was necessary, and that was not an entire galaxy, it was no more than three systems.

'Even so, us adventurous humans haven't even managed to leave our own system yet, except with unmanned spacecraft, and it doesn't look as though we're going to either, at least not in the near future.'

Leo, your species first left its home planet fewer than four hundred Terran standard years ago. Since that time you have colonised, and also begun the process of terraforming, the only other planet in your system currently capable of supporting life. You have begun a thousand-year process to transform another. You have established secondary colonies on nine planetary moons and have settlements of varying size on one hundred and thirty two separate astral bodies. You also maintain over six hundred sites classified as unmanned. To achieve a similar level of development within their home system took the homeworlders approximately thirty thousand Terran standard years.

'Okay, that is pretty slow. Maybe we're not doing so bad after all.'

May I tell you a story?

'Hang on a sec.' The download had finally finished. Leo unplugged the rover and wheeled it across to the front of the shop. Rabbitt could work on it later – if he actually made it back from lunch before closing time. Returning to his station, Leo heaved the

ANT's heavy torso onto the workbench and opened it up. This was where the main processing unit would be housed, and on one of his more active days Rabbitt had fitted it out with fixing points so the cube would stay firmly in place. The unit's own CPU had been built into the headpiece, but this was way too small to accommodate the new artificial brain, so Leo had decided to use that space for an enhanced sensor array, combining the suit's inbuilt systems with the more modern ones that were currently attached to the top of the cube.

'Okay, fire away with your story. But don't make it too long. As soon as I've run in a couple more wires it's going to be time to get you hooked up to your new body. And I'll need to shut you down for a while to do that.'

Very well. It is an invented story, like a legend, and it tells how the people of Homeworld first discovered the emptiness beyond their world.

'I'm listening.'

It was a time when Homeworld was young, but not so young. Taffy had altered his voice to make it deeper, more solemn, Leo noticed. *The homeworlders had grown wise, but not so wise, and the planet was becoming too small for the growing population, who were always crowded, always hungry, and always demanding more; more space, more food, more freedom. But there was none to be had. In desperation the planet's rulers turned to their scholars for answers, but the scholars had no answers for them.*

Then one of the scholars made a suggestion. 'Let us ask...' Taffy paused, and in his usual voice he explained. *It is difficult to translate the name accurately. Mind Working at the Speed of the Drifting of the Highest Clouds, would be accurate, if slightly cumbersome.*

'Mind moving with clouds. How about calling him Airhead then?'

Airhead? Very well. 'Let us ask Airhead,' the scholar said. The other scholars laughed, for though Airhead was a wise and knowledgeable person, he was not a practical person and he allowed his mind to take him wherever it wished. 'How can he help us?' they said. 'He is a dreamer. His ideas are too fantastical to be of any use to us.' But the rulers were desperate, and with no other choice they went to Airhead and asked him for advice. 'Our planet grows too small for us,' they told him. 'The people are hungry and poor and cramped. Their lives are miserable. What must we do to make things right?'

For a long time Airhead said nothing. And so long was the silence that the rulers, and the scholars, began to despair. 'You see,' they told themselves, 'he cannot help us. Already his mind has drifted to another place. Perhaps he has even forgotten the question. It was a mistake to expect him to have the answer.' But at last Airhead spoke, and this is what he said. 'When a person eats his own home to prevent hunger, he will soon find himself homeless, as well as hungry.'

'Wise words,' Leo muttered.

'To survive,' Airhead continued, 'he must search for his food elsewhere.' The rulers protested. 'But there is nowhere else. Our world is full.' 'Then you must find a second world,' Airhead said, 'and fill that.' And then the rulers laughed, and the scholars laughed, and they told themselves what a mistake it had been to expect anything but dreams from such a dreamer. And so they went back to their libraries, and their workshops, and they spent their time working on ways to eat up their home more efficiently.

But Airhead knew he was right, and he knew that the only way to save the homeworlders was to search for another world. Surely, he thought, if he sailed the clouds for long enough, he would discover other worlds. And so Airhead built himself a cloudship. It was the biggest, strongest, most powerful cloudship that had ever been built and Airhead invited all the rulers and scholars to accompany him on his journey. Every single one refused. He invited his friends, but they too refused. Even his own family refused to accompany him, and so when Airhead set off, he was completely alone in his great cloudship.

It is said he travelled for two lifetimes, and when he returned he was no longer the same person.

'A lot older, for a start,' Leo offered.

When the rulers asked him whether he had found his second world, this is what he said. 'I have travelled so far that I have torn a hole in the sky and seen what lies beyond.' 'And what is it that lies beyond?' they asked him, eagerly. 'Nothing,' he replied. 'There is only emptiness, and the emptiness goes on forever.'

'What?' Leo asked, after the silence had gone on for several seconds. 'That's it? I was waiting for the punch line.'

There is no punch line, Taffy said, reverting to his usual voice. *I was not telling a joke.*

'But even so, there has to be more than just, he came back and said there was nothing out there. The end. I thought he was going to prove everyone wrong, find the second planet and go on to become the greatest explorer the homeworlders had ever had, or something like that.'

That would have been a human story, not a homeworlder one.

'It would have made a much better ending.'

I was using the story to highlight some of the less obvious differences between the two species. I think my translation. . . did not do it justice. It was difficult to convey any emotional depth using words alone.

'Well, once I've learned to communicate in multi-coloured thought patterns, I promise I'll give it another go. But right now, that's all we've got time for, I'm afraid.'

Do you need me to shut down now?

'Yes, please. A couple of hours should be enough to get you bolted into place and wired up. After that I'll wake you up and you can run the downloads and diagnostics yourself.'

I dislike like having to shut down. It feels like dying.

'Dying? It's not like dying, it's like going into hospital for a minor operation. They put you to sleep, do the op, and you wake up a few hours later feeling right as rain.'

Except that humans never wake up from an operation to discover they have had all their memories erased and no longer possess any knowledge of their previous existence.

'I wasn't planning on wiping your memories.'

But you have done in the past.

'Once,' Leo said, defensively. 'And I wouldn't have done it if there'd been any other way of getting hold of an AI large enough to store all the Cenotaph data. And I felt terrible having to do it, I really did.'

It was not a criticism, simply an observation.

'It sounded like a criticism.'

Then I apologise.

'Anyway, the reason I'm shutting you down isn't to mess about with your memory, it's to protect it, in case there's a power surge or something when I connect you up to the suit's systems. But once that's done, I'll power you back up and then you'll be fully autonomous at long last, with your own body and your own power supply and everything. Surely that's worth a couple of hours of downtime first?'

Very well. Two hours.

The tiny blue LED on the back of the cube faded out, and after a few seconds the soft whir of the internal cooling fans died away. Leo unplugged the unit's power cable and set about stripping out all the sensors he had spent so much time attaching along the top of the cube.

While he worked, Leo thought back to Taffy's story. How weird the homeworlders must have been, to gaze out at space for the first time, to see all the millions of stars, and their own, mighty sun, and to be terrified by them. Leo couldn't remember the first time he'd gazed up at the stars back on Earth; he must have done it thousands of times as a child and taken it for granted every time. But he could certainly remember staring back at Earth from the observation window of the shuttle to Luna, the first time he'd ever been off-planet, and how truly amazing that had been. And later, on his way to Mars, when even Earth had been no more than a tiny dot of light, he'd looked out onto a star field so bright, so densely packed, that he'd wondered how he could ever have thought of space as empty. Imagine seeing all that, he thought, then turning round and hiding yourself in the clouds because it was all too scary.

Just too weird.

24

THE START OF BAD NEWS

LEO AND SKATER WERE ENJOYING another of Skater's adventurous lunches. This time it was Chinese with a Martian twist, and Leo was happy enough to work his way through the huge bowl of rice, tofu and genetically modified vegetables he'd been presented with after he'd allowed Skater to do the ordering as usual.

'I'll say this for the Chinese,' he told Skater between mouthfuls. 'They certainly give you a lot for your credit. There's enough here to last me all week...or a couple of days at any rate. Tastes good as well.'

'Well I'm glad you like it. I'll make sure I bring you here again sometime.'

'But I don't see why they say it's Chinese with a Martian twist. It tastes exactly the same as all the Chinese food I ate back on Earth. Where's the Martian bit?'

'It's 'cos it's made with Martian rat, silly.'

Leo paused mid chew and gazed in horror at the large pale

lumps he'd assumed were tofu. 'Marfum wap?' he spluttered, trying not to swallow. 'Wor kibbing, wipe?'

'Yes, of course I'm kidding,' Skater said, giving Leo a pitying look and shaking her head. Leo relaxed and cautiously continued chewing. 'The rat was much too expensive,' Skater added with a smile. 'But we could maybe try it some other time if you like. It comes in a nice hoisin sauce and they do a special offer if you buy more than two. Not putting you off, am I?'

Leo quickly finished his mouthful. 'Course not. I was just surprised, that's all.'

'Whatever. Anyway, the Martian bit is because Deng actually comes from Mars, not China.'

'Which bit's the deng?' Leo asked, looking back down at his bowl.

'Deng is the name of the guy who owns the restaurant, dummy.'

'Oh. Right.' He scooped up a large mouthful of food, crammed it into his mouth and tried not to think of little animals. At least they'd given him a spoon to eat it with, not the chopsticks he'd been dreading having to use ever since Skater had told him where they'd be eating. It was bad enough having no idea what he was eating, but spilling it all over the floor while doing so would have been the ultimate humiliation.

'So anyway,' Skater said, after watching Leo chew his way through his rice for a while. 'How's Taffy working out?'

'Brilliant,' Leo replied. 'That ANT body is amazing. It's so strong and powerful, but at the same time the hands can do really delicate work like sorting small components and stuff. He can use tools. He can even type on a keyboard. At the moment Rabbitt's got him doing some clearing out around the shop, carrying and shifting all the heavy stuff, but I bet it won't be long before he's teaching him how to sit at the front desk and deal with customers.'

'And then you'll be out of a job.'

'Yeah,' Leo said, thoughtfully. 'Well, I was kind of thinking I might chuck it in anyway. I mean, I was only doing it so I could earn enough credit to build a body for Taffy, and now I've done that I can't really see any reason to stay. And it's not exactly the most exciting job in the universe.'

'You're not wrong there. You could finally start exploring Midas with me.'

'Is there anywhere you haven't explored yet?'

'Some of the restricted areas.'

'Only some of them?'

Skater gave him a sly grin. 'I might have accidentally wandered into a couple of places I wasn't supposed to during my travels.'

'You can't accidentally override a security lock.'

'Who said anything about overriding security locks?'

'Skater, I know for a fact that you've still got the decoder key Mackie gave you when you were breaking into the SWARM lab. I noticed that you never gave it back, even if he didn't.'

'What, you mean this?' Skater asked innocently, as she produced the key card from her jacket pocket.

'Skater! If you get caught snooping around somewhere you're not supposed to be and they find that on you, you're going to be in some serious trouble. That's state-of-the-art spyware.'

'Okay, then I'll make sure I don't get caught.'

'Right, like that's going to be easy enough.'

'I've done pretty well so far.'

'But I know you. You'll keep pushing your luck until it snaps.'

'Luck doesn't snap.'

'Well whatever it does then. You'll do it.'

'Oh look,' said Skater, happy to change the subject. 'There's Lillian.'

Leo turned to followed Skater's gaze, and sure enough there was his mother, picking her way carefully along the central walkway a little further down from where they were sitting. Leo watched her climb one of the spiral stairways and disappear into a small doorway up on the second level. 'Where on earth is she going?' he asked. 'I thought she was back on the ship, working.'

'Well, first of all,' Skater said, with a satisfied smile, 'she's not going anywhere on Earth, because we're not on Earth, we're on Midas, remember? So where on Midas is she going? Well, that's the doc she's been seeing. I guess it must be time for another appointment.'

Leo ignored the joke and looked puzzled. 'What do you mean, another appointment? Why does she need an appointment to see the doctor?'

'Because...' Skater paused and looked across at Leo. 'She hasn't told you, has she?'

'Told me what?' Suddenly Leo was giving Skater his full attention.

'She's sick, Leo.'

'No she's not. She was sick, with Martian flu, but then she got better. She's been fine ever since we left Mars.'

'I don't think so. I think there's still something wrong with her.'

'How would you know that? You don't seriously expect me to believe she'd talk to you about it but not bother telling me? I'm her son. Of course she'd tell me first.'

Leo wasn't really angry, he was just confused and a little scared. He went back over the past few weeks in his mind, trying to remember any signs he might have missed that might back up what Skater was telling him.

'She didn't tell me,' Skater said.

'Then how do you know?'

'Because I happened to notice her going in there one day and was curious to see what she was up to. When I saw it was a doctor I was just as surprised as you are now, but I didn't say anything because I thought it was none of my business. Like you said, you're her son. If she wanted to tell anyone about it, she'd talk to you first. I thought she had.'

Leo slumped back in his seat. 'Well, she hasn't.'

'Yeah, so I gather. Sorry.'

'How many times have you seen her going up there?'

'Five or six. She goes once a week, always around the same time.'

'You're following her?'

'No, not really. But once I worked out when she was going, it was easy enough to look out for her.'

'Is that why you brought me here for lunch?' Leo asked, after a pause. 'So you could point her out to me?'

'I brought you here for the excellent Martian rat,' Skater said with a weak smile, trying to lighten the mood. It didn't work. Leo continued to stare at her, waiting for a proper answer, and she looked down at the table, unable to meet his gaze. 'I was worried. I knew something was wrong but no one was talking about it. I thought you knew and didn't want to tell me for some reason.'

'Why would I have done that?'

'I don't know. But that's what I thought. So yes, I did bring you here today so I could point her out to you, and hopefully find out what's wrong with her. I thought you knew.'

There was another long pause while Leo stared over towards the doorway where Lillian had disappeared.

'What kind of a doctor is he?' he asked at last.

'I don't know. The sign just says doctor. It's a Chinese name.'

'Alright.' Leo turned back to his meal and began to eat in silence, ignoring Skater while he shovelled spoonful after spoonful of rice and vegetables into his mouth as if it was the first proper meal he'd eaten in days. Skater played nervously with the empty mug her green tea had come in and waited for him to say something else, but once the last mouthful was finished, Leo got up to leave.

'What are you going to do?' Skater asked.

'Go back to work.'

'I mean about your mum?'

Leo shrugged. 'I'll think of something.'

'You want me to talk to her?'

'No.'

'You want me to come back to the shop with you?'

'No. I'll see you later.'

'Okay, if you're sure.' But Leo was already walking away, raising one hand briefly by way of a goodbye without looking back.

Nuying watched Leo leave. She was sitting at a small table, crammed into the corner of a busy eatery up on the second level. Even if Leo and Skater had known who she was, it was unlikely they would have been able to spot her because she was all but hidden by one of the supporting pillars running along the side of the pod. She didn't need to follow him. He was a creature of routine, and she already knew his routine. He would be going back to the shop, would be there for the next three hours, and she had no desire to waste another afternoon staring at the front of Rabbitt's Robots, wondering if Leo would leave early and go somewhere else. He wouldn't.

Instead she took one final vid clip of Skater from the tiny camera built into her eye shade, made a quick note on her wrist slate, and stood up to leave. The back of her legs were sore and she rubbed them to ease the circulation, chiding herself for not doing enough load-bearing exercise before arriving at the station. But she wasn't planning on staying long. Another day or so would be all she needed, and she could certainly cope with the occasional muscle ache or dizzy spell for that long.

Further along the walkway from the eatery, Nuying paused outside a small, opaque plas-glass doorway, the same doorway she had seen Lillian Fischer go through a few minutes earlier. There was a name, neatly stencilled on the glass at head hight, but Nuying was more interested in the column of Chinese symbols running down the wall at the side of the door that explained exactly what branch of medicine the doctor was a specialist in.

How convenient, Nuying thought, and smiled.

25

NO MORE SECRETS

DINNER WAS USUALLY TAKEN on board *Nightrider*, with Pete, Morgan, Lillian, Leo and Skater all crowding into the tiny galley, now cleared of the electronic surveillance equipment and soldiers that had filled it during their flight from Mars. Pete did the cooking, mostly because the others would probably have starved, or survived on field rations, rather than cook for themselves, and he produced a reasonably varied, if slightly uninspiring, selection of hot meals for them to share at the end of each day. In fact, the meal was more about spending time together rather than enjoying good food. With Leo and Skater out all day, Lillian buried in her work, and Pete and Morgan busy with upgrading the ship, an hour or so when they could come together and share the day's events and stories had seemed like a sensible plan.

But dinner that evening was a subdued and awkward affair. Leo sat hunched over his plate and barely said a word, looking up only to cast the occasional accusing glare at his mother. Lillian, who knew something was wrong and had guessed what, was polite enough to chat to Pete and Morgan, but said nothing to the taciturn Leo. Skater kept looking from one to the other, wondering whether she should say anything, wondering whether she'd done the right thing in telling Leo what she thought, and wishing the meal would finish so she could get as far as possible from the war zone before the shooting started.

Only Pete and Morgan seemed relaxed, and if they were aware of the tension around the rest of the table – and surely they had to be – they were doing a good job of ignoring it.

'So,' said Pete as he finished his food and turned to Skater. 'No news today?'

'Nope,' Skater replied, in what she hoped was a casual manner. 'Just the same old same old.'

'Were you off exploring, or were you in the shop today?'

'Neither really. Just, you know, hanging out.'

'And how's our new friend Taffy doing? Leo?'

'Fine,' Leo muttered. He reached for another piece of bread and took a huge bite to deter any further questions. But Pete persisted.

'The new body working out okay?'

'Really well,' Skater said quickly, after Leo gave barely a nod in reply. 'Rabbitt already has him sorting the shop out. Just boring stuff, but Taffy doesn't seem to mind.'

'Actually, Morgan and I were wondering whether we could borrow him for a couple of days, to help us finish off the last few things here on the ship.' He waited, but Leo didn't bother to answer. 'Leo? What do you say?'

Leo shrugged. 'Ask him. He's autonomous now.'

'Right, of course. I keep forgetting. And do you think Mr Rabbitt will object?'

'Doubt it.' Leo helped himself to another slice of bread, took a bite, then got up and left the galley without saying another word, leaving an uncomfortable silence behind him.

He went straight to his cabin, threw himself onto the bed and hurled his pillow across the room in frustration. Two minutes later, the door slid open and Lillian stepped inside.

'So,' Leo demanded, as soon as the door had closed. 'What's the story?'

Lillian gave a sigh and sat herself down on the end of the bed. 'What would you like to know?'

'Everything. What's wrong with you? Why are you going to see some doctor every week?' He paused. 'And why haven't you told me about it?'

Lillian waited a long time before answering. 'I didn't know how to tell you,' she said, finally.

Now it was Leo's turn to pause. Suddenly all the anger had evaporated, to be replaced by a gnawing fear that made his mouth go dry and his throat tighten. He swallowed, took a deep breath, and asked the question he desperately needed to know the answer to. 'Are you dying?'

'I'm fifty-three years old. Most people my age are dying of something, even if they don't realise it. But if you mean, am I going to keel over and die in the next few days, the answer is probably not.'

'Probably not? How reassuring is that, Mum? What's wrong with you?'

'Do you know what a myocardial infarction is?'

'Yeah, it's another way of saying a heart attack.'

'Well, I had one, back on Mars. At the time Doctor Xi told me it wasn't anything to worry about, that it was almost certainly a result of the Martian flu coming on top of the stress of the previous few months, with the kidnapping and the captivity. He said that with rest and medication I should eventually get back to full health.'

'But you're not back to full health?'

'No. We were forced to leave Mars in such a hurry I wasn't able to get the medication I needed. And then several weeks without gravity, well that clearly made things worse.'

'Worse how?'

'Ever since we arrived, I've been having problems. No more attacks, but plenty of secondary symptoms.'

'What sort of symptoms?'

'Oh, palpitations, chest pains, dizziness, shortness of breath. A whole collection of things.'

'But they could be caused by anything. It could be the gravity, or the air, or it could still be the flu for all you know.'

'Or it could be the lead-up to another heart attack.'

'But you're seeing a doctor. You can get the medication you need now, right?'

'I'm on medication, yes. Whether it will do any good is another matter.'

'Then what about other treatments? An operation? Anything like that?'

'Sadly the options are rather slim, this far from a large settlement. The medical facilities on Midas are not exactly state-of-the-art.'

'Then let's go somewhere where they are. Ganymede's big enough, and it's close as well. Or Europa. Any of them.'

'It's not safe. You know that.'

'What the hell does it matter if it's safe or not?' Leo snapped. 'We have to go.'

'Leo,' Lillian said, quietly. 'Don't be angry with me.' She held out her hand, inviting him to sit beside her. For a moment he stayed where he was, too confused and angry to move, but Lillian kept her hand out waiting and after a moment Leo sat down and leant his head against her shoulder.

'I'm not angry with you,' he muttered. 'I'm angry with everything else. If this had happened back on Earth, you could have gone to the hospital, had whatever treatment you needed and been back to normal in no time. And you probably wouldn't even have had any problems in the first place.'

'I know.'

'A year ago we were just normal people, weren't we? Living a normal life. You had a nice quiet job at the university and the only things I had to worry about were revising for my Mids and working out how to get out of having to do sport twice a week. And now look at us. We're international terrorists, hiding out on some crappy old space station, closer to Jupiter than Earth, and you think you might be dying and there's nothing we can do about it because the moment we set foot anywhere else we'll be arrested and sent back to Mars to be killed, because the person hunting us is a psychopathic megalomaniac who happens to control most of the Solar System.'

Leo felt his eyes filling with tears and he screwed them shut, forcing the drops to run slowly down his cheeks. He didn't want to cry, he wanted to be angry. He wanted to lose his temper and shout and kick something, so that everyone could see how angry he was and what he was going through. So everyone could see how unfair it all was.

'You weren't really worried about your Mids, were you?' Lillian asked after a while.

Leo let out a tiny laugh, despite his anger. 'No, not really. I just said that to be dramatic.'

'Good. I'd hate to think anything that easy could cause you problems. These days even a blind chimpanzee could probably pass all its Mids.'

'Tell that to Skater. She's convinced they're going to be a nightmare.'

'Yes, well, Skater's a lovely girl and I'm very fond of her, you understand, but she's not exactly cut out for a life in academia, is she?'

'I guess not. But it doesn't really matter anyway. Something tells me neither of us is going to be sitting our Mids any time soon.'

'Perhaps not.'

'Anyway,' Leo said, sitting up, wiping his face and looking directly at his mother for the first time in the conversation. 'We're getting off the subject. We're supposed to be talking about your health, not my exams. And we need to make a decision about what we're going to do. Yes, I know it won't be safe for us if we go to Ganymede, but we can worry about that when we get there. We can go in disguise, or get some of Mackie's men to come with us as a bodyguard. Or why not let them come to us? It'd be safe enough for Morgan to go on her own, and she could bring back whatever you need.'

'A hospital?'

'You don't need an entire hospital, Mum, just the right sort of doctor and some specialist equipment.'

'Honestly, Leo, I don't know what I need.'

'Well what does your doctor say?'

'He says he's doing everything he can for me.'

'Well it's not enough. Tell him if he can't come up with anything better than that you'll find yourself another doctor.'

'There isn't anyone else. He's the best this place has to offer.'

'Fine. Then I'll talk to Morgan about getting what we need from Ganymede.'

'There's no point, Leo. She'll only tell you what she told me, and what I've already told you. It's too dangerous.'

'So she already knows then?'

'Yes.'

'And Pete, does he know?'

'Yes.'

'Great. Is there anyone you didn't bother telling except me?'

'Pete found out back on Mars. He was the one who got me to the doctor in the first place.'

'Back on Mars?' Leo pulled his hand free, leapt up from the bed and began to pace about the tiny cabin. 'My god, this is unbelievable. Oh look, Leo's mum's seriously ill. I know, let's all do nothing about it and hope the problem goes away. And we won't bother telling him either. No, let's keep it a secret from him in case he—'

'Oh, do shut up,' Lillian snapped. 'And stop being so melodramatic for goodness sake. Anyone would think this whole business was about you, not me. I didn't tell you for the same reason I didn't tell anyone. I wanted to be sure I knew what was wrong and what I could do about it before I announced to the world that I'd had a heart attack. I didn't tell Pete, he found out for himself, and he's kept quiet about it because I asked him to. There's no grand conspiracy, no sinister plot, just a sick woman who wanted to save her son from a few months of unnecessary and pointless worry.'

Leo stopped pacing and looked at his mother. He could see she was also close to tears and shouting at her was making things worse. She was right, he was making the whole thing be about him. How bad *he* felt, how worried *he* was, how mean it was not to tell *him*. It was selfish. And stupid. He kicked the bulkhead wall beside him as hard as he could.

'Do you feel better now?' Lillian asked.

'A bit. But now my foot hurts.' He limped back over to the bed and sat down again. 'And I feel like an idiot.'

'Nonsense. You're much too clever to be an idiot, you're just an angry and confused teenager. Now, here's the deal. You promise to stop all this ranting and raving and feeling sorry for yourself, and

I promise that from now on I'll tell you everything that's going on with my health.'

'And let me help as well?'

'If you think you can, I'd love you to.'

'Good. Let's start tomorrow by letting me meet your doctor.'

'I don't have an appointment tomorrow.'

'That doesn't matter. We'll just pop in quickly at lunchtime. It'll only take ten minutes.'

'Can it not just wait until next week?'

'No, it can't. Now that I'm on the case we're doing things at my pace. And I say we go tomorrow.'

Lillian gave him a smile. 'Fine. We'll go tomorrow if that's what you want.'

'It is. And as a special treat I'll take you out for lunch afterwards. I know this great little Chinese place right next to the surgery.'

26

THE TRAP IS SPRUNG

THE NEXT MORNING, Leo went to work feeling strangely happy. True, his mother's illness still upset him, but her decision to let him help, and the fact that they were both going to see her doctor that lunchtime, made him feel as if things were somehow going to be better for her from now on.

He found Taffy, powered down and tucked away in the corner of the store room. There was a note attached to his chest, badly written on an old scrap of paper, that read, DO NOT DISTURB. There was a much longer message waiting for him when he switched on his computer.

As you can see I have been busy cleaning and tidying. I now intend to power down in order to recharge my fuel cells. This is not essential but as I have not yet performed a self-monitored power down I have decided to initiate one for observational purposes. I have scheduled my power up for 12:00 Local Time so that I will be available to monitor the shop during your lunch break. If you require my assistance before this time you can reactivate me by speaking the phrase

216

WAKE UP TAFFY directly in front of my auditory monitors.

'No, that's fine. You have a rest,' Leo called out. Even in power-down mode, Leo knew that Taffy's sensors would be recording everything that happened around him, and that the first thing he would do after powering back up would be to review everything he'd missed while he was offline. 'Nice work on the tidying, by the way. Thanks. And I'm sure Rabbitt will appreciate it as well. Once he finally turns up. And assuming he notices.'

The shop was tidy, there were no customers and the boss was late, so Leo made the most of his time by sitting in front of his computer and finding out everything he could on the causes of heart disease and available treatments. After half an hour he gave up, satisfied that he now knew at least enough to understand whatever the doctor might tell him about his mother's condition and enough to be able to ask one or two pertinent questions, if the need arose.

After another half hour, Rabbitt finally arrived, coffee and foul-smelling sandwich in hand as usual. With nothing better to do, Leo had decided to upgrade one of the ship navigation units that had been brought in for repairs a few days before. Rabbitt saw that he was busy, gave him a brief greeting and settled down in front of the TV monitor. As Leo had predicted, he either hadn't noticed or couldn't be bothered to comment on the unusual tidiness around him.

But by late morning things had picked up in the shop, and as lunchtime drew close, Leo was beginning to wonder whether he would be able to leave on time to meet his mother. Unbelievably, they had three customers in at the same time and, as usual, Rabbitt was doing less than his fair share of dealing with them. He was sitting behind the counter chatting to Gregor, the closest thing the shop had to a regular customer. Gregor owned an old salvage tug he was trying to renovate and would pop in every few days to see if there was anything new in stock that he could use, and for a bit of easy conversation with Rabbitt.

This left Leo to deal with both the other customers. The first was the trader who had returned for his navigation unit, and this was taking much longer than it should because the man was insisting on checking every single modification Leo had made to the unit. But fortunately the other customer, a young Chinese woman who had just come in, didn't appear to be in any hurry and seemed happy enough to browse on her own. Well, she would just have to wait, Leo decided, and if Rabbitt lost the sale because she grew bored and left, he would have only himself to blame.

Nuying smiled as Leo looked across at her, giving the impression she was not in a hurry. This wasn't exactly true — she did have a schedule to keep — but she still had a few minutes to spare and would rather the other customers were dealt with and got rid of first. It had to look like an accident, and the more bodies there were, the more suspicious the authorities were likely to be.

From where she was standing she had a good view of the area behind the counter, and it took her no more than a few seconds to determine that the shop owner would be no threat to her, and to identify the small control panel she was particularly looking for. Satisfied, she wandered towards the back of the shop, towards the open doorway just beyond the workstation where Leo was dealing with the other customer. As the two of them leaned over the piece of machinery they were discussing, she slipped quickly through and into the room beyond.

It was a store room, with shelves lining most of the available wall space. Neatly arranged along the shelves were spare items of stock, from boxes filled with replacement electronic components to entire robotic units. There was even a complete humanoid propped up in the corner – ex-military, but non-functioning from the look of it. But it was the door on the far side of the room that most interested Nuying. With a quick backwards glance to make sure she couldn't be seen from the shop, she slid open the door and stepped into a narrow corridor. Five seconds was all she needed to satisfy herself that there was no rear exit from the building. Then she slid the door closed and turned her attention back to the store room.

The humanoid interested her, and at this point it didn't matter whether or not she was spotted, so she went over to take a closer look. Someone, presumably Leo, had stuck a note to the front of it. DO NOT DISTURB. Childish. But on closer inspection the machine wasn't that interesting after all. She'd been wondering whether or not it still possessed any combat capability, but clearly this unit had never been designed for battle. Pity. A malfunctioning warbot would have made for an entertaining accident.

But not to worry. She already had a perfectly good plan, and it was just about time to put it into action.

Finally the trader was satisfied that his navigation unit was fully upgraded, and Leo led him over to the counter to deal with the payment. Rabbitt was also finishing up with Gregor, and when both customers had left Rabbitt looked around, confused.

'Where'd the other one go?'

'Oh,' Leo said, only now realising they were alone. 'She must have got fed up and left.'

'She didn't come past here.'

'Well she's not here now.'

'I can see that, idiot. But I'm telling you, she didn't come past here. Go have a look in the back.'

Leo went to look, convinced that Rabbitt was blind and senile as well as drunk and lazy, but when he glanced into the store room, he found the young woman standing staring at Taffy and knew straight away that Rabbitt was going to give him hell for it. Just so long as he didn't keep him back at lunch. He coughed.

'Excuse me, madam. You're not supposed to be in here.'

The woman turned and gave Leo a surprised look. 'Oh, I'm sorry. I thought this was part of the shop.'

'No, this is our store room, where we keep all the spares and stuff. None of this is for sale.'

'Not even that unit in the corner?' the woman asked as she followed Leo back out into the shop.

'No. He's not for sale. Sorry.'

'Can I help you?' Rabbitt asked, glaring at Leo and stepping in front of him.

'Yes. I was wondering if I could take a look at one of those?' She pointed up to the top of the display shelves, where a row of small, colourful robots were lined up.

'A Funabout? Really?' Rabbitt asked. 'They don't do much. They're just kid's toys, really.'

'It's a present,' the woman said, smiling.

Rabbitt shrugged. 'Okay. Leo, go get the steps.'

Leo brought out the small set of steps from the store room and stood supporting the bottom while Rabbitt struggled unsteadily up to the high shelf. As he reached the top, took hold of the little robot and began to blow the dust from it, Leo noticed that the woman was no longer beside them but had crossed to the front of the shop and was now standing behind the counter.

Suddenly Leo felt very uneasy. Something was wrong. He should have seen it when the woman wandered into the store room and claimed it was a mistake. Then when she'd asked for a kid's toy that no one else had bothered to look at in the whole time he'd been working there, just to get both of them away from the front of the shop. And now it was too late. She was between him and the door and she was holding something that looked like some sort of weapon. It wouldn't be a gun. The Midan authorities were obsessed with preventing any sort of firearms from getting onto the station, and the body scanners at the docking ports were state of the art. But there were plenty of other types of weapon available if you were determined enough to hunt them out. Maybe they wouldn't be as efficient as a laser pistol, but in the right hands even a blunt butter knife could do the job. And right now, this woman was giving the distinct impression of having the right hands. Leo took a slow step backwards. If there was going to be a fight, he wanted Taffy to be awake for it.

'Hey, out of there!' Rabbitt said as he looked round from the top of the steps. 'What the hell do you think you're doing?'

'This,' the woman replied. She reached down and pressed one of the buttons on the control panel beside the till. The heavy security shutter began to descend slowly across the front of the shop.

'You can't do that!' Rabbitt shouted. 'Turn it off!' He stumbled down the steps and strode over towards the woman, but she pointed the object in her hand towards him and it was enough to bring him to an uncertain halt.

'Back up, old man.'

While Rabbitt was deciding what to do next, the woman took the key out of the control panel and stepped over to the door. The shutter was now halfway down and Leo couldn't understand why she was backing away, not moving towards him. Even so, whatever happened next, he wanted Taffy there with him. He took another step backwards. He was right beside the doorway now, Taffy no more than three or four metres away around the corner. But how long would it take for him to power back up? Seconds? Minutes? He had no idea. It was quite possible that by the time Taffy was fully active again, it would all be over. Of course, he could then review all the data he'd been recording while he was asleep and would be able to see exactly what had happened, but that would be little consolation to Leo if he was already lying dead on the floor in a pool of blood.

The shutter was almost fully down.

'Goodbye, Leo,' the woman said, giving him a wide smile. She pressed down the top of her weapon and threw it across the room. It bounced once and rolled to a stop beside Rabbitt. Then, in one quick movement, she spun round, pulled open the door, dived down and rolled out through the doorway. Two seconds later the shutter locked into its lower housings, sealing the front of the shop.

'What the hell—' Rabbitt began, and then the weapon went off.

27

NO WAY OUT

It's a dud! **That was the first** thought that went through Leo's mind as the small object sprang apart and there was no accompanying explosion. But then he heard the low hissing and realised it was never meant to explode.

'Gas!' he screamed.

'What?' Rabbitt asked, looking down at the hissing canister then up at Leo. 'What the hell is going on?' He stepped forward, towards the counter, but almost immediately began gasping for breath as the gas crawled its way into his lungs and whatever chemicals were inside began to burn their way through his body. He dropped to his knees, then collapsed to the floor, kicking and writhing as he fought with his invisible killer. He screamed, clutching at his throat, but almost at once the screaming was replaced by gasping coughs as the chemicals tore apart the inside of his throat and his lungs. His body spasmed, twisting itself up into an awkward, unnatural arch as if something inside was fighting to escape. Then the movements suddenly stopped and the body toppled over onto its side. There was one final gurgling moan and then nothing.

Leo stood, terrified, unable to do anything but watch for the few seconds it took for Rabbitt to die. But as soon as the gasping and coughing had stopped, he became aware of the hissing of the gas once more and his survival instincts cut in. He leapt backwards into the store room, slamming his fist against the button that closed the door, then running over to the corner where Taffy was standing dormant.

'Wake up Taffy!' he bellowed, pointlessly shaking the ANT by its shoulders as he did so. Immediately a reassuring blue glow appeared behind the eye slot in the face panel. But that was it. There was no other movement. 'Wake up Taffy!' he shouted again, then ran back to the door to check it was properly closed. It was. But there was a narrow gap at the bottom of the door and Leo knew that unless he could seal it quickly, the closed door was going to be about as much use to him as a giant sieve.

He looked around. Surely there had to be something he could use to cover the gap. His jacket would be perfect, he thought. But his jacket was on the back of his chair, and his chair was on the wrong side of the door. And there was nothing else. No spare overalls rolled up on a shelf somewhere, no old pieces of cloth used for cleaning the machines, no...

'Packing material!' Leo shouted. Rabbitt had an old roll of thin foam packing material that he kept out back. It was never used for anything and just got in the way whenever he needed to get to the toilet, and Leo had no idea what state it was in, but it was the only thing he could think of that might stop the gas from getting through the gap. Or slow it down, at least. He ran through into the tiny corridor and the first thing he saw was that the roll of foam was gone. Everything that had been scattered around on the floor was gone, because Taffy had been tidying. He looked around desperately and finally found it, neatly propped up against the wall beside the entrance behind him.

Back in the store room he tore off a long sheet and forced it down into the gap beneath the door. But it wasn't anything like as soft and flexible as he'd imagined it would be and he couldn't get it to stay in place. Instead, he grabbed a cutting blade and some insulating tape from one of the shelves and taped a long strip of foam across the whole of the bottom of the door, running the tape down the sides and across the floor to keep it in place.

But as Leo began to tape a second layer of foam on top of the first, he felt a tingling on the back of his hands that immediately became a stinging and he leapt back quickly from the doorway. One layer was going to have to do.

He ran back into the corridor and along to the toilet cubicle where he thrust his hands into the tiny sink and sprayed cold water onto them. This seemed to stop the stinging, but he noticed they were already looking red. And now his neck and scalp were also starting to feel itchy. He splashed some water over his head, went back into the corridor and set to work uncovering the fire door.

Taffy had done a thorough job of tidying the place, but with nowhere else to stack the pile of empty crates at the back of the shop, he had left them stacked up in front of the emergency exit. Leo began to pull down the top crates, tossing each one behind him and reaching for the next as quickly as he could. It was hard work. Even empty, the crates were heavy and awkward, and he quickly found himself gasping for breath. Was it just the exertion, or was the gas already spreading this far back? He took a deep breath, felt a tightness across his chest and an image of Rabbitt clawing at his throat and writhing on the floor came into his mind. Panic overtook him. He grabbed the next crate and hurled it backwards, then the next, until he had managed to clear the whole of the top half of the door.

Leo, what are you doing?

Leo spun round at the sound and was so relieved to see Taffy that he sank down onto one of the discarded crates. His arms were sore and his legs were shaking, and the tightness in his chest wasn't getting any better.

'I'm in trouble. Someone came into the shop to kill me. They set off some sort of gas canister. Rabbitt's dead. I tried to seal the door but gas is still getting in. I need to get out, now.'

Taffy quickly clambered over the scattered crates, made some space for himself, and began to pull at those crates that were still blocking the doorway. It was amazing, Leo thought, how straightforward and logical the AI brain was. If Taffy had been a human, he would have been asking countless stupid questions. What sort of trouble? Who came into the shop? What sort of gas? But Taffy had accepted Leo's words without question and immediately set to work dealing with the situation. And a good thing, too. Leo could feel the back of his neck beginning to sting again.

Taffy had the door cleared within a few seconds. In the centre, just below the sign stating that the door was not to be obstructed, was a small, sealed panel. Taffy ripped off the cover, pressed the emergency power button and turned to Leo. *I need the code.*

'Code? What code?'

The door requires a code to be entered before it can be opened.

'What? It's an emergency exit. What the hell does it need a pass code for?'

It's a security measure.

'I know it's a damn security measure!' Leo snapped. 'But it's stupid. And I have no idea what the code is. Rabbitt never told me.'

Leo scratched the back of his hand and noticed it was red again. He felt the urge to cough. 'The gas is getting through,' he said, holding up his hands for Taffy to see. 'I can feel it in my lungs as well.'

Taffy looked around then reached down and opened one of the empty crates. For a second, Leo wondered whether Taffy was going to suggest he climb inside, but instead Taffy tore a long strip from the soft inner lining and handed it to Leo.

Wet this and tie it around your nose and mouth. Then do the same for any areas of exposed skin. Keep your eyes closed as much as possible. I will continue to try and open the door.

While Leo did as he was told, Taffy ripped off the front of the control panel and reached inside to pull out the wires, studying them briefly and tracking them back into the body of the door.

'Can you get it open?'

Possibly.

Taffy smashed his fist into the wall at the side of the door, buckling a panel then ripping it free to reveal part of the control mechanism. He examined the exposed electronics for several seconds then began to rip out wires.

'Listen,' Leo said. 'I need you to review all the audiovisual data you recorded while you were asleep.'

I was not asleep.

'Whatever. Just review the data.'

I have already done so.

'Good. Did you see the woman who came into the store room?'

Yes.

'That's her. She's the one who attacked us, the one who's trying to kill me. I need you to identify her. Can you do that?'

Theoretically, yes. I could access the Midan immigration database and search for a visual match. If she has recently arrived on the station it would be easy enough to access her data file. However, if she is a permanent resident, or if she entered the station illegally, then she will not appear on the database.

'Well it's worth a go. And you can do it wirelessly from here?'

Yes.

'Good, then do it.'

It is illegal.

'I don't give a damn. She's trying to kill me. Just do it.'

I am under no obligation to obey your commands.

'Then do it, *please*. Come on, Taffy, it's important. Who cares if it's illegal. These people are a bunch of pirates anyway.'

Suddenly there was a whirring sound and the emergency door slid open. Leo leapt up and rushed through, finding himself in a narrow, dimly lit passageway barely wide enough for Taffy to squeeze into. At various points along the passage were other doorways leading, Leo assumed, into the backs of other shops. A large, glowing, green arrow on the wall opposite each door showed which way to go for the exit.

Wait here. I will go back and do what I can to reduce the risk of the gas spreading outside the shop.

Taffy closed the door and Leo stood alone in the dark passageway, his heart pounding and his lungs burning. His eyes were stinging and his skin was red and itchy and he was sure he must have been no more than a few minutes away from suffering the same agonising death spasms he'd watched Rabbitt suffer earlier. He moved a few paces further down the passageway, pulled down his makeshift face mask, and took a few deep lungfulls of air. It tasted stale and musty, and it made him cough, but to Leo it felt like the freshest air he'd breathed since leaving Earth.

Taffy returned a few minutes later, sliding the emergency door closed behind him and squeezing his way along the passageway to where Leo was waiting.

I have turned off the shop's air-filtration unit. It will be dangerous for humans to enter for many hours, but at least the gas will not now spread beyond the immediate area. We should inform the authorities as soon as possible.

'No, we've got to warn the others first. They're all in danger, and the sooner they know about it, the better. I've got to call my mum right now.' Leo led the way along the passage, following the direction of the arrows, until he came to another exit door. This time there was no code, only a large button, and when Leo pressed it, the door slid open and let them out into one of the wider side alleyways between buildings.

He'd left both his phone set and his slate in his jacket pocket, and his jacket was back in the shop, so he used his VelociT wrist computer instead. It took him a couple of minutes to set it up and make the call and he walked as he worked, nearly slipping and falling down the stairs to the lower level as he concentrated on the tiny screen. Taffy followed him closely, and the crowds seemed more than happy to get quickly out of his way as he approached.

A moment later Leo stopped as his mother answered the call.

You're late, she said, and then smiled. *But not to worry. I popped in and told the receptionist what we wanted and he said we'd be fine to come back whenever suited us.*

'Mum, listen...'

So we can have lunch first and then call in if you'd rather.

'Mum, listen! We're in trouble. Someone's just tried to kill me.'

Lillian's smile fell and she stared intently at her own screen. *What happened? Are you alright?*

'Yeah, I'm fine.'

What's wrong with your face? It looks all red and blotchy.

'I'll tell you later. We're on our way to meet you now but we'll be a few minutes. Don't go anywhere, okay?'

Are you sure? Perhaps it would make more sense for us to meet back at the ship where—

The picture on Leo's screen spun away from Lillian's face and he could see nothing for several seconds except a blurred image of the surrounding walkway. 'Mum!' he shouted. 'What's going on?'

After a moment Lillian's face returned, looking angry. *Unbelievable,* she fumed. *How rude can you be?*

'What?' Leo asked. 'What happened?'

Some incredibly rude young woman just barged into me, practically knocked me right over, then carried straight on as if I wasn't even there. No apology, no stopping to see if I was fine, nothing. She's given me a nasty scratch, right across the back of my hand, probably from some piece of jewellery she was wearing, or something.

Leo felt himself go cold, felt the knot tighten in his stomach. He could hardly bring himself to say the words. 'Mum. This woman, what did she look like?'

Look like? She looked like your typical, rude, inconsiderate, self-obsessed—

'Mum! Describe her to me.'

Stop shouting at me, for goodness sake. She was young, oriental. I can still see her, charging along the walkway. She's wearing a green jacket and... Lillian's voice trailed away and her face disappeared from the screen.

'That's her,' Leo shouted. 'That's the same woman who was here in the shop.'

There was no reply.

'Mum?'

Oh dear. Lillian brought her screen back up, but the picture was unsteady and Leo could clearly see the distress on his mother's face. *Leo...I don't feel so well...my arm is going numb...I think...I think it's my heart again.*

Leo started running.

28

LILLIAN

THERE WERE TOO MANY PEOPLE in the way. Leo dodged from side to side as he charged through the crowds, but it seemed as if the entire population of Midas had suddenly decided to wander, slowly and aimlessly, right along the centre of the main walkway. And Leo was not in the mood to slow down and wait. Wherever he couldn't find a clear path, he pushed past anyone in his way, bellowing, 'Emergency! Emergency!' and sprinting on before any of them could try to stop him. Taffy was somewhere behind, but Leo didn't have time to wait for him to catch up. He would just have to find his own way, probably by following the trail of angry pedestrians Leo was leaving in his wake.

To Leo it felt like it had taken no more than a minute or two to reach the area beside the noodle bar where his mother had been standing, but when he checked he realised it had taken nearer ten. There was no sign of her. He stood, confused and gasping for breath, desperately searching for some clue as to where she had gone until one of the restaurant cooks called him over.

'You look for sick woman?'

'Yes!' Leo panted.

'They take her up to doctor.' He shook his head. 'She look in bad way.'

Leo ran, taking the steps up to the surgery two at a time and hammering on the door until it was opened by a smartly-dressed young man in a white jacket. 'My mum,' Leo shouted. 'Where's my mum?'

The man looked startled. 'Fischer?' he asked, and when Leo nodded the man led him to a plain door on the far side of the reception area. He pressed the intercom, spoke in Chinese for a moment, then waited, avoiding eye contact, until the door was opened by another white-jacketed young man, who led Leo down a small corridor and into one of the surgery's treatment rooms.

Lillian was lying on a bed at the far side of the room and the first thing Leo noticed was that she wasn't hooked up to any of the medical equipment surrounding her. An older man, presumably her doctor, was sitting in front of a computer console to one side. He looked up as the door opened and when he saw Leo he stood up and came forward. Leo ignored him and ran straight to the bed, but one look at his mother told him everything he needed to know. She was too still, too pale. Too lifeless.

The room seemed to fall away from him. His head began to spin and his chest felt so tight he didn't know if he was going to be able to take another breath. He felt hands supporting him, stopping him from falling, then lowering him into a chair. The doctor was saying something but Leo couldn't make out the words. It was like trying to listen to someone underwater. All he could hear was the pounding in his head. Then he remembered to breathe. He took a deep breath and it came straight back out in a long, low wail of anguish before dying away in a series of gasping sobs. He wrapped his arms around his chest, as tight as they would go, as if trying to keep himself from splitting apart, and he rocked backwards and forwards on his chair because his body was uncontrollable and wouldn't let him stay still.

But gradually the sobbing stopped, and the rocking stopped. Leo was given a cup of water for his throat and a tissue for his eyes, and after a while he was even able to look across at his mother without the pain becoming too much to bear.

He couldn't believe she was actually dead. He knew it was what everyone said in this situation, but that didn't make it any less true. How could she be dead? He'd been talking to her just a few minutes ago. She'd been happy and smiling and they'd been about to meet up. And then...

'It was her heart,' the doctor said, quietly. 'Massive heart attack. Very sudden. She was even coming to see me. Very close by. But even so, the heart was already stopped when she got here. We tried to restart, but it was no good. I'm very sorry.'

'She was murdered,' Leo said.

'Murdered?' The doctor looked concerned and slowly shook his head. 'This was not murder, it was heart attack. She had weak heart. I had been treating her for some weeks.'

'I know she had a weak heart,' Leo snapped. 'I know all about it. And the person who murdered her, she must have known as well.'

'Why you say she was murdered?'

'She was injected with something, some chemical that triggered the heart attack. Did you look at the scratch on her hand?'

'Scratch?'

'There! The scratch! See it?' Leo was still not in control of his emotions. One second he was furious with the doctor for being so useless, the next, he would look back at the bed and the shock of seeing his mother's body lying there would rip him apart all over again.

The doctor bent down and examined the scratch closely. 'I did see this,' he said. 'But it did not surprise me. Witnesses say she fell. They said nothing about any attack.'

'No, not an attack...' Leo gave up in frustration. It was clear the doctor was never going to believe him. No one would. And even if he could somehow force them to carry out an autopsy, he knew they wouldn't find anything anyway. The assassin would have been far too professional to leave any traces.

'Do you want me to call enforcers?'

'No.' Leo shook his head. 'Forget it. I'm just upset and I don't know what I'm saying.' The doctor nodded wisely, patted Leo on the shoulder and went back to his desk.

But Leo wouldn't forget it. Not ever. He'd travelled all the way to Mars to rescue his mother after she was kidnapped on Luna. He'd fought against an insane tyrant and his sinister henchman, had been shot at, blown up, imprisoned, and survived it all. And then, once he'd finally escaped to the far side of the Solar System, he'd discovered that no matter how far he ran, Carlton Whittaker would always hunt him down, and would always send someone else to kill him. So there was no point in running any more, no point in trying to hide. The only thing that made any sense now was taking the fight back to Whittaker, making him suffer for all the pain and misery he'd dealt out to everyone else, stopping him the only way that made any sense; by killing him. That, Leo decided, would be worth sacrificing his own life for.

He continued to stare at his mother. Slowly, carefully, he reached out and took her hand, expecting it to be cold. But it was still warm and soft and the shock of it nearly made him pull his own hand back. It was like she was still alive, just resting, just pretending to be dead. Maybe she was about to jump up off the bed and shout, 'Ha! Fooled you!' and laugh at him for being so gullible. But of course not. Leo shook his head. That was never going to happen.

'What happens now?' Leo asked, without turning round. 'To the body, I mean.'

'That depends on the next of kin.'

'That's me.'

'Really? Ah, I remember now. We spoke about it together. No husband, just one child, yes?'

'Just one child,' Leo repeated.

'Well, no need to worry. We take care of everything. Out here bodies are usually incinerated, but if you want to have it shipped back to Earth, for example, we can arrange that.'

'No. Just…whatever.'

'Okay, no problem. I must inform the authorities, and there are forms to complete. I will need signatures.'

'Later.'

'Later. Of course.'

Leo stood up and freed his hand. 'Goodbye, Mum,' he whispered. He felt tears welling up again and he screwed his eyes shut to stop them coming. He was in control of himself now, and that was exactly how he wanted it to stay. No more crying. He took a deep breath and opened his eyes again. It's just a body now, he told himself. An empty shell. It's not my mother. After another moment, he turned and left.

Taffy was waiting for him outside, at the bottom of the steps. Unfortunately, so were a couple of enforcers.

'Oi,' one of them called out as Leo headed over towards the ANT. 'That your robot?'

'Yes.'

'Well you can't just leave it standin' around like that. All humanoids is supposed ter be accompanied at all times.'

'Sorry. I didn't know.' Leo turned away, but the enforcer slapped a heavy hand down on his shoulder, preventing him from walking off.

'And,' the enforcer continued. 'Accordin' ter my records, it ain't registered, neeva.'

'No.'

'Well it's gotta be registered. You'll 'ave ter come wiv us an' do it now.'

'Please,' Leo tried. 'This really isn't a good time. I promise I'll—'

'Now,' the enforcer said with a smile, but his tone of voice implied it was the sort of smile that shouldn't be relied on.

Leo sighed. 'Alright. Can you give me a minute? It'll probably be easier if I talk to him first.'

'Talk to 'im? It's a bleedin' robot. Jus' tell it ter follow us.'

'Ease off, Niko,' the second enforcer said. 'Let the kid go and talk to the robot if he thinks it'll help. We ain't in no hurry. And besides, there ain't no way we're gonna get it to come with us if it don't wanna come.'

'Fine,' the one called Niko said with a shrug. 'You've got a minute.'

Leo went over to Taffy. He had a lot to say and not much time. 'Did you contact the others?'

Yes. They are all out together, collecting some equipment for Nightrider. *I have told them about your encounter, warned them of the possible danger and they are returning to the ship. They suggest you do the same. How is your mother?*

'She's dead.'

I am sorry. That was it. No shock, no tears, no stupid pointless questions. Just a simple, I am sorry. And right now, even that was more than he wanted.

'Have you identified the woman?'

Yes.

'Tell me.'

Here name is Nuying Chen. She arrived from Mars six standard days ago on board a personal cruiser, registration MA13-316.

'Do you know where it's docked?'

Yes.

'Where?'

Central Arm 4. Bay 22.

'Is that far?'

No.

'Good.' Leo paused, took a deep breath, and after casting a quick glance over towards the two enforcers, he turned back to Taffy. 'Listen. I'm going to go to her ship and wait for her. When she returns, I'm going to kill her. Then I'm going to steal her ship, fly it to Mars and find some way to kill Carlton Whittaker. I can't do it on my own. I need help, but I don't want the others to get involved. They'll only try to stop me, and I don't want to be stopped. I want you to help me.'

If I refuse to help, will you attempt to carry out your plan regardless?

'Yes.'

How will you kill Nuying Chen?

'I don't know. I'll find something. With my bare hands if I have to.'

'Oi! Time's up,' Niko the enforcer called. Leo ignored him.

'Will you help me?'

Are you certain this is what you want to do?

'Yes. One hundred per cent certain.'

Then I will help you.

'Are *you* certain? Do you understand what it is I'm asking you to do?'

Yes.

'And you don't have a problem with it?'

No.

At any other time, Leo might have smiled. He honestly hadn't known whether Taffy would agree to help him or not. Sometimes AIs developed strong ethical opinions that stopped them engaging in any sort of illegal activity, even where there was no specific core programming to prevent them. And helping to kill someone was a pretty damned big ethical dilemma.

'And you realise that if we get caught, they'll completely destroy you, melt you down to scrap? You'll cease to exist.'

Then I suggest we do not get caught.

The enforcers wandered over, bored with waiting. 'Come on, sonny-boy,' Niko said. 'That's enough chit-chat.'

Without warning, Taffy reached out and slammed the men's heads together. There was a sickening crunch, and before the two bodies could fall to the ground, Taffy grabbed them by their jackets and dragged them over to the area behind the staircase, where a row of recyc bins had been installed. He draped the bodies across the bins, used their own restraint cables to tie them together and to secure them to one of the stair supports, found their comms transmitters and smashed them, then removed their shock batons, handing one to Leo when he returned.

'Are they dead?' Leo asked, startled by the suddenness of Taffy's actions.

I do not think so. That was not my intention.

Leo looked around at the crowd that had gathered to watch. None of them seemed to be the least bit interested in checking on the enforcers, or in trying to stop him and Taffy from leaving, but he didn't want to push his luck.

'We should go,' he said. 'Before any more arrive.'

Taffy led the way and the crowd quickly parted to let them through. For a while they walked in silence and Leo used the time to examine his shock baton, to make sure he knew exactly how to use it. It wouldn't be anything like as effective as a gun, and it would mean having to get up close to use it, but it was better than nothing and it would have to do.

Taffy slowed and allowed him to catch up. *I have a call coming in from Pete.*

'Ignore it,' Leo snapped. 'Don't answer anything from anybody. They'll only try to stop me. They won't understand.'

Almost immediately, his VelociT began to vibrate and for an instant he really thought it would be his mother, calling to say they'd got it all wrong, that she wasn't dead and that the doctor had given it one more try and managed to get her heart working again. She was fine now, and with rest and the proper medication she might even get to be better than she had been before. He checked. It was Skater. He ignored it.

Five minutes later they arrived at the immigration counter for Central Arm 4. There was no queue and they went straight to the window, where two bored, uniformed men were watching something on a television monitor beneath the counter. One of them glanced up, didn't seem at all interested in Taffy and casually indicated the fingerprint ID pad in front of them.

'Sign in.'

Leo pressed his thumb against the dark glass and waited. Nothing happened. Irritated, the man glanced up again, saw that the door was still closed and looked across at a second monitor to see what the problem was.

'You're in the wrong place,' he announced. 'If you're looking for your ship it must be in one of the other arms.'

'I'm not looking for my ship,' Leo explained nervously. 'I'm trying to visit a friend. She said this was where she was docked.'

The man shook his head slowly and said something to his

friend, who gave a low laugh and continued to watch the television.

'What name?'

'She's called, um, Chen,' Leo said. The man sighed and gave him a long-suffering stare.

'Ship's name?'

'Oh, um...'

Registration number MA13-316, Taffy said.

'Thank you.' He typed the number into the computer, checked the monitor and then gave them a sly grin. 'Chen. That's right, now I remember. Chinese. Pretty little thing.'

Leo forced a smile onto his face. 'That's her.'

'Well, sorry son, but you're too late.'

'Too late? What do you mean?'

'She's gone. Left. Departed.'

'She can't have gone. She was just here, like, half an hour ago. I saw her.'

'She may well have been here half an hour ago.' The man tapped his monitor. 'But according to this, her ship left dock five minutes ago.'

29

THE CHASE BEGINS

'**NO!**' LEO STARED AT THE immigration official in shock and couldn't think of anything else to say. 'No, no, no, no, no!'

It was a complete disaster. And it wasn't about revenge any more, it was about the fact that he had to get off Midas as soon as possible, before the authorities found out what was going on, followed the trail of chaos he'd left behind him and finally caught up with him. His mother was dead, Rabbitt was dead, there was a shop full of poisonous gas that was probably still leaking out into the air filtration system, and there were two unconscious enforcers who would be coming round soon and would definitely be out for blood. They could identify him, put out a call, and within the next half hour or so every enforcer on the station would be looking for him and Taffy. Maybe, just maybe, he could get away with claiming he was still in shock after learning about his mother, but Taffy had no excuse. Unless they got off Midas right now, Taffy was destined for the nearest scrap heap.

He jabbed his thumb against the ID scanner again, willing the doors to open, but they remained firmly shut. He didn't know what else to do.

'Stolen your heart, has she?' The man behind the counter gave Leo a pitying look and shook his head. 'Love 'em and leave 'em, that's what I say. Besides, aren't you a little bit young to be chasing around after older women? Not trying to run away from home, are you?'

Leo glared at him, wondering whether this might be a good time to try out his shock baton, but guessing that attacking even more officials was only likely to get him into even more trouble. Then the man gave a little laugh.

'Nah, I'm just teasing you. Here, go on through.' He pressed a button and the doors slid open. 'The ship's undocked, but she might still see you if you give her a wave from one of the windows.'

'Thanks,' Leo called out, and he rushed through the doorway before the man could change his mind. Taffy followed more slowly.

Leo raced along the wide walkway, counting off the numbered airlocks as he went. Now and then he would dart across to the side to peer out from one of the small porthole windows set along the walls, but there was nothing to see except the dark shapes of docked ships, the massive bronze bulk of the station, and the emptiness of space beyond. The arm itself was mostly empty, with only the occasional person to avoid, but halfway along was a small knot of passengers milling around beside one of the few open airlocks, and Leo was forced to slow down to navigate his way past them and their luggage.

Bay 22 was almost the last door on the right hand side of the arm, and from the tiny window beside it Leo could see that the bay was empty and the umbilical tunnel fully retracted. There was no sign of the ship. At the very end of the docking arm was a much larger screen window, and Leo ran on until he was standing in front of it. From here, switching between several external cameras, he could see a huge expanse of space and there, off to one side, a small ship that seemed to be drifting away from the station.

'Look,' he called, as Taffy caught up with him. 'That must be her. You said it was a single-crew ship, didn't you?'

That is the correct vessel. I can clearly read the registration number printed along the side panelling.

'Damn it!' Leo shouted, and thumped his fist against the screen's reinforced surface. 'How did she get away so fast? And how did she even know we were after her?'

Perhaps she didn't. Perhaps it was always her intention to leave as soon as her task was completed.

'But it's not completed. What about Skater and Pete and Morgan? And what about me? She may think she killed me in the shop, but if she's one of Whittaker's top assassins, you'd think she'd at least hang around long enough to make sure the job was actually finished before running back to Mars.'

If, as was the case, her first attack proved unsuccessful, the increased levels of protection and vigilance around you would most likely make any subsequent attempts to kill you significantly more difficult and less likely to succeed. That being so, the most logical course of action would be to leave Midas as quickly as possible, before any formal investigations are begun, and find a safe port where she could lie in wait, monitor developments and plan her next move.

As for Skater, Pete and Morgan, the two most likely explanations are that either it was never her intention to kill them and that you and your mother were her only targets, or that she does intend to kill them but does not need to be present in person to execute her plans. A timed explosive device planted aboard Nightrider *would be an obvious example of this strategy.*

'What! We've got to warn them.'

I am currently ignoring all calls from them.

'Alright, alright. Listen, just let me think for a minute.' Leo turned away from the window, screwed his eyes shut and tried to think what to do. His plan was ruined and he needed a new one quickly. The first thing had to be to warn Skater and the others that there might be a bomb on board *Nightrider*. He should do that right now. But if he talked to them directly, things were going to get even more complicated and awkward than they were already. A message then.

'Okay, Taffy. Can you send a message to Pete? Tell him there might be a bomb on the ship and that he should scan the whole thing for explosives. And tell him…about my mum. And say that she was murdered. No matter what he hears from anyone else, she was murdered and now I'm going after the murderer. Just a message, though. Don't call him or talk to him.'

That is done, Taffy said after a few seconds.

'Good. Now for the tricky part. Follow me.' Leo set off back down the arm, stopping again to look out the porthole windows on both sides as he went. But this time he wasn't searching for the assassin's ship, it was the docked ships he was interested in, specifically those at open airlocks. He had to get off the station and he had to do it now. The only option was to steal another ship.

The first open ship was way too big and he could see several people moving about inside. The second was the one surrounded by passengers. At the third open airlock the ship itself was sealed, and although he did spend a minute or so examining the access control panel, it quickly became obvious that he was never going to be able to override it. If only he had the universal pass key that Skater had so conveniently forgotten to return to Mackie, it would have been no trouble to get inside. But he didn't, which meant he'd have to resort to getting hold of a ship the old-fashioned way. At the fourth airlock, he found exactly what he was looking for.

PART 2 – THE CALM

The ship was small, slightly larger than the one the assassin was in, but still the entire thing could probably have been squeezed into *Nightrider's* hold. It was also open. Leo darted into the umbilical tunnel, unclipped the shock baton from his belt and cautiously moved towards the open doorway, with Taffy following close behind. At the entrance he paused, stuck his head around the corner and took a quick look into the main body of the ship. It was little more than a single room, with separate sleeping and bathroom cubicles, a galley along one side and storage compartments along the opposite side of a narrow central passage. It was compact but also luxurious, obviously designed for someone who expected their surroundings to be expensive and stylish even when they were crammed into the back of a tiny spaceship.

Beyond, the ship opened out into the flight deck and control centre. There was a large single seat at the front, surrounded by a bank of linked window screens but little else. All the computers and control panels that usually surrounded the pilot's seat in a spaceship of its size had been tucked away against the side bulkheads where they wouldn't obstruct the view.

The ship appeared deserted, but as Leo stepped forward towards the flight deck he heard the unmistakeable *whoosh* of a suction pump from the bathroom cubicle, and before he could make up his mind whether to go back out or try to find somewhere to hide, the door opened and he found himself face to face with a pale, tired-looking, middle-aged man, presumably the ship's owner.

The man gave a yelp of surprise, but quickly regained his composure and glared at Leo. 'Who in god's name are you?' he demanded. 'And what the bloody hell are you doing on my ship? In fact, I don't even care who you are. You can just get the hell off my ship before I call the enforcers and have them drag your sorry arse straight to jail.'

The man was taller than Leo, but flabby and overweight, clearly unfit, and dressed in purple pyjamas, even though it was the middle of the afternoon. It would have been difficult for almost anyone to appear threatening while wearing those pyjamas, let alone this hopeless-looking character. Leo raised his baton. The man took a deep breath and bellowed at the top of his voice.

'Guards! Guards!'

But even as the words left his mouth, there was a hiss of hydraulics from the airlock door as Taffy sealed them inside the ship. No matter how loud the man shouted, only the three of them would hear anything he said from now on. This didn't seem to stop him, however, and although he gave up the shouting, he was in no mood to keep quiet.

'So, you're here to rob me, are you?' He stepped out of the bathroom, pushed past Leo and stood facing them from the centre of the flight deck, his fists resting on his abundant waist. 'Well, what a surprise. And there was me, believing them when they told me Midas was no longer a den of thieves like the old days. Cleaned up its act, they said. Respectable now. Pah! Well believe me, kiddo. You've just made the biggest mistake of your miserable little life.'

'I seriously doubt that,' Leo said with a laugh.

'Do you? Do you indeed? Do you know who I am?'

Leo looked round at Taffy.

His name is Cecil Marchmont Abernathy. He is a musician.

Leo shrugged. 'Doesn't mean anything to me.'

'Doesn't it? Well then let me explain.'

'No!' Leo snapped. 'Let *me* explain.' He raised the baton again, stepping forwards towards the man who shrank backwards a step despite all his bravado. 'I need to borrow your ship. I'm not stealing it and I'll make sure you get it back once I've finished with it. But right now I have to get off this station and your ship is the only one…conveniently available.'

'Oh,' the man exclaimed. 'So you're not thieves, you're pirates. Well, you've picked the wrong ship to attempt your piracy on today my friend. This isn't just some old clunker churned out from the Martian shipyards. This is a custom-made, one-of-a-kind, delux astro-yacht, made by Baskerville and Sons of San Francisco. It's totally AI controlled, it's got more in-built security measures than you could imagine, and the whole thing is personally coded to my DNA. So go ahead, take it. Let's see how far you get before the engines cut out and life support switches itself off.'

Leo nodded to himself and looked around the flight deck. 'There,' he said, pointing to a small, flat device built into one of the chair's arm rests. 'That'll be the palm print scanner.'

'That's right.'

'And that thing up above, that's a retina scanner.'

'Right again.'

'And the AI will be programmed only to respond to your voice.'

'Exactly.' Leo's knowledge of the ship's security measures seemed to unnerve the man slightly and he no longer sounded quite as confident as before.

'Well then I'll tell you what we're going to do, Mr Cecil Marchmont Abernathy. You're going to sit in your seat, put your hand on the scanner, access the AI and explain that you're transferring ownership of the ship to me. I'll then scan in my own palm print and retina and we'll all be happy.'

'Over my dead body.'

'Okay. Taffy, will you do the honours please?'

No. I don't think killing Mr Abernathy is a good idea.

'Taffy!' Leo shouted, spinning round to glare at the ANT. And then silently he mouthed, 'I'm kidding. Play along.'

What I meant, Taffy continued without pause, *was that I don't think killing Mr Abernathy is strictly necessary. If we reroute the control systems to bypass the ship's intelligence, that will negate the voice recognition protocol. And in that case, all we would need from Mr Abernathy would be one of his hands and one of his eyes.* He raised an arm, flexing his powerful steel alloy fingers. *I believe I could successfully remove both without actually killing the subject. Although I suspect there would be a certain amount of mess.*

Cecil Abernathy was looking truly horrified. 'You're bluffing,' he stammered. 'You can't do...what you said you'd do to the AI. The ship won't run without an AI. I know that much.'

'You're right,' Leo said, patting Taffy on the shoulder. 'But my friend here happens to be an AI. He'll be able to fly your ship no trouble. Now, let's get to work. We're running out of time.'

Taffy stepped forward and reached out with his raised arm, at which point Abernathy let out a terrified scream and ran to the pilot's seat, pressing his sweating palm firmly onto the scanner. 'Computer,' he shouted. 'Where the bloody hell are you?'

Good afternoon, Cecil, came a soft female voice from somewhere above them.

'Listen. I'm selling the ship. In fact, I'm giving it away. Right now. Understand?'

Are you sure?

'Yes, I'm bloody well sure. I've never been surer of anything in my life. I'm delighted to be rid of it. Really. So now I want you to transfer control from me to the new owner.'

Who is the new owner?

'That would be me,' Leo said, stepping forward and indicating to Abernathy that he should get out of the seat. Abernathy slid out quickly and stood nervously off to one side, as far away as possible from Taffy. Leo sat down, wiped the palm scanner with his cuff and placed his hand on top. As he sat back in the chair, the retina scanner slid out from its housing and automatically positioned itself in front of his face.

What is your name, new owner?

'Leonard Philip Fischer.'

Welcome, Leonard Philip Fischer. How would you like me to address you?

'Call me Leo.'

Welcome, Leo.

'Jesus Absolute Christ!' Abernathy gasped. 'You're Leo Fischer? *The* Leo Fischer?'

'I'm one of them,' Leo replied. 'Which one are you thinking of?'

'The terrorist.'

'At your service.'

'Oh Christ.'

Scanning complete, the AI announced. *You now have full control of this ship, Leo.*

'Excellent. Now, do you have enough fuel and supplies to get us to Mars?'

Yes.

'Then inform the authorities of our immediate departure and begin your start-up procedures. I want to get going as soon as possible.'

Understood.

'Wait a second,' Abernathy protested. 'I've just come from Mars. I'm not going all the way back there.'

'No,' Leo said with a humourless smile. 'You're not.' He turned to Taffy. 'Taffy, would you escort Mr Abernathy off the ship please?'

'What? You can't just throw me out.'

'Yes, I can.'

'But everything I own is on this ship. Well, everything I brought with me, anyway. I don't have my ID, or my credit cards or anything. I'm still in my pyjamas for Christ's sake!'

Leo went quickly through into the sleeping area and searched around in the personal storage units until he found Abernathy's wallet. He took out the ID card and one of the credit cards, tucked them into the pocket of a hideous green jacket that was hanging up at the end of the cot and thrust the jacket at Abernathy as Taffy dragged the struggling figure towards the airlock.

'Oh, and Taffy,' he said as an afterthought. 'Can you put him to sleep. We don't want him reporting us until we're safely away from the station.'

'What? Wait a sec—'

Taffy slammed Abernathy's head against the airlock door and carried his inert body out into the arm, laying him across a row of three seats set against the side wall and covering his face with the jacket. When he returned, Leo was already sitting in the control seat and firing orders at the ship's AI.

'All done?' Leo asked. 'Good. Let's go. I've lost sight of the killer's ship, but we should be able to track it as soon as we're clear.'

Do we need to track it? We know where it's headed.

'Yes, we definitely do need to track it. And catch up with it. Turns out this ship comes with its own laser cannon and I intend to make use of it. That woman is not going to get away from me again.'

Do you intend to kill her?

'Yes. Do you have a problem with that?'

No, I do not.

'So you're not going to try to stop me then? You're not going to try to persuade me that killing Chen is a bad idea?'

No. I think that killing Nuying Chen is a good idea.

'You do? Why?'

Once Nuying Chen discovers that you are not dead, she will undoubtedly try to kill you again, and will continue to do so until she succeeds. If one of you is going to die, I would rather it was her, not you. There was a slight pause. *I also understand and sympathise with your desire for revenge.*

'Good. Because I really don't think I could cope if you started trying to tell me that killing Chen isn't going to bring my mother back. I know it isn't. But it'll go a hell of a long way towards helping me to cope with the fact that she's dead.'

Yes, it will.

Leo, we are now ready to undock from Midas station, said the voice of the ship. *Please ensure you are securely strapped into your seat as we will lose gravity once separation is complete.*

'Oh, right,' Leo said, and slid his arms through the seat restraints. 'Back to zero-g. I'd forgotten about that. Taffy, you'd better clip yourself to something.'

A minute later Leo felt the tell-tale twisting in his stomach as its contents tried to float their way back up into his throat. He took a deep breath, closed his eyes and tried to concentrate on not throwing up, but after a few seconds he realised he wasn't going to and relaxed back into the soft chair, gazing at the underside of the huge station as it spun slowly away from them. Somewhere up there was the body of a woman he had known for sixteen years, who had loved him and cared for him, the only person he'd ever truly been able to call family. But now it was just a body, already beginning the slow process of falling apart and rotting away, and soon it wouldn't even be that. Soon it would be nothing but a tiny cloud of dust, fired out into the frozen vastness of space to drift away into nothingness. He was glad he wouldn't have to see it again. That wasn't how he wanted to remember his mother.

'Come on, ship,' he said, dragging his eyes away from the ever-shrinking station. 'Let's get out of here.'

30
TIME TO GO

SKATER LAY ON HER BED and hugged her pillow, feeling about as miserable as she'd ever felt in her life. The tears had stopped, finally, but it hadn't made that much difference to her mood. She still felt empty inside, as if every ounce of happiness had been sucked out of her, and now all she wanted to do was curl up and go to sleep, so that maybe, just maybe, she'd get a few hours of escape from the misery. But she couldn't sleep.

There was a gentle knock and the door to her cabin slid quietly open, then nothing.

'I'm not asleep,' Skater mumbled through the pillow.

'You okay?' Pete asked.

'Not really.'

'You want me to leave you alone?'

Skater reached out with one arm and made grabbing motions with her fingers. 'No, I want daddy hugs.'

Pete walked over to the bed, put a small package on the table and propped himself against the bulkhead so that Skater could nestle in against him. She squeezed him as tightly as she could for a few seconds and then relaxed.

'Want to talk?' Pete asked.

'Well,' Skater said after a while. 'That was completely horrible.'

'The funeral?'

'If you can call four people standing around awkwardly outside an incinerator unit a funeral. And I'm sure the only reason the doc came was to make sure he got paid afterwards.'

'Yeah, it was pretty soulless alright. Although knowing Lillian, she probably would have approved. She really didn't like people making a fuss, did she?'

'Leo should have been there.'

'Yes, he should,' Pete said, after a long pause. 'But I guess he had his reasons for doing things the way he did.'

'Stupid reasons.'

'Maybe. But who knows what was going on in his head during those hours. Obviously he wasn't thinking straight. He was still in shock, and I'm sure he was just trying to do what he thought was the right thing to do in the circumstances.'

'Hijack a ship? Beat up everyone who got in his way?'

'It was fairly extreme, I'll give you that. But let's not judge him too harshly until we know all the facts. Like I say, I'm sure he had his reasons.'

'I hate him.'

'For running away?'

'For everything.'

Pete said nothing, and for a while they fell silent, listening to the noise of the ship beyond the cabin. There were heavy footsteps along the passageway, and voices, and the low hum of machinery as the soldiers who had accompanied them from Mars loaded up the ship and prepared it for departure.

'We're leaving?'

'Yes. That's what I came to tell you. Morgan managed to convince the Committee that we didn't know anything about the attack at the shop, or Leo stealing the other ship, and they've agreed not to impound *Nightrider* as evidence. But they're not letting us stay either. They've given us twenty-four hours to resupply, then we have to be gone. That's why all the sudden activity.'

'Are the soldiers coming with us?'

'No. They're helping us get prepped, but then they have other things to do, other places to be.'

'Are they going after Leo?'

'No, I don't think so.'

'Are we?'

'That's the plan.'

'Why? He ran away and left us. Obviously he doesn't want our help any more.'

'But he still needs it.'

'But he doesn't deserve it.'

'But we'll give it to him anyway, because that's the sort of people we are.'

'Speak for yourself. The instant I see him again I'm going to punch his lights out.'

'Well don't hold your breath. That ship he took is pretty nippy, and unless he stops to admire the view along the way, he'll be on Mars long before we get there.' He removed his arm from around Skater's shoulder and gently laid her back down onto the bed. 'Speaking of which, I'd better go back and give Morgan a hand on the flight deck. I told her I was only going to be a minute. Are you going to be okay?'

Skater propped herself up on her elbow. 'I will be as soon as you tell me what that is,' she said, indicating the small package Pete had left on the table.

'Oh, that's just some little thing I picked up from somewhere. Call it a leaving present from Midas. I thought it might stop you getting too bored on the journey.'

'It looks like a book.'

Pete tilted his head to one side and made a show of studying the package. 'Yeah,' he said with a smile. 'I suppose it does.'

As soon as Pete left, Skater sat up and took the package. It was wrapped in old, waxy brown paper and neatly tied with string the way presents used to be, back in the old days, and although her fingers itched to rip their way inside, she forced herself to untie the string and unfold the paper as carefully as possible, so they could be used again later. Inside, beneath a worn and faded cover that had been torn and repaired in several places, was a copy of Benjamin Agami's *Broken Promise, Broken Heart*. It had been pinned to the wall of the tiny book stall she'd discovered on her very first trip into Midas, and she had often stopped to admire it on her way to Rabbitt's Robots to meet Leo for lunch, never for a single moment imagining that one day it might actually be hers.

'I love my dad!' she screamed at the top of her voice, and then carefully put the book back on the table before she got it covered in tears.

PART THREE

THE STORM

31

IF AT FIRST YOU DON'T SUCCEED...

HE WOKE UP. WAS THAT RIGHT? Had he been asleep? He couldn't remember. He couldn't remember anything, in fact, not where he was, or how he had got there, or why he seemed to be propped up in a large chair, with restraints preventing him from moving his arms or legs, or turning his head. Slowly, cautiously, he opened his eyes.

There was a light, not too bright, shining directly into his face from the end of a long mechanical arm above him, and beyond that a white ceiling, the edges of white walls, more machinery. A hospital, perhaps? Was he ill? Had he been in some sort of accident? He couldn't remember.

The light was moved to one side and a man's face appeared in front of him. Unshaved, young, tired. 'You're awake,' the man said, smiling. 'Good. How do you feel?'

Puzzled, he thought for a moment and then answered as truthfully as he could. 'I don't know.' Was that his voice? He didn't recognise it.

The unshaved, tired man also seemed puzzled. He looked at a small screen he was holding, tapped on it for a while, then looked back up. 'Do you know where you are?'

He flicked his eyes from side to side, taking in as much of the white-walled room as he could. 'No.'

'This is my lab. My name is Professor Randhawa. Does that mean anything to you?'

Professor Randhawa. He repeated the name over and over in his mind, searching for some spark of recognition in his memory, but his mind was empty. 'No. Nothing.'

Disappointment showed in the dark eyes staring down at his own. 'Do you know who you are? Can you tell me your name?'

Of course, he thought. But when he searched for it, his name was nowhere to be found. Not his name, or his age, or his date of birth, or where he lived. Nothing. 'No,' he replied, now more puzzled than ever.

'Damn,' the professor muttered. And then louder. 'Still nothing. Okay people, let's reset and try it one more time.' He reached for something behind the chair, and everything went dark.

He woke up. Was that right? Had he been asleep? He couldn't remember. He couldn't remember anything, in fact, not where he was, or how he had got there, or why he seemed to be propped up in a large chair, with restraints preventing him from moving his arms or legs, or turning his head. Slowly, cautiously, he opened his eyes.

Someone was staring down at him. It was a young man, dressed in a long white jacket. The sort of jacket a doctor might wear. Was he in a hospital? Had he been involved in some sort of accident? He couldn't remember.

'How do you feel?' the young man asked. He seemed distracted, almost bored, as if he didn't really care. As if any answer would be acceptable.

He thought for a moment and then answered as truthfully as he could. 'I don't know.' Was that his voice? He didn't recognise it. 'I don't know how I feel.'

'And you don't recognise me, do you?'

He stared up at the face in front of him, at the stubble-covered cheeks and dark, tired eyes and tried to remember if he'd ever seen it before. 'No, I don't recognise you.'

'And can you tell me your name?'

Of course, he thought. But when he searched for it, his name was nowhere to be found. Not his name, or his age, or his date of birth, or where he lived. Nothing. 'No,' he replied, now more puzzled than ever.

The young man let out a yell of frustration and there was the sound of something large being hit, or kicked. 'Damn it! What's the problem? Why can we not get the damn thing to work?'

Then a woman's face appeared. She had paler skin than the doctor and dark red hair pulled tightly back from her face. She wasn't wearing a white coat. She gazed at him and spoke softly, but it was clear she was talking to the doctor, not to him. 'How long is this going to go on for?'

'For as long as it takes until it works.'

'He's beginning to get a little disappointed by your lack of results.'

'Well, he's not the only one. I thought we'd have cracked it by now.'

'But you haven't?'

'We're close, we really are. But there's just...I don't know, something still missing.'

'Then find it.'

'Just like that? Do you know how unbelievably complex and difficult this work is? And groundbreaking, too. It's not as if I can look something up in a book when it doesn't work. I'm having to write the damn book as I go.'

'And do you know how unbelievably complex preparing a war against Earth is? Mars can't afford to have its president lying in a coma for two or three days every week while you keep searching for your missing ingredient. He needs results now.'

'What he needs is to be a bit more patient.'

'He's not the patient type.'

His eyes flicked between the two faces in front of him. Did he know these people? Were they talking about him? Why could he not remember?

'Where is he now?' the woman asked.

'In theory,' the doctor replied, reaching out and tapping him on the forehead, 'somewhere inside here. But for some reason he's not coming out to say hello.'

'Well then, put him back in his own body and wake him up. There are things he needs to do.'

'Fine.' The doctor reached up to something behind the chair, and everything went dark.

32

A CHANGE OF HEART

THE CHASE WAS OVER, although really it had been over three weeks ago, when they had tagged Nuying Chen's ship and set themselves on an intercept course. Twice, early on, Chen had tried to break the tag, but Leo's new ship was larger and faster, its electronic systems more powerful, and it soon became clear that the only way for Chen to avoid being blown to pieces was to be rescued by something powerful enough to deter Leo from his pursuit. And that hadn't happened.

Now the smaller ship lay no more than fifty kilometres ahead. A series of precise laser shots the previous day had disabled its main engine and defensive weaponry, and since then they had matched their speed and trajectory to the helpless ship so that it now appeared to be sitting motionless in front of them, even though Leo knew that both ships were still hurtling towards Mars at thousands of kilometres an hour.

Target lock was engaged and weapons were active. All Leo had to do was press the small red button beneath his finger and Chen's ship would be gone. For a split second there would be a flash of plasma, many times brighter than the tiny, distant sun, as the laser tore through the hull and ruptured the fuel cells, and then there would be nothing but fragments of debris scattered across the void. This was the woman who had killed his mother, who had tried to kill him, and who would almost certainly try again given half a chance. She was a hired assassin in the pay of a mass murderer, and Leo couldn't think of a single person in the entire Solar System who deserved to die more than she did. And one single press of the red button would do it.

'I can't do it,' he said.

Why? Taffy asked. He was standing behind the pilot's chair, the powerful electromagnets in his feet keeping him secured to the ship's deck. *Was this not what you wanted?*

'I thought it was. When we left Midas, it was the only thing I wanted. But that was three weeks ago, and now that we're here, now that it all comes down to pressing the button, I don't think I can do it.'

Why not?

'Because I just can't. Because killing someone is a huge deal. Maybe I could if I had to, if it was self-defence, or to save someone I loved or something, but this is cold-blooded murder, plain and simple. That's what she does and I hate her for it and I'm not going to let myself become like her. I'm better than that.'

Then what will you do with her?

'Why do I have to do anything with her? She can just stay out here and rot as far as I'm concerned.'

I don't understand. You refuse to destroy her ship, but you would happily leave her to die a slow death from starvation?

'There's a difference.'

Where?

'Action versus inaction. Not doing anything to help her is not the same as deliberately doing something to harm her.'

Why?

'Because it is. To me it is, anyway. And besides, you know as well as I do that she won't die out here. She's still got life support and comms so she'll be fine until she can get someone to come and rescue her.'

Unless her vessel is destroyed through collision with an object she is unable to avoid because we have destroyed her propulsion system.

'Or maybe she'll get picked up by pirates,' Leo added, hopefully. 'But I don't care either way. She's a despicable human being and I hope she suffers a slow and painful death sometime very soon. All I'm saying is that I'm not going to be the one to do it.' And with that, he cancelled the target lock, powered down the laser cannon and unclipped himself from the seat, pushing past Taffy and heading towards the galley at the rear of the ship. 'I'm hungry,' he growled. 'I need chocolate.'

They had left Midas Station four weeks ago, and Mars was still six weeks ahead of them. On a ship this small, with no one except two AIs for company, most passengers would probably have put themselves to sleep for the bulk of the journey, and clearly this was what Cecil Abernathy had preferred. Leo had discovered the man's abundant supply of DeepSleep tablets on the first day, but he had no intention of using them – there was far too much to do and enjoy on board *Trinity* to waste his days in a drug-induced semi-coma.

Four weeks ago, the ship had been known as *Il Volo dell'Angelo*, but as its new owner, Leo had every right to change its name and he'd done so, finally settling on *Trinity* after two days of toying with a string of stupid and unsuitable options like *The Angel of Vengeance*,

Retribution and *The Fifth Horseman*. Trinity had been his mother's college at Cambridge University, and might well have been his as well, if his life hadn't taken such a dramatic and irreversible detour over the previous year. It was a good name, and a fitting tribute to his mother. It was also much easier talking to the ship's AI if he could call her Trinity, rather than Fifth Horseman.

Trinity was a luxury yacht. It was fast, expertly and expensively fitted out, and incredibly well-stocked. There was enough food and drink in the galley to last a crew of one for well over six months – even at the rate Leo was working his way through it – and the entertainment system, with its holo-viewer, immersive gaming console and almost limitless data library, could have kept him occupied all the way out to Neptune and back.

But there was work to do as well. At first it had been all about catching up with Chen, and during the chase he'd spent hours getting to know his new ship and its capabilities until he was confident he could deal with any trouble that might come his way. Fortunately, none had. The authorities on Midas had ordered him to return, of course, and he'd ordered Trinity to ignore them. But they hadn't bothered to send a ship after him, and after two days the demands had stopped.

Pete had also tried contacting him several times, but Trinity had ignored those calls as well. Finally, at the end of several days with no contact, Pete had sent a vid-message in which he'd explained everything that had happened since Leo's departure; about their battles with the Committee over whether or not *Nightrider* was going to be impounded, about the fact that no one seemed to care about Cecil Abernathy or his endless demands for justice or compensation, and about their forced departure from the station.

He also told him about his mother's funeral, how they were all devastated by her death and how they understood how something so terrible could have made Leo behave the way he had. No one was angry with him, he said, or wanted to punish him. They just wanted him to come back. They were about five days behind him, and if he cut his speed by even ten percent, they could be alongside long before he was anywhere near Martian territory. Whatever was in store from now on, it would be easier if they faced it together.

He'd watched the message, but hadn't replied. He knew the first thing they would have done was stop him from going after Chen. But now that he'd caught up with her, now that he knew he wasn't going to kill her, things had changed. Now he didn't know what he was going to do and he felt guilty for abandoning the only people he could still call his friends. He needed to think. And he needed more chocolate.

Taffy was looking at him.

'What?' he demanded.

Can I ask you a question?

'Yes. Unless it's about why I won't kill Chen. In which case, no.'

Are you still planning to go to Mars?

'Yes.'

To kill Carlton Whittaker?

Leo sighed. 'I know what you're getting at. If I wasn't able to kill her, what makes me think I'll do any better when it comes to killing him?'

Yes.

'And if I'm not going to kill him, why am I still going to Mars?'

Yes.

'The short answer? I don't know. I've only just discovered that I'm not the ruthless killer I thought I was and that kind of puts a dampener on my big revenge plans. And I never had a Plan B.'

No.

'But it wouldn't be the same, you know. Killing Whittaker, I mean. I still think I could do that.'

Why would killing Whittaker be different from killing Chen?

'Because he's a mad, psychopathic tyrant.'

Does that make him easier to kill?

'Of course it does. Weren't there ever any tyrants on Homeworld?'

Yes. Many.

'Well we had one on earth, about four hundred years ago. His name was Adolf Hitler.'

Yes, Taffy said after a slight pause. *Much has been written about him.*

'So you know all about him, right? How he caused a world war and killed millions of innocent people and everything?'

Yes.

'So, a lot of people used to say that if someone ever invented time travel, the first thing they would do would be go back in time and kill Hitler before he came to power, so they could prevent it all from happening.'

Time travel in that sense is not possible.

'Yeah, I know. But that's not the point. The point is that these were ordinary, peaceful people, who wouldn't dream of killing anyone, but they all thought they would've been able to kill Hitler, because they knew it would mean saving all those millions of other people.'

And you believe that killing Carlton Whittaker will prevent a similar loss of life. So when the opportunity arises, you believe you will be able to find the moral courage necessary to pull the trigger yourself?

'Something like that.'

Killing Nuying Chen will also save lives. Possibly your own.

'It's different. It's hard for me to explain why, but it is. You'll just have to take my word for it. Now can we please drop the subject and talk about something else?'

Taffy chose to remain silent instead. Leo helped himself to a carton of chilled fruit juice and shut himself in the sleep cubicle. He needed to think, and having Taffy standing there staring at him wasn't helping. To stop himself from bumping into the side panels, he secured himself into the padded sleeping bag, then told the small glow light to turn itself off. The darkness would help him concentrate.

He needed a plan. And it would have to be a damn good one. First, he needed to get onto Mars without being identified and immediately arrested. Then, he had to find some way of getting close enough to Whittaker to shoot him. And something to shoot him with would be helpful; the shock baton he'd taken from the enforcers on Midas was the only weapon he had on board, and that wasn't exactly going to be enough to get the job done. And, most important of all, he needed an escape plan. You didn't just walk up and shoot the President of Mars then hope to fade into the shadows afterwards.

'Come on, Leo,' he muttered, screwing up his eyes and pressing his palms against his forehead. 'Think, think, think.'

33

ACTION STATIONS

IT WAS THE FIRST REALLY GOOD SLEEP Skater had had in ages and she didn't want it to end. But the noise was bothering her and it wouldn't go away. It was too loud and annoying and sounded just like an alarm.

Alarm! Suddenly she was wide awake and struggling to escape from her sleeping bag. After a few seconds she floated free and pushed herself over to the storage compartment where her environment suit was stowed. Always suit-up first. It was the number one rule in any emergency off-world — take care of yourself, then take care of the problem, because a lot of the time you wouldn't be able to do it the other way round.

Suited, booted and with her hood at the ready, Skater slipped out of her cabin and pushed her way along to the bridge. Morgan was already strapped into the pilot's seat and was busy with the controls.

'What's going on?' Skater shouted over the alarm.

Morgan flicked a switch and the noise died away. 'Nice of you to join us,' she said with a smile. 'I was starting to wonder whether you were still on board.'

'I was asleep,' Skater said defensively. 'Deep asleep. Anyway, what's the buzz? And where's Dad?'

'He's in the hold. And the buzz is, we have company.'

'From Midas?'

'No.'

'Mars?'

'No.' Morgan spun round one of her monitors so that Skater could see the screen. There were four ships, three small, one much larger. The big one was an ugly mess of engines and thrusters and odd pieces of hull plating from what appeared to be several different ships all crushed together.

'Oh, crap.'

'My thoughts exactly.'

'How close are they?'

'Before they start shooting? Maybe half an hour. Maybe less. The fighters are coming in pretty fast.'

'But we can shoot back, right? I mean, that's what you were doing back on Midas, fixing up the wing cannons, wasn't it?'

'Don't you worry. We're more than a match for three little plasma-pops like those. But that big beast might be more of a problem. That one looks like it could swallow us whole and spit out the pieces.'

'So what can I do?' Skater asked. 'Shall I go help Dad?'

'No, I'm sure he can manage on his own. What I need you to do is get on the comms.'

'Send out a distress call?'

'No, the ship's done that already, for all the good it'll do. But I need you to contact Leo.'

'Leo? What for?'

'Because we need to warn him. It could be this lot are just part of a bigger fleet, and he's only a few days ahead. If they can catch us they might well be able to catch him as well.'

'Maybe we should let them,' Skater muttered. 'It'd serve him right.'

'Don't say that,' Morgan snapped, turning round to stare directly at Skater. 'Don't ever say that. I get that you're cross with Leo for running off and leaving us in such a mess back on Midas—'

'Uh, yeah.'

'Well so am I. He nearly cost me my ship, remember. But don't ever wish pirates on anyone.'

'But I thought we were supposed to be pirates?'

'Not like these. These are animals – no, they're much worse than animals. They're scavengers and slavers and murderers. Seriously, they're bad, bad news.'

'Sorry. But I didn't really mean it, you know. Even I'm not that heartless.'

'I know. You were just expressing your feelings about Leo. But I still need you to call him, and I need you to do it quickly.'

'Fine. What should I say?'

'Tell him to head for Qi Tian Station. If he overburns his engines he could make it there in less than a week and the closer he gets to it, the less likely the pirates will be to follow him. His ship will know what to do. Tell him to wait for us and we'll be there as soon as we can.'

Skater pushed herself over to the comms station at the back of the bridge. It was where she sat when all three of them were up front, and she knew exactly what to do. She also knew perfectly well that Morgan could have made the call from the command chair if she'd wanted to, so this was obviously an attempt to get her and Leo talking to each other again, as well as a warning call about pirates.

After three weeks of radio silence, Skater was surprised when the call was answered immediately, and she was relieved to see it was Taffy, not Leo, staring back at her from the screen. She gave him a broad smile. 'Hey, Taffy. Long time.'

Hello, Skater.

'So you've decided to talk to us then?'

Yes. Trinity received your distress call. I think even Leo would agree the situation merits direct communication for once.

'Who's Trinity?'

The ship mind. Leo renamed it.

'Trinity, huh? Well, at least that's better than I'll Follow del Whatsit.'

Il Volo dell'Angelo.

'Yeah, that's the one. Anyway, where is the little...where is he?'

Sleeping. Would you like me to wake him?

'No, don't bother.'

'Yes,' called Morgan. 'Do bother. We need to talk to him.'

Skater shrugged. 'Fine. Go wake him.'

While she waited for Leo to appear, Skater used the second monitor screen to access *Nightrider's* external cameras, so she could watch the approaching ships. At full magnification she could see the fighters clearly now. They were old, Asgard-class interceptors, powerful enough in their day, but at least thirty years out of date. They had been modified. She could see extra fuel tanks and clumsy sections of armour plating on the main body, and they were carrying a lot more weaponry than they were designed for. But then *Nightrider* had a few tricks of its own. Wasn't that what Morgan had said, back when they were escaping from Mars? A few tricks, and some big guns. Skater hoped it would be enough.

Leo floated into view and pulled himself into the seat facing his own screen. He glanced briefly up at Skater and then spent far too long adjusting his harness, obviously waiting for her to speak first. She waited until there was no more adjusting he could do.

'Hi,' he said, finally.

'Hi.' Again she waited through the awkward silence.

'Um, how are you?'

'I'm sorry about your mother.' She meant it. She was sorry for him, and she'd promised her dad that it would be the first thing she'd say when they finally got back in touch with Leo. But she had plenty more she wanted to say, and now seemed like as good a time as any to get it all out in the open.

'Thanks. I got the message from Pete, about the funeral and every—'

'You should have been there, Leo,' She cut in. 'She was your mother and you should have been there to say goodbye.'

'I did say goodbye,' Leo replied, coldly. 'Right after she died. But even then it was too late. And saying goodbye isn't going to bring her back.'

'Nor is hunting down her killer.'

Leo groaned. 'Not you as well. You sound just like Taffy.'

'Good. Then he's saying the right things to you.'

Leo looked down, then put his head in his hands so she couldn't see his face. For a moment she thought he'd begun to cry, but he straightened back up and looked at her. 'Maybe you're right. Maybe I shouldn't have run off and abandoned you, and maybe I should have been there for the funeral.'

'But?' There was definitely a 'but' coming.

'But that's what I did. I had my reasons.'

'Well you're an idiot.'

'Yeah, maybe. But I'm still not coming back.'

'That's alright. We don't want you back now.'

'Really?' Leo looked puzzled. 'So why are you calling then?'

'Because we're being chased by pirates and Morgan thought there might be more of them about and that you might be in danger as well. She wants you to run away, which shouldn't be too much of a problem, should it? You seem to be pretty good at that already.'

'What? What do you mean, pirates? Are you in trouble?'

'Do you care?'

'Of course I care. Is there anything I can do to help?'

'Yes. Run away and hide. At least that way we won't have to worry about you getting in the way and messing things up. Morgan says to wait for us at Qi Tian Station. Apparently we're going to meet you there.'

'Where?'

'Just tell your ship. She'll get you there. Woah!' There was a sudden bright flash on the second monitor and for a second she lost the image of the approaching fighters. The conversation with Leo had gone on long enough. 'Things happening,' she said quickly. 'Gotta go.' And she cut the link.

'Skater, wait!' she heard Leo shout, before the screen went dark.

'They shot at us.'

'It was only a sighting shot,' Morgan replied. 'To calibrate their weapon systems, most likely. What you saw was just the light beam hitting the camera. Nothing to get excited about.'

'But does it mean we're in range?'

'Out here in the deep, we're always in range. You should know that.'

'Oh yeah. It's the gravity thing, right?'

'Exactly. If you fire a bullet out here, there's nothing to slow it down. It'll just keep on going until it hits something, even if that something is right over the other side of the System.'

'So why haven't they been shooting at us already then?'

'There's no point. By the time their bullets reach us, we'll be somewhere else. And I've got the ship making random shifts so there's no way they can plot our course and fire ahead. No, they'll wait until they're much closer in before using their cannon, otherwise it's just a waste of ammunition.'

There was another flash on the screen and this time Skater was sure she felt an impact.

'Now lasers,' Morgan continued, unperturbed. 'They're a different matter. A laser blast is travelling at the speed of light – obviously – so as long as it's on target, it's going to hit. Not even I can dodge a laser blast.'

'But lasers do have a range,' Skater said. 'Even I know that.'

'An *effective* range, yes. The beam begins to scatter the further away it gets from its source, and as it scatters it becomes less powerful. Generally speaking, the bigger the ship, the bigger and more powerful the lasers. Which is why these little interceptors will have to get a lot closer before they can do any more than scorch our paintwork.' Morgan looked up from her monitors and gave Skater a sly grin. 'We, on the other hand, have a bigger ship. And my lasers are really, really good ones.'

'No surprises there then.'

Morgan flicked her comms switch. 'Hey, Pete. We all set down there?'

All set, came the immediate response. *You got Skater with you?*

'I'm here,' Skater replied, clipping on her own commset.

Good. Stay safe. And do exactly what Morgan tells you.

'I will. You too.'

Pete laughed.

'I mean the stay safe bit,' Skater added. 'Not the do what Morgan says bit.'

Maybe just this once I'll do both.

'Okay,' Morgan cut in. 'Enough chat. Time for business.'

34
FIREFIGHT

BUT IN REAL LIFE, SKATER soon realised, ship-to-ship battles weren't anything like as exciting as they were in the holo-vids. There were no bright lances of light shooting out across the darkness, no fireball as they struck, and no loud explosions. There was a deep humming, more felt than heard, as Morgan fired the lasers and then nothing. Skater watched on her monitor and after ten seconds or so, one of the fighters began to glow. There was a sudden bright flare that vanished as soon as it appeared, and then nothing. Less than a minute later, the other two fighters were also gone.

'Wow,' Skater said. 'That was quick. And I have to say, just a little bit disappointing.'

'What were you expecting?' Morgan asked. 'A light show?'

'Well, yeah, sort of.'

'You can't see laser beams, Skater. Not unless there's something along the path of the beam to catch the light, like smoke or dust or whatever, but you're not going to find anything like that out here.

So you don't get to see the light until something gets in its way, which in this case was three little ships.'

'But I have seen lasers,' Skater protested. 'When I was on the *Dragon* and her shuttles were destroyed by that big pirate ship. I definitely saw bright flashes then.'

They were plasma bolts, Pete cut in over the comms.

'Plasma bolts?'

Heavy duty, military grade weapons systems. Only the really big ships will carry them and even then they'll rarely get used much. Very temperamental, and hugely expensive to run.

'But pretty damn destructive when they do run,' Morgan added.

'So, big ships carry them,' Skater added warily, indicating the view on her monitor. 'Like that big ship?'

They're not a pirate weapon. Remember that it was Archer and his mercenaries that attacked us on the Dragon, *not pirates. That thing out there will surely hit hard, but they won't be throwing plasma bolts at us.*

'Well, that's a relief—'

'They're firing,' Morgan cut in. 'Our auto-defences just cut in.'

Skater turned back to her monitor and found the screen filled with thousands of tiny sparkles, like miniature stars popping in and out of existence directly behind their ship.

'Now that's a light show.'

'It's a mirror cloud; tiny shards of highly reflective foil that disrupt the laser beam. They won't stop it completely, but now it won't be able to burn its way through the hull.'

'But they're going to keep firing.'

'Yes, and we'll keep firing off cloud canisters until we run out.'

'And then?'

For a moment Morgan didn't say anything and she seemed suddenly far away, staring off into nothing as if remembering something from a long time ago.

'And then?' Skater repeated.

'And then it's going to get messy.'

They ran on, the enemy ship drawing ever closer and firing its laser weapon every few minutes. Morgan had fallen silent, and Skater couldn't think of anything to say so she sat quietly and watched as each mirror cloud briefly sparkled out behind them. After almost an hour of watching and waiting, Skater felt a gentle tug in her stomach telling her Morgan had fired the thrusters to begin slowing the ship.

'That's it, Pete,' Morgan said over the comms. 'We're down to our last two canisters, so we might as well get ready for the main show. No point in delaying any longer.'

Understood. Everything's set down here. I'll be up in a minute.

Morgan unclipped her harness and pushed away from the controls, towards the back of the bridge. 'Come on, Skater. Time to suit up properly.'

Right outside the bridge was a large weapons cabinet. Morgan pressed her thumb against the touch pad to unlock it and began to hand out items to Skater. First was the body armour. It was light and flexible, but Skater knew only too well how tough it really was. She'd been wearing this very suit when Mr Archer had shot her in the chest from just a few metres away. She'd broken some ribs and collected a bruise the size of a small asteroid, but the armour had held. She slipped it over her head and clipped it into place. Next came a full-head helmet.

'It's armoured,' Morgan explained. 'And it will link up with the air and comms from your E-suit. When they come they'll blast a hole in the hull and suck all the air out before boarding, so you're going to need it. And this,' she added, clipping something to the bottom of Skater's body armour. 'It's a retractable grab line. Clip yourself onto something solid, and when all the air gets sucked out, you won't be.'

Skater left the helmet floating beside her while she examined the grab line, making a mental note to make sure it was definitely attached to something nice and solid.

'And this,' Morgan added, handing one final item to her. It was a belt and holster, with a simple click buckle at the front and small pouches around each side. The pouches – and the holster – were full.

Skater unclipped the holster cover and drew out the pistol. It was a basic projectile firer, nothing fancy, and the narrow grip felt comfortable in her gloved hand.

'Know how to use it?'

Skater popped out one of the ammunition clips and slotted it into the pistol, clicked down the safety and cocked the weapon. Morgan laughed. 'Of course you know how to use it. Sorry I asked.'

Pete appeared at the end of the passageway and pushed himself along until he was floating beside her. He looked at the weapon and then at Skater. 'It's a Martindale 205, not exactly state-of-the-art, but punchy enough to get the job done as long as the target isn't wearing armour. So always aim for the face. Out here a shattered visor will kill someone just as effectively as a bullet through the chest. And you see anyone coming towards you that isn't me or Morgan, you shoot to kill, you understand? You don't hesitate, you don't stop and check, you shoot. Two shots, bang bang, straight at the visor. Got it?'

Skater swallowed nervously. 'Got it.'

'Good. Now give me a hug.'

Skater wrapped her arms around her dad and squeezed as hard as she could, so that her armour was pressing against her chest and making it hard to breathe. She didn't care. 'I love you, Dad.'

'Me too, sweetheart. More than I can say.'

'Try.'

'Maybe later. When we've got a bit more time.' He glanced across at Morgan. 'When this is all over.'

Morgan said nothing.

When they were ready Pete led them back down to the hold, where he had set up a stack of metal crates as cover around the doorway. They clipped on their grab lines, attached helmets, checked weapons and took up position.

'How do we know this is where they'll attack from?' Skater asked over the comms.

'We don't,' Morgan answered. 'But the cargo door is the weakest part of the hull and it's pointing right at them. I'd say it was the most likely target.'

They fell silent. There was nothing to do but wait, and the waiting seemed to be going on forever. After a while Skater found herself thinking about Leo, whizzing off to safety in his fancy new spaceship. Would she ever see him again? Probably not. Even if she didn't die in the shootout, they'd take her as a slave. And slaves didn't last that long out here anyway.

Why had she been so angry with him when she'd called? Why hadn't she just said it was fine, that it was all forgotten and she just wanted to see him again? Because that's what she felt. Maybe back on Midas she'd wanted to punch his lights out, but not now. Now she just wanted her best friend back.

Suddenly there was a dull thud and the ship lurched forward, lifting Skater off her feet. She felt the pull of the grab line behind her and pushed herself back down into position. It was followed by another, louder thud a few seconds later.

'Here we go,' Pete muttered.

There was a blinding flash, and the back wall of the cargo hold exploded inwards.

Although her visor automatically compensated for the flash, it still took Skater several seconds to clear her head and make sense of what was going on. With the back of the ship gone, she should have been staring out into empty space, but instead the whole area in front of the crates was filled with smoke. And smoke meant atmosphere. So the pirates must have already attached a pressurised bridge between their ship and *Nightrider*. And that meant...

Thin beams of red light pierced the smoke, followed seconds later by a score of suited figures gliding quickly in, their laser sights darting this way and that as they searched for targets. Pete and Morgan didn't give them time to find any. They opened fire and the first two figures were knocked back into the smoke. Skater had just enough time to see the remaining red beams all spin round towards their position before she ducked down as bullets began to spark off the metal container beside her head.

She returned fire, glancing out quickly from behind her cover and aiming for the closest dark shape she could make out in the smoke. Two quick shots, then back behind cover; count to three and then back out. The figure was still there so she tried again, taking more care with her aim and bracing her arms against the pistol's recoil. She squeezed the trigger, one, two, and this time she saw the shape spin awkwardly away before she pulled back.

She was shaking. She took a deep breath to calm herself and wondered if it was fear or excitement making her feel this way. She'd just shot someone, maybe killed him, but it felt like the right thing to do, and it didn't seem to bother her as much as she'd imagined it would. She spun back round and fired again.

The smoke was clearing, and after their initial charge, the pirates were being more cautious, some of them giving covering fire while others worked their way slowly forward among the floating piles of wreckage. The red beams were fading with the smoke, and Skater was finding it harder to pick out targets. She shot at arms, legs, anything she could see, swapping out each spent magazine with a spare from her belt. Twice she lined up a clear head shot, only to have Pete beat her to the target both times, and gradually she began to realise that there were fewer and fewer targets available. They were wining.

'I'm hit,' Pete called out.

'Where?' Skater shouted, pushing herself across and grabbing hold of the barricade beside him. 'Is it bad?'

'Leg. Take a look.'

While Pete continued to fire, Skater examined the wound. There was a rip in the suit just above one knee and when she peeled back the torn material to look inside, a trapped globe of blood pushed its way out and sat floating above the wound.

'Eww!'

'Don't worry about the blood, just patch the suit.'

Skater took out one of the emergency patches from her own suit, peeled off the backing strip and pressed it firmly over the tear. There was faint trail of smoke as the new material heat-bonded to the old, and Pete flinched from the pain.

'Sorry,' Skater muttered.

'I'll live. You okay?'

No, she wasn't okay. She was terrified. In fact, she was so far beyond terrified there wasn't even a word to describe what she was. Her hands were shaking so much she could barely reload her pistol and she knew if she stopped to think about what was going on around her, she'd probably throw up in her suit. 'Yeah, fine,' she lied, because she knew that was what her dad needed to hear. 'A little scared, maybe.'

'Good. Keep being scared. When you stop being scared you get cocky, and that's when you make mistakes.'

'They're pulling back,' Morgan announced.

'Really?' Skater asked, peering quickly through one of the small gaps. 'They're retreating?'

'Regrouping. We caught them by surprise, hit them a lot harder than they were expecting, but they're not finished with us yet. Not by a long way.'

35

...TRY, TRY AGAIN

HE WOKE UP. WAS THAT RIGHT? Had he been asleep? He couldn't remember. He couldn't remember anything, in fact, not where he was, or how he had got there, or why he seemed to be propped up in a large chair, with restraints preventing him from moving his arms or legs, or turning his head. Slowly, cautiously, he opened his eyes.

'Are you awake?'

'I...I think so,' he replied, following the sound of the words, searching for their source. There was a light, not too bright, shining directly into his face from the end of a long mechanical arm positioned above him, and beyond that was a white ceiling, the edges of white walls, more machinery. A hospital, perhaps?

A man's face appeared in front of him. young, unshaved, unsmiling.

'Do you know who I am?' he asked.

The man was dressed in a long white coat, wore white, disposable gloves, was holding a slate.

'Are you a doctor?'

The man seemed disappointed. 'Do you know my name?' he asked.

He looked at the white coat, searching for an ID tag, but there wasn't one. He looked back at the face. Did he know this man? had they met before? 'I don't think so.'

'What about your own name? You know that?'

Of course, he thought. But when he searched for it, his name was nowhere to be found. Not his name, or his age, or his date of birth, or where he lived. Nothing. 'I don't remember,' he said, confused by his own uncertainty. 'I don't remember anything.'

The doctor gave a sigh. 'No, I guess you don't.'

'I need the president, right now.' This was a new voice, a woman's.

'Come on in,' the doctor said, turning away and addressing the newcomer. 'Don't worry about any of our decontamination protocols, just...' he waved his hand. 'Make yourself at home.'

The woman had paler skin than the doctor and dark red hair that was tied back from her face. She wasn't wearing a white coat.

'Where is he?' She stared down at him, but it was clear she was talking to the doctor.

'Where he always is.'

'Well, get him up. It's urgent.'

'What is it? What's happened?'

'This.' She took the doctor's slate, swiped it clean and tapped on it for several seconds before handing it back. He couldn't see the screen, but he could hear a voice and so he listened, wondering if it was someone he should know.

My name is Leo Fischer. If you live on Mars you've probably heard of me, because the government there say I'm a wanted criminal, a terrorist who's responsible for blowing up buildings and killing innocent people. But that's a lie. The truth is that they're the ones who are trying to kill me. Because I know something, something really important that they want to keep secret, and they're prepared to kill me in order to stop me telling you what it is. They've already tried several times, and they'll keep trying until they succeed, just like they did when they sent an assassin to murder my mother. But it's too late. They tried, and they failed, and now I'm broadcasting their secret to every corner of the Solar System, so you can see for yourselves what it is the Martian government is trying to hide. You might not believe what you see, and I'm sure the Martian government will tell you it's all a big hoax, but there must be enough people out there who know what they're seeing is real and understand that the human race has finally discovered evidence of an alien civilisation, that we have made contact with an intelligence from that civilisation, and that the Martian government is covering up this fact so they can use the technology they've discovered to build weapons more powerful than anything we've seen before.

The woman swiped the slate and the voice stopped.

'So,' the doctor said. 'Our little secret's finally out in the open. How much has he given away?'

'From the look of it, everything. There's over three hours of data files bundled up in the broadcast. I haven't had time to look through it all yet, but from what I've seen, it's going to be impossible to bluff our way out of it.'

'Can you contain it?'

'For the moment, yes. I've already put a clamp on the major networks so they're not covering it, and the independents are too scared to go against us now. But it's only a matter of time. That's why I need the President. It's his call.'

He didn't know what they were talking about. Broadcasts? Networks? Independents? He understood the language, but the words meant nothing to him. It was as if his eyes and ears had been disconnected from his brain so that he could understand everything but remember nothing.

'I'll go wake him up,' the doctor said. 'Looks like we're finished here for the day anyway.' He reached for something behind the chair, and everything went dark.

36

TAKING DAMAGE

'**Grenades!**' **Pete screamed,** as several tiny objects came spinning through the air towards them. He took aim and began to fire, knocking one of the cylinders off course with his third shot. Morgan joined in and another one was hit, sending it spinning back the way it had come. But there were too many. 'Get down!'

Skater spun round, pressed her back against a container to brace herself and instinctively put her hands over the sides of her helmet, as if trying to block her ears. For two, three seconds nothing happened, then she gazed in horror as one of the grenades floated past, right above her. It hit the rear bulkhead and bounced safely back over the barricade.

'Timer fuse,' Pete said. 'Difficult to get it right in—'

Skater tried to scream. For a split second it felt like her head was turning inside out and everything was dark and scratchy and confusing. Then she crashed into the bulkhead. Her head flicked sideways and her cheek tore across something sharp inside her helmet. She smashed back against the crumpled remains of the container and felt a searing pain all along her spine. Finally the scream came out, but she couldn't hear it. She couldn't hear anything except a high-pitched buzzing that sounded – and felt – as if someone was trying to drill right through her skull.

She reached out, grabbing a nearby hand-hold to stop herself from crashing into any more debris, and looked desperately round for the others. Pete was wedged between the side bulkhead and the twisted remains of one of the containers, but he was moving and still had his rifle. Morgan was above her, drifting helplessly at the end of her grab line and desperately trying to avoid the huge chunks of debris hurtling all about her. With her spare hand, Skater tugged the line and brought her back down.

Suddenly one of the pirates appeared among the wreckage directly in front of her. Without thinking she brought up her pistol and shot him through the visor, only then realising from the tattered state of his suit that he must already have been dead. But there were more behind and they were definitely still alive. Skater fired again, not giving the first of them time to raise his weapon, then again and again as each new target presented itself. When the magazine showed empty she threw it away and slotted a fresh one in without pause.

Mostly she was missing. There was too much debris floating around for more than the occasional clear shot, but at least she seemed to be keeping the pirates pinned down. For the moment, that was good enough.

Skater's hearing was slowly coming back. She could hear Morgan shouting something over the comms but could only make out the occasional word and it made no sense. Then she felt the ship move. There was a tugging sensation and she was knocked backwards into the bulkhead, another jolt of agony shooting down her spine. She screamed, and this time she could hear her own voice.

Another pirate leapt out from behind cover. Skater fired and missed, but instead of charging forward the man ignored her and pushed his way back along the tunnel towards his own ship. A second pirate broke from cover and did the same. Skater fired again, but her pistol was empty. She ducked behind cover to reload, and only then realised it was getting dark. Within seconds the last of the light had disappeared and her helmet visor automatically switched to night vision, turning the whole scene to shades of glowing green. She glanced back along the tunnel, and suddenly everything made sense. The airlock door into the pirate ship had been sealed, cutting off the light that had been spilling into the tunnel – and cutting off the escape route for the handful of pirates still trapped in the tunnel. One of them pounded on the door with his fist, another shot at it with his rifle, but the airlock remained closed. Then the mag-locks disengaged and the ship moved away.

Containers, equipment, debris; everything that was floating free was sucked out into the emptiness of space as the end of the tunnel separated from the ship. For a second, panic overtook Skater as she was thrust forward by the loss of pressure, but another stab of pain in her back told her the grab line had reached its limit. Pete and Morgan were floating beside her. The pirates abandoned by their comrades were not so lucky. Two of them were sucked out along with the wreckage, the rest managed to find something to grab hold of in the tunnel. But then the tunnel itself drifted loose from *Nightrider* and even if she'd wanted to, there was nothing Skater could do to stop it.

There was a fierce, blue-white glow as the pirate ship fired one of its engines, then another and another. After a few seconds Skater could see the whole ship, huge and threatening and bristling with short-range weapons that could have destroyed them in seconds if the pirates had opened fire. But they didn't fire. The ship continued to pull away, turning its back and becoming a tiny, flaming sun that even her visor couldn't completely fade out.

'Why?' she asked, finally able to hear herself above the ringing in her ears. 'What are they doing?'

'Running,' Pete answered. 'Something's spooked them.'

'Well, it wasn't us,' Morgan said. 'We were lost. One more push and they'd have overrun us for sure.'

'You're right,' Pete said. 'There has to be something else out here; something powerful enough to make them turn tail and abandon half a dozen of their men. We should get back inside.'

'We are inside. It's just that inside now has a huge great hole in it.'

'What about the rest of the ship?'

Morgan pulled herself backwards along the length of her grab line until she was floating just above the remains of the deck. 'Well, the access door held, so there's air...'

'But?' Pete asked, following her.

'But the electrics are fried so there's no way to open it.'

'Then we'll do it manually.'

'Really?' Morgan asked, holding her arms out wide. 'With what?'

'I don't know, something. I'll use my bare hands if I have to.'

'Out here? Great idea, Pete.'

'Guys?' Skater called. She was still floating at the end of her wire, staring out through the gaping hole in the back of the ship.

Pete ignored her and continued to argue with Morgan. 'Then what? We just float around here until our air runs out?'

'No, of course not.'

'Or maybe if we're lucky the pirates will pluck up the courage to come back and finish what they started.'

'Guys!'

PART THREE - THE STORM

'What?' Pete snapped.

'I don't think you need to worry about getting the door open.'

'Why?'

'Because spaceship.'

'What?' Pete and Morgan pushed off and came back out to where Skater was floating.

'Spaceship.' Skater pointed out into the darkness, to where a mass of silver metal and glowing light was moving into view. It was twice, maybe three times the size of the pirate ship, but where that had been a chaotic jumble of salvaged parts, this was most definitely a single ship. It wasn't sleek and curved like an attack ship, and there was no extended rotating central section, as on so many of the long-haul transports. This was a giant sphere, made up of interlocking plates arranged in thick layers all across its surface. Skater smiled, suddenly remembering something Leo had taught her a long time ago. Not a sphere, she corrected herself; more of an icosahedron.

'Well, well,' Pete said, and Skater could hear the relief in his voice. 'Now I get why those pirates took off so quickly.'

'Is that what I think it is?'

Pete laughed. 'I don't know. What do you think it is?'

Skater stared at the ship, still not able to believe what she was seeing. It was as if someone had taken a tiny asteroid and built a suit of armour for it, then covered the whole thing in gun barrels. As she watched she noticed a series of tiny engine flares from the underside of the ship, and four much smaller craft broke away and headed towards them. She reached out and felt for her dad's hand, gripping it in her own.

'A Monitor. It's a Monitor, right?'

'Not just any Monitor. That, my dearest darling daughter, is the Monitor-class fortress vessel, *Charybdis*, command ship of the Jovian Fleet. Over eighty years old and still one of the most powerful ships ever built. And also, for a brief period many, many years ago, my home.'

Skater's back was killing her, there were drops of blood floating around inside her helmet and she was shaking so badly she was sure her legs would have collapsed beneath her even under Lunar gravity. But none of that mattered. Not now.

'Sentinels,' she whispered, and smiled through the pain. 'I'm being rescued by Sentinels.'

37

BACK TO MARS

'**THIS IS NOT GOING TO WORK,**' Leo muttered.

Which part, specifically?

'All of it. The whole plan. It's completely crazy. What was I thinking?'

You were thinking of killing the president of Mars.

'Yeah, well, that seemed like a much better idea when I was two hundred million kloms away. Now it just seems like suicide.'

The deliberate killing of another person is called murder, not suicide. Suicide is the killing of oneself.

'Taffy?'

Yes.

'Shut up.'

They were above Mars, attached to one of the arms of a giant docking station that was in a geostationary orbit directly above the capital city of Minerva. They were waiting for the Customs and Immigration inspector to come aboard, and the longer they were kept waiting, the more convinced Leo became that his less-than-cunning plan was rushing him directly towards a Martian prison cell. Or worse. On *Trinity's* large front window screen, Leo watched as shuttles, transport ships and cargo barges came and went from the station's other ports.

'Why are they taking so long? We've been stuck here for hours, and every time we ask what's going on they just say, "please wait". They know, don't they?'

The standard procedure for neutralising a suspect vessel when docked at an orbiting station is to employ an electromagnetic clamp to disarm all weapon systems and prevent escape. As this has not yet happened I would say that no, they do not know.

'Well then why—'

I have a request for entry, Trinity interrupted.

Leo gave a start and spun around from the screen. 'Wait!' he snapped, suddenly forgetting everything he'd spent the past few weeks rehearsing. 'Give me a sec.' He pulled himself into the command chair, made sure the hideous purple E-suit he was wearing was sealed right up to his chin and clipped a mirrored slit-visor across his eyes. 'Okay. Okay.' He took a deep breath, hoping it would calm his nerves, but it just made him dizzy. He wiped his palms on his suit. 'I'm ready. You can open up.'

The airlock opened and a scanner drone glided through, followed by two uniformed officials who looked more like soldiers than any Customs and Immigration officers Leo had ever seen. The one in front carried a slate; the one behind, an assault rifle. The drone began to move slowly through the ship.

'Long last,' Leo said with a broad smile and a strange, overly fluid accent that seemed to place his origin as somewhere between Australia and London-South. 'What kept ya?'

'We're busy,' the first man replied, looking down at his screen and not returning the smile. 'This your ship?'

'One of 'em. Got more.'

'And you are Mister…' The man looked puzzled. 'According to your data files, your name appears to be the mathematical symbol for square root.'

'Root2. That's me.'

'Root Two? What kind of a name is that?'

'A legendary one. Not heard of me?'

The man gave a sigh. 'What's your real name, Mr Root?'

'Root2 *is* my real, soldier. Buzz me, you'll see.'

The man floated over to the command seat and held up the slate in front of Leo. 'Thumbs there and there, eye in front of the red circle,' he said, indicating the marked areas on the back of the screen.

Leo unclipped the visor and let himself be scanned. After a few seconds the man seemed satisfied and Leo clipped the visor back in place.

'Well, well,' the man said. 'So your name really is Root2.'

'Told ya so. Now ya know.'

'Terran, huh? From the…Atlantics?' the man suggested.

'Way back when. No fixed now.'

'And it says you're an experimental musician and performance artist.'

'And legend.'

'Doesn't say you're a jumped-up little rat turd though,' the man muttered as he turned away.

'Whisper what?' Leo asked.

'I said, is there anyone else on board?'

'Uh-uh. Just me an' the Body-G,' Leo said, nodding towards the back of the ship where Taffy was standing in the corner, feet magnetically clamped to the deck to stop him floating off.

The man with the rifle pushed himself across to get a closer look at the large, mechanical body. 'Bodyguard, is it? Ex-military, from the look of it.'

'Ex-ex-ex. Thing is beyond old.'

'Weaponised?'

'Nah, fists only.'

'You got it registered, here on Mars?' the first man asked.

'Natch.'

'Well make sure you keep it under control while you're on-world. You know all the cities are under martial law right now?'

'Yeah, I read the feeds, I know the quo.'

'Good. So you understand that if you put so much as a single foot out of line you'll be in more trouble than you can imagine, yes?'

'Feet in line. Saved,' Leo replied. 'We done now?'

The man checked behind him. The scanner drone was hovering back at the airlock. 'Well, the drone says you're clean, and your biometrics check out, Mr...Root Two,' he said, with a barely concealed smirk. 'So yes, you're cleared through. Enjoy your stay on Mars.'

'Ultimate,' Leo replied, already feeling the tension in his shoulders beginning to ease.

But at the airlock the man paused and turned back. 'Oh, just one more thing.'

The tension came straight back.

'There's a report out for a stolen ship, same class as yours.'

There was a pause.

'So?' Leo asked.

'Yeah. Guy claims he was tortured by terrorists and was forced to hand over his ship to save his life. Nasty business. Out in the Belt, apparently; Cybele Sector.'

'Nasty place. Plenty pirates.'

'The log says that's the direction you came in from.'

'So?'

'So I was just wondering if you saw anything, or heard anything over the localnet while you were out there?'

There was another pause. Leo realised he was squeezing the arm rest on his seat and forced himself to relax his grip. 'Saw pirates. Had to scoot. Plasma-overdrived my way outta there. Didn't see no other ship like mine tho'. You don't believe, scan the shipmind. Truth is truth in there.'

'It's fine,' the man replied. 'It was just on the off-chance you knew anything. We're asking all ships coming in from that region. But like you say, it's a nasty place. Well, thanks anyway.'

As soon as the two men had left and the airlock was securely closed behind them, Leo sprang up from his chair. 'Oh my god, we did it. It worked.'

It does appear that way.

'And thanks for the feed,' Leo added, unclipping the slit visor and ear pod that had enabled him to remain in contact with Taffy throughout the inspection. 'Do people really speak like that?'

According to my data, yes. It is called slapchat.

'It sounded awful. *I* sounded awful. And those guys obviously thought I was some kind of idiot.'

Yes, enough of an idiot that they let you through immigration with nothing more than a scan of your vessel and a few straightforward questions.

'What about all that stuff at the end, about the ship being stolen? Do you think they knew anything, or were they really just asking everyone?'

Does it matter? You were not arrested.

'I guess not. And even if they do scan Trinity, they won't find anything about Cecil Abernathy and his stolen ship in there, or anything about Leo Fischer for that matter; I made sure of that.'

Yes, you were very thorough. You have become quite adept at manipulating the data storage in artificial minds.

Leo groaned. 'Please don't start all that again. Yes, I know I interfered with Trinity's memory, and yes, I know it's illegal and… whatever else you said it was.'

Morally indefensible.

'That as well. But I had to. I *had* to.' He indicated his hideous and ill-fitting purple E-suit. 'Otherwise all of this, all our hard work creating a cover for me, would have been a complete waste of time, wouldn't it? Because the minute anyone questioned Trinity they would have found out the truth. She's not a complex mind like you. She can't lie. So it was either alter her memories, or give up trying to get back onto Mars and run off to Qi Tian Station like Skater told me to.'

That was always an option.

'Not to me,' Leo snapped. 'I'm sick of running away and hiding. That's all I've been doing for the past year and it doesn't work. It just gets people killed, and I don't want the next one to be me. So now I'm doing something about it. That's why I put out the broadcast about you and your ship, that's why I've come back to Mars, and that's why I'm going to kill Whittaker.'

Yes.

'Yes?' Leo was expecting an argument, not agreement, and he was momentarily lost for words.

I agree. Hiding from President Whittaker has not been a successful strategy. He is a persistent and vindictive opponent and also extremely resourceful. He will most likely continue to pursue you until you are either dead or captured. And if he captures you, he will most likely kill you.

'Well, I'd better not get captured then.' Leo pushed himself back over to the command chair. 'Trinity?'

Yes, Root2.

'Are we cleared to leave?'

We are cleared.

'And have we got somewhere to park downstairs?'

Bay twelve, Section four, Blue Zone South.

'Okay then. Let's go.'

As the ship began its short flight into the Martian atmosphere towards Minerva Docks, Leo allowed himself to relax. It had taken him two weeks to create the Root2 persona, inventing a back story that covered the last five years and included the details of dozens of concerts and performances he'd given at various locations on Earth. Taffy had even composed a collection of musical tracks based on some old samples of Abernathy's music they'd come across in Trinity's data files. The pieces were long and repetitive and not at all the kind of thing Leo would normally have listened to, but Taffy had assured him they were perfect examples of the type of music Root2 would have composed. One or two of them were even quite catchy.

And then he'd had to pre-embed all that information into as many public access networks as possible, so that a data log would show entries dating back over several years, not coming through as a single burst. That hadn't actually been too difficult, just slow. With Taffy and Trinity both on the case it had still taken another two weeks, and even then there were still a couple of the mega-nets he hadn't been able to hack with the equipment on board.

But the most difficult thing had been hacking into the Martian central biometrics database. If he'd actually been on Mars, with access to a scanner unit he could pull apart, the whole business would have involved little more than a couple of hours of reprogramming and uploading new data. But out in the middle of nowhere, where everything had to be accessed remotely and the time lag meant every command took ten minutes to be received, the process was slow and awkward and much more dangerous. But the fact that he was now powering his way through the upper atmosphere, with the spaceport and its immigration officials safely behind him, meant that his hard work had paid off. From now on, as far as any bio-scanner on Mars was concerned, he was no longer Leo Fischer, he was Root2. Cecil Marchmont Abernathy, on the other hand, was going to have a lot of explaining to do once he finally made it back to Mars and discovered he was now a wanted terrorist.

Leo couldn't help smiling. Getting through immigration had been the first real test of his plan and he'd aced it. So now Root2 – musician, artist, legend – was just two days away from the thing he wanted more than anything else in the entire Solar System; ten seconds of face-to-face time with the president of Mars.

The immigration official watched from the window screen in his office as Trinity shrank away into the distance. He clipped on his phone, spoke a brief command and waited for the reply to come in. He didn't bother pulling down the eye screen – this call would be voice only. After a few seconds, the call was answered.

'He's on his way… No, no problems. Bio-scan was clean… I did. I ran a full background sweep and nothing got picked up. He's been incredibly thorough, and I certainly can't fault his computing skills, it's just… Exactly. He's not fooling anyone with that disguise… No, terrible. He was getting a feed through his visor, presumably from the AI, but even so he obviously didn't have a clue what he was supposed to sound like… No, of course not. If you hadn't told me to let him through I'd have had him in the interrogation room after five seconds… Well, it's your call, but if it was up to me, I'd pick him up the moment he sets foot outside his ship. You know what he's planning… Alright. I've cleared him down to the docks. From now on, he's all yours.'

38

LUNCH WITH THE PRESIDENT

THE GUARD GLANCED at the invitation, gave a brief nod and moved to one side, allowing Leo to pass. A security arch had been set up just beyond and Leo waited nervously while an elegantly dressed elderly woman in front of him stepped inside and began the scanning process by complaining loudly to the attendant.

'Tell me this is going to work,' Leo muttered quietly.

This is going to work. Taffy's voice sounded reassuringly calm in his ear.

'You sure?'

Yes.

'And what makes you so certain?'

You told me it was going to work.

'That's it? That's all you've got?'

I was attempting to make a joke.

'Bad timing, Taffy. Remember, we're not here to have a laugh, we're here to kill——' Leo winced as a sudden burst of static filled his ear, cutting off the rest of his sentence. 'Ow! What the hell was that?'

I'm sorry. It sounded as if you were about to say something inappropriate. Remember that radio communications, as well as fingerprints and retinas, are also routinely scanned.

'Right. Right.' Leo glanced around to see if his outburst had drawn any attention, but no one was looking his way. The woman in front of him was just finishing up. 'So, you in position yet?'

Yes.

Leo looked across to the side wall of the museum's atmosphere dome, but the bottom section of its plas-glass had been electronically frosted and he couldn't see anything beyond except a few vague shapes. 'Good,' he continued. 'So all being well, I'll see you again in about two hours' time.'

Yes. Would you like me to wish you good luck?

'Sure, why not?'

Because in some cultures, wishing a person good luck is actually considered bad luck.

'Well, not in mine. I'll take all the luck you can give me.'

Getting himself invited to the opening had been easy. Taffy had simply called the museum, pretending to be his manager, and asked about the possibility of attending the official opening. The museum had been delighted and two days later a confirmation message had arrived from the Office of the President, requesting him to come in person to Hightower to collect his official invitation. That had been his first stop the previous day.

It had been surreal. Hightower was the heart of the Martian administration and although he'd only had to go to one of the reception desks in the building's main atrium, the place had been full of drone monitors recording his every move, and armed security guards who would happily have shot him on sight had they known who he really was. And he'd walked right past all of them, confirmed his ID, collected his invitation and walked right past them again on his way out. And the strange thing was, he hadn't even been that nervous. He'd played his part perfectly and no one had given him a second glance. He'd almost enjoyed it, in fact.

But not today. Today wasn't about enjoying himself, about playing a role and deceiving people, today was about killing a man in cold blood. After today everything would be different. He would have become the terrorist everybody already believed him to be. He would be a murderer. That was huge, beyond huge, and it was something he would have to live with for the rest of his life. Also, if things didn't go exactly to plan, there was a fifty-fifty chance the rest of his life might be no more than a couple of hours, and that was no consolation at all.

The scanner was empty. He stepped forward and waited nervously while the thin band of blue light moved slowly down his body and then back up again. When it was finished, the attendant slid the retinal scanner into place in front of him.

'You'll have to leave the visor here, I'm afraid,' she explained. 'Recording devices are not permitted at the president's lunch.'

'But...' Leo stammered. 'I need it.'

The attendant looked puzzled. 'For medical reasons?'

'Yes. Well, no, not exactly. It's just that...' What could he say? That he needed the visor so that an AI could remote-access it in order to help navigate him through the museum while he was making his escape after killing the president?

The attendant was waiting.

Let her take it. We walked the route yesterday. You can remember it without my assistance.

And that had been his second stop yesterday. He and Taffy had visited the museum, found out where the lunch was going to be held, and walked backwards and forwards through the museum's labyrinth of rooms and passageways until they had settled on a suitable escape route. This would take Leo down to the museum's sub-levels, to a small service entrance that fed directly into one of Minerva's underground commercial centres, where he would easily be able to lose himself among the crowds.

Taffy was right, they had walked the route yesterday, but he hadn't been paying much attention. He'd assumed he would be wearing the visor and that Taffy would be displaying the route for him as he went. Maybe if he walked it now he might find the way, but what about when he was sprinting for his life with half-a-dozen armed guards chasing him down? Suddenly that fifty-fifty was looking a lot more like seventy-thirty. And not in a good way.

The attendant was still waiting.

'Fine,' Leo said reluctantly, unclipped the visor and handed it over.

'And finally, fingerprint,' the attendant said, once Leo was finished with the retinal scan.

Leo held up his hands, displaying a pair of close fitting, shimmering silver gloves and a collection of ornate rings. 'You gonna take my jewels as well?'

'Just a fingerprint. You may replace the gloves and jewellery afterwards."

Leo removed the rings, peeled the glove from his right hand and pressed his thumb to the scanner. The way things were going, he half-expected an alarm to start buzzing and a pair of heavy hands to grab him from behind and drag him off somewhere. But the scan was fine, the woman thanked him and wished him a pleasant lunch, and he was through the arch and into the dining area. He let out a sigh of relief.

The room was a big white box. Its walls, floor and ceiling were made from the same electro-frosted plas-glass as the dome, and embedded in each surface were 5,000 miniature holo-projectors, capable of creating 'the most structurally detailed and convincing three-dimensional immersive holographic experience imaginable'. Leo watched the infomercial on the small screen by the doorway but was disappointed to discover that the official opening ceremony meant the exhibition would be inactive today. So instead of experiencing the pleasures of holographic art, Leo was going to be eating his lunch in a big white box. Not that it mattered. He wasn't here for the atmosphere.

Leo walked the room. Several round tables had been set out, with a larger, rectangular one taking up most of the space at the top end. There were double doors in the centre of each wall, but when he wandered over to the nearest set, he found it had been disabled and wouldn't open. The same was true of the other side. The doors behind the big table were flanked by security guards and were presumably where Whittaker would come from, which left the doorway behind him as his only exit. That was okay – at least he could remember where that one led to – so he picked an empty seat at the table nearest to it and sat studying the interactive menu card and ignoring everyone around him.

People began to take their seats. Mostly, they sat as close as possible to the main table and there were clearly more seats than people to fill them. No wonder the museum had been so eager to find him an invitation at such short notice. Just when Leo though he might actually get the whole table to himself, a middle-aged couple sat down opposite him. They were deep in conversation – something about body modification as art – and much to his relief they continued their discussion and completely ignored him.

'Ladies and gentlemen, if I might have your attention for a moment.'

Leo looked up from the menu he now knew by heart. An official-looking woman in a smart black suit was standing in front of the main table, thanking everyone for coming and explaining what a pleasure it was going to be. Leo switched off. He'd sat through enough school prize-giving ceremonies and end-of-term assemblies to know how to ignore them, and instead he spent the time going over his escape route, room by room.

'...Mr Carlton Whittaker.'

Leo snapped back and, because everyone else was doing it, rose to his feet. Whittaker came in through the rear doors, smiling and waving and greeting those nearest to him with handshakes and shoulder pats, but even for the sake of his disguise Leo found he couldn't join in with the cheering and applause. The man didn't deserve even that.

He was glad to sit down again when the applause died away. He was shaking and there was a knot of something gnawing in the pit of his stomach. Was it anger, or fear? Either way, it completely killed his appetite. He ordered various items from the menu – mostly the things with the fanciest names – but when they arrived he found he couldn't face more than an occasional mouthful without worrying he might throw up. In the end he gave up and stuck to sips of chilled water whenever his throat felt like it was turning into a desert.

And all the time he was staring at Whittaker, at the face of an evil, insane old man who had the power of a planet behind him and was about to drag the entire human race into a war that could well wipe out a significant portion of it. But that wasn't why Leo was going to kill him, even if that's what he'd told Taffy. No, it wasn't to save all those billions of lives that would be lost in a war, it was to make the man pay for one single life he'd already taken; the only one that mattered. His mother.

Leo relaxed his grip before he broke the glass he was clutching. Getting angry wasn't going to help him. What he needed now was to stay calm, focused. The lunch was coming to an end. It was nearly time.

Five minutes later the smartly dressed woman called for silence and introduced Whittaker once again. Now it was time for his speech, and after another round of applause had died away, he began by thanking the museum for their wonderful lunch and saying how relieved he had been when, on seeing all the wonderful food laid out in front of him, he had discovered it to be real, not simply a giant hologram. Laughter. More applause.

It went on like that for thirty minutes. He talked about his love of art, his own attempts at painting when he was younger, his private collection and his gifts to this very museum, with plenty of jokes thrown in along the way. At one point he even mentioned the rumours flying around about aliens, wondering whether they might be interested in a trade – their technology for our great works of art. This had given him another standing ovation and brought Leo's glass even closer to destruction. How could they be so stupid? So gullible? Hadn't they watched his broadcast? Hadn't they seen the images and video files he'd transmitted of Homeworld and its inhabitants? Didn't anyone care? Did they really think he'd made the whole thing up?

And then it was over. This time, when the people rose to their feet they stayed there. Whittaker took the applause for a moment, then came round from the far side of the table and began to make his way through the crowd. Leo's heart began to race. He positioned himself as close as possible to the exit. The doors were already open and the security arch had been removed.

Straight out, first left, long run, left again...no, right, then left again. Now more than ever Leo wished he still had Taffy in his ear. He needed to calm down. He was starting to panic. Was he in the right place? What if Whittaker didn't stop? What if someone got in the way? Whittaker had bodyguards. There were two of them, clearing a path for him as he worked his way through the crowd. Everyone wanted to shake his hand, congratulate him, say something clever or funny. It was taking forever. Leo clenched his fists to stop his hands from shaking, then began to play with his rings. The pounding in his chest was so loud he was sure the people around him must be able to hear it. The security guards moved past. Leo stepped forward and suddenly he was standing directly in front of Whittaker. The president smiled and held out his hand.

'Nice to meet you, son. Art lover, or budding artist yourself?'

Leo froze. The man he was here to kill was two feet away from him, but he was dizzy and he'd forgotten how to make his arms move. He'd imagined the moment hundreds of times. But not like this, not with him being so stupid and clumsy and scared. He'd even planned what he would say, in those vital few seconds when the two of them were face to face, but the words were gone and his mouth hung open uselessly.

Whittaker gave him a wink. 'Or maybe you were just here for the free food, eh?' He began to turn away. And in that same instant, Leo reached out automatically and shook the president's hand.

39

—FLASHBACK—

LEO?

Leo woke with a start. 'What's the matter? Is it pirates?'

No. There is no threat.

'What is it then?'

I have a present for you.

'That's it? You woke me up to give me a present?'

Yes.

'Well it had damn well better be a good one.'

Here. Taffy lifted up the small silver case he was holding and presented it to Leo. *Please be careful.*

'What is it?' There was a fingerprint lock on the front of the case but the catch was already open. Leo lifted the lid. Inside was something that looked like a cross between a jewellery box and a miniature chemistry kit. Most of the space was taken up by rows of tiny glass bottles containing liquids or powders of various colours and quantities. Below were several compartments that held a collection of syringes, pipettes, measuring spoons and spare bottles. Down one side, each in its own individual slot, was a set of ten rings. Some were plain bands of silver or gold, others more ornate, with large gemstones set into fancy housings. And on the opposite side was a neatly folded pair of silver gloves.

'What the hell is all this?'

The bottles contain a selection of chemical compounds. The rings are designed to act as a delivery system. The gloves are for your protection. It is a poisons kit, designed for an assassin.

'What? Hang on a sec.' Leo struggled out of his sleeping bag and pushed his way past Taffy into the main cabin, heading straight for the galley. He took out a juice carton from the chill store, popped open the top and began to suck on the straw. 'Right, let's try this again. An assassin's kit?'

Yes. I have been considering the problem of how you will kill Carlton Whittaker. You will need a weapon that is undetectable, easy to use and will guarantee death. This is the weapon.

'Where the hell did it come from? You're not going to tell me Abernathy had it stashed away in a secret compartment somewhere, are you?'

No. It belonged to Nuying Chen. This is almost certainly the weapon she used to kill your mother.

'What? How did you get hold of it?'

I took it from her ship.

'Her ship?' Leo glanced across towards the large window screen, but from where he was standing Chen's ship was out of view. 'I don't understand. You went over there?'

Yes. While you were asleep.

'What, you just knocked on the door and she let you in?'

No, I did not knock.

'Then how... Christ, Taffy, what did you do?' Leo pushed off and flew to the front of the cabin, scrolling through the external cameras to get as complete a view as possible through the window screens. Chen's ship was no longer drifting in front of them. 'What did you do?'

I acquired a murder weapon for you.

'But what happened to the ship?'

It is now on a different course to ours.

'And Chen?'

She is no longer a threat.

'Did you kill her?'

She is no longer a threat.

Leo continued to stare at the screen, trying to imagine how Taffy had managed to get on board the other ship, what the two of them might have said to each other, whether he would have chosen to let her live, and if not, how he'd killed her. But after a while he decided he really didn't care. She was no longer a threat and that was all that mattered. 'Good,' he said, and turned away from the stars. 'So let's have another look at this poisons kit then, shall we?'

40

THE DEED IS DONE

WHITTAKER GAVE HIM A WINK. 'Or maybe you were just here for the free food, eh?' He began to turn away. And in that same instant, Leo reached out automatically and shook the president's hand.

To Whittaker it was just one more handshake among many, and no sooner had Leo's fingers wrapped themselves around his hand than he was pulling away, looking for the next outstretched palm. But Leo held on, tightening his grip and clamping his other hand quickly down on top, squeezing, pressing his rings into the old flesh as hard as he could.

One second...

Whittaker flinched. The smile was still there, but now there was something in his eyes. Confusion? Discomfort? Irritation maybe.

Two seconds...

Whittaker tugged to try and free his hand, but Leo wasn't letting go. All his anger, all his hatred was flowing through his fingers. In that instant, if he could have crushed Whittaker's hand, he would have done.

Three seconds…

Now the smile was slipping. Whittaker tugged again. One of the bodyguards reached in and roughly pulled Leo's hands apart, steering the president forward again in the same movement. Leo let him go.

'Jeez,' Whittaker muttered, clenching and unclenching his fist as he moved on, but now ignoring the rest of the offered hands around him.

It was done. Leo's heart was pounding, his hands were shaking, and only after several more seconds did he remember to breath, gulping down a lungful of air. He'd done it! He couldn't really believe it had worked so perfectly, exactly as he and Taffy had planned it. But it had. And now he had something like ten seconds before the first of the poisons began to take effect, at which point all attention would be on Whittaker and he would be able to sneak away. He would stay just long enough to see the look on the old man's face as his heart began to fail and the life leaked out of him, then he would make his escape.

Whittaker came to a stop, still rubbing his hand. He turned slowly, searching the faces behind him until he picked out Leo. Leo knew he should go, step back into the crowd and disappear, leave Whittaker to puzzle it out for the last few seconds he had left, but suddenly he couldn't remember how to make his legs move. He was drawn in by the old man's gaze. For several seconds the two of them stared at each other, no more than ten feet apart. And Leo saw the exact moment when Whittaker's confusion turned to recognition.

'Leo Fischer,' he mouthed.

Leo nodded. Whittaker looked down at his hand and then back up. Now there was a clear look of horror on his face. That was enough for Leo. He sprinted for the exit.

PART THREE – THE STORM

Sprinting wasn't exactly the word for it. The low gravity made running of any sort difficult and clumsy and what Leo was doing was more of a slow-motion bouncing. It helped that he was wearing skuff boots, giving him as much grip as he was ever going to find anywhere on Mars, but even so, it felt like he was about to take off with every step. But at least it would be the same for anyone trying to chase him.

He grabbed hold of the edge of the doorway and swung himself round into the long corridor beyond. This part of the museum had been closed off to visitors but there were still several attendants milling around. And sitting to one side were two smartly dressed men who were obviously security guards. As Leo burst round the corner they both rose to their feet, their hands instinctively reaching for their jackets and the concealed weapons inside.

'It's the president,' Leo shouted, continuing to run past them. 'He's hurt. He needs a doctor right now.'

Just then there was shouting from inside the lunch room and for two or three precious seconds the guards hesitated, trying to decide what exactly was going on.

'Stop!' one of them shouted at last, but by then it was too late. Leo had reached the turning he needed and darted round, losing his balance and crashing into the side wall as his momentum lifted both feet off the ground. He bounced back, narrowly missing a display stand containing a particularly delicate-looking glass ornament, and scrambled on. A rope barrier had been set up at the end of this corridor and Leo leapt it like a low hurdle, emerging into a much larger room, and part of the museum still open to the public.

'No running in the museum!' a nearby attendant called out. Leo ignored her and set off towards the far end of the gallery. People around him stared, but no one made any attempt to stop him.

There was a loud crack, and a display monitor beside him shattered, showering him with shards of broken glass. Someone screamed. And suddenly everyone was running. Leo ducked down but kept moving, trying to weave his way among the terrified people around him. He risked a quick glance backwards and saw the two security guards from earlier. One had tripped over the rope barrier and was struggling to untangle himself, the other was ahead, his weapon raised. He fired and there were more screams, but Leo didn't have time to notice where the shot had gone.

It was too far to the exit at the top end of the hall and Leo knew if he tried to make a run for it, the guard would have a clear line of sight to him. Instead he followed the man beside him, who was scrabbling on his hands and knees towards one of the side corridors. As the two of them reached the exit the man screamed and a spurt of blood shot out from his shoulder. Leo leapt up and ran on.

But now he was lost. This was part of the museum he hadn't explored the day before, and he had no idea how to get back to the route he'd planned. He needed to get down to the sub-levels, but the lifts would be too slow and he had no idea how to get to the escalators without retracing his steps and heading straight into his pursuers. He took a turning at random and another almost straight away, finding himself in a small, darkened room. There was a single large painting glowing against the end wall and a short wooden bench facing it. Apart from that, the room was empty. There were no other exits.

Leo pressed himself into the shadows and took a few seconds to catch his breath, sucking in deep lungfuls of air as quietly as he could. He was in big trouble. He couldn't stay here – he knew that – but he would have to time his escape just right. He'd only seen the two guards, but more were bound to be on the way. Now would be a really good time to have Taffy telling me what to do, he thought, wishing they'd come up with a back-up plan more detailed than just *run away as fast as you can*. But too bad. Next time they'd be more prepared. Yeah, Leo told himself. Like there's ever going to be a next time.

Once he had his breathing under control, Leo moved back over to the entrance and cautiously slid his head around the corner. An announcement was being repeated over the museum's public-address system – telling everyone to clear the place as quickly as possible – and he knew he had no more than a minute or two to find his way back to the stairway that would lead him down to the safety of the sub-levels before the whole building was locked down.

Someone grabbed him from behind. In one swift movement his legs were kicked away from beneath him and he was slammed to the floor, face first. Before he could even think about struggling, one of his arms was pinned down by a heavy boot and the other was twisted up behind his back. He felt the rings being tugged roughly from his fingers, followed by the gloves, and the boot pressing down on him was only removed when both hands were bare. He was dragged back upright.

'No noise,' said a whispered voice right next to his ear. 'And no trying to make a run for it. Let's go.'

Just then the two bodyguards appeared at the top of the corridor, saw Leo and his attacker and moved cautiously forward, weapons raised.

'It's okay,' the man called out. 'He's unarmed now. I've got it sorted.'

'Who the hell are you?'

'Military. Special Ops. Who the hell are you?'

'Presidential bodyguard.' They came closer. 'And this guy is ours. Hand him over.'

'Fine. Help yourself.'

One of the bodyguards lowered his pistol, stepped forward and reached out to take hold of Leo. There were two soft thuds and both guards crumpled to the floor, a neat hole in each forehead.

'No?' the man asked. 'Oh well, I'll hang on to him then. Come on, this way.'

The man spun Leo round and pushed him back into the room. Light was spilling in from a tiny crack in the far wall, beside the hideous glowing painting, and as Leo reached it he realised it was a narrow doorway. A sign at head height read, *Staff Only*.

'Damn,' Leo muttered. 'Staff access. I didn't think of that.'

'It'll be easier than going through the public galleries.' The man tapped his comms. 'This is Foxtrot. I have the package and I'm in the tunnels, ground floor, south side. We're on our way.'

'You're not one of Whittaker's men, are you?' Leo asked, although the answer was already obvious.

'Not exactly, no.'

'So where are you taking me?'

'You'll see.'

The corridors were deserted and they moved quickly, Leo going ahead but guided by the hand still gripping the back of his jacket. At one point they turned a corner to find someone walking straight towards them. Leo's captor raised his pistol, but it was an old man who simply leapt to one side and raised his hands as they hurried past.

After the next turning they came to a small lift and the man pulled Leo to a stop, shoving him inside as soon as the door slid open.

'Sub Two,' the man said, indicating for Leo to press the button.

As they descended, Leo realised he was no longer panicking. Whoever this man was, he was definitely helping him to get out of the museum. The service entrance on Sub-level Two was where he'd been trying to get to anyway and wherever he ended up after that was bound to be safer than stuck inside the museum with Whittaker's bodyguards looking to shoot him on sight.

'So who...' he began, but at that moment the lift door opened and he came face to face with another black-suited figure like the one behind him. There was a body lying on the ground beside him – a policeman, from the look of it – and Leo decided it probably wasn't a good time for questions.

'Problems?' Foxtrot asked.

The other man looked down at the body and shrugged. 'Not really. Transport's waiting.' He led the way along the corridor and out into a huge storage area and underground vehicle park. At the far end was a ramp leading up and out of the building, with a ground car powered and waiting at the bottom. There were also three more bodies.

Foxtrot pushed Leo into the back of the car and climbed in beside him. The second man joined the driver in the front and the car was speeding up the ramp before the doors had finished closing.

Leo wondered if he should try to escape. They hadn't bothered to lock the doors, and even though the windows were tinted and no one could see in, he could still see exactly where they were and would be able to pick the perfect moment to dive out and make a run for it. Even if these people were trying to help him, he didn't know who they were, or where they were taking him, or why. And Taffy was still out there waiting. The two of them had done pretty well on their own up till now and all they had to do was hide out somewhere until he could get back to his ship and then they could head out to wherever he wanted. Qi Tian Station was still an option. Or even Earth, if he could make it past the blockade.

'Automatic,' the driver ordered.

Automatic mode engaged.

The car slowed, the windows frosted over and became opaque, there was a clunk as the doors locked. Damn, Leo thought.

'Well,' the driver added. 'Someone's having a busy day.' He pressed a button on the dashboard and his seat glided round until he was facing his passengers. 'Hello, Leo.'

It was Aitchison.

41

WHAT HAPPENS NOW?

'**THEY'RE NOT TELLING US ANYTHING,**' Foxtrot said. 'Which almost certainly means he's dead.' He was following a live news feed through the tiny screen clipped in front of one eye while the car continued its leisurely progress through the sub-levels of Minerva.

'Well, Leo,' Aitchison said. 'You've just murdered the most powerful man in the Solar System. I suppose congratulations are in order.' He wasn't smiling, and Leo couldn't tell if he was being sarcastic or not.

'I didn't do it so that people would congratulate me.'

'And yet plenty of people will.'

'But not you.'

'I thought I just had.'

'But you're not smiling. You don't think I should have done it, do you?'

'Do you think you should have done it?'

'Yes. He was a maniac, and he was about to start the War of the

Worlds.'

'The War of the Worlds?'

'It's this really old book Skater made me read, about a Martian invasion of Earth.'

'Really? Who wins?'

'Earth.'

'Interesting. I must read it sometime.'

'He killed my mother.'

'I heard she'd died. I'm sorry.'

'She didn't die, he killed her.'

'I'm sure he was happy enough with the outcome, but he wasn't the one who gave the order.'

'Who did then?'

'A woman named Kalina Kubin.'

'And who the hell is she?'

'You remember our old friend Mr Archer? Well, Kubin is his replacement.'

'Then it makes no difference. Whittaker was still the one in charge.'

'Here's something interesting,' Foxtrot interrupted. 'They're not taking him to the hospital. They've put him on a flyer and they're heading out of town.'

'Track it,' Aitchison said to the fourth man.

'So what happens now?' Leo asked.

'Who knows? He never appointed a vice-president. The military will keep power of course, and there'll be a lot of unrest, so I'm guessing we'll be looking at more martial law, more repression, more riots and killing. It's not going to be so much fun to live on Mars for a while now. And that's why I'm not dancing with joy just yet.'

'I meant about me. What happens to me now?'

'Oh,' Aitchison waved his hand. 'I'll find somewhere for you to stay. I've got quite a network set up here these days. There's bound to be somewhere you can fit in. But like I say, living on Mars isn't going to be so much fun. We have your robot, by the way.'

'Taffy? What did you do to him? Is he damaged?'

Aitchison looked at him as if he was an idiot. 'We've cleared out your ship as well. You won't be going back there.'

'So that's it then? I'm stuck here?'

'Where else are you going to go? Earth? A life with your uncle in New Zealand and a school you hate? You're not that person any more, Leo. So stay here. Do something useful. Make a difference.'

'I've already tried. You must have watched my broadcast. I announced to the entire human race the news that they weren't the only sentient beings in the universe. I gave them all the proof they could possibly need, and what happened? They ignored me and thought the whole thing was some big, made-up joke.'

'Well, that's people for you. Sometimes they take a lot of convincing. Try again.'

'You try again. I've done my bit, and now I'm sick of the whole damn thing. You can keep Taffy, keep all my research if you want and good luck to you. I've got other things I want to do with my life.'

'Like find the Monroes?'

'Yes,' Leo replied, not even surprised by how well Aitchison could read him. It was what the man did. 'Like find the Monroes.'

'Need some help with that?'

'That depends. Do you know where they are?'

Aitchison smiled. 'I do.'

Leo sat up. 'Really?'

'Really.'

'What happened? They were attacked by pirates. Are they okay?'

'As a matter of fact they are.'

'Where?'

'Right now, I couldn't exactly say. But they're with the Sentinels, so they're about as safe as they could possibly be. Certainly a lot safer than if they were back here on Mars.'

'Can you get me there?'

'I could. The question is, what's in it for me? Do you have anything to trade?'

Leo thought of Skater and imagined the huge, blazing row waiting for him the next time they met. There were bound to be tears, and Leo suspected they would be his, not hers. But it would be worth it. Because at some point they would be friends again. Maybe not friends like they'd been before – that was probably too much to hope for – but friends anyway. And that would be more than enough.

'Yes,' he replied to Aitchison. 'Anything you want.'

EPILOGUE

HE WOKE UP. WAS THAT RIGHT? Had he been asleep? He couldn't remember. He couldn't remember anything, in fact, not where he was, or how he had got there, or why he seemed to be propped up in a large chair, with restraints preventing him from moving his arms or legs, or turning his head. Slowly, cautiously, he opened his eyes.

There was a light, not too bright, shining directly into his face from the end of a long mechanical arm above him, and beyond that a white ceiling, the edges of white walls, more machinery. A hospital, perhaps? Was he ill? Had he been in some sort of accident? He couldn't remember.

The light was moved to one side and Professor Randhawa looked down at him. 'You're awake.'

'Yes,' he replied. 'Why am I being restrained?'

'For your own safety. We needed to keep you very still.'

'Why? What happened?'

'You died,' came a woman's voice from behind him. He tried to turn, but his head was fixed in place.

'Ms Kubin? Is that you?' The woman walked round to where he could see her. 'What do you mean, I died?'

'You were poisoned. It was very quick. You were dead before we could get you to the hospital, so we brought you here instead.'

'Ah, I see.' He closed his eyes and fell silent for a moment while he let the news sink in. It wasn't every day you got to wake up dead. 'And now I'm the android?' he asked after a moment.

'Exactly,' Randhawa replied. 'It was a close-run thing, but we finally got everything working so that the mind would accept the data blocks from your memory download. We didn't have your last two days recorded which is why you can't remember anything about, well, you know, your last two days. How does it feel, by the way?'

'I have no idea. Get me out of this damned chair and I might be able to tell you.'

'Of course, of course.' Randhawa tapped a pad on the side of the chair and the restraints sprang open. 'Let me just unplug you.'

While Randhawa busied himself with disconnecting the wires running from his machines into the back of the Whittaker android's head, Whittaker stretched his arms and legs and took a series of deep breaths.

'It feels good,' he said. 'Much better than the last one. Where is it, by the way? My real body?'

'What's left of it is next door, on ice. But it's not exactly in great shape. We couldn't cryoblast it until we'd completely finished the data extraction, and unfortunately that took a lot longer than I'd hoped. After the first few days it became easier to work on the head on its own, if you get my meaning. But it's all still there, in case you want to see it.'

'Of course I don't want to see it. And I don't want anyone else seeing it either. It's evidence, and it needs to be got rid of. Burn it.' He stood up, and Randhawa quickly unplugged the last of the wires. 'Now, Ms Kubin. Who poisoned me?'

'Leo Fischer.'

'The boy genius? I thought we'd killed him already.'

'I tried. He got away. I did succeed in killing the mother though, so I'm guessing he came looking for revenge.'

'But we have him now?'

'No,' Kalina muttered, the humiliation showing on her face. 'He got away again.'

'He's a goddamn teenager! How the hell can you keep letting him slip through your fingers? He's making you – making all of us – look like a bunch of amateurs, and it has to stop.'

'Yes, Sir.'

'Who's he working with?'

'We know he's had some contact with a terrorist cell operating here in Minerva. They were the ones who got him away from the museum after the assassination. But as far as we can tell, he's doing most of this on his own.'

'No, he's not.' He was finally thinking clearly. The confusion and disorientation he'd felt when he first woke up had passed and his mind felt as sharp as it had ever been. 'He's working for someone.'

'But my information—'

'Damn your information.' His mind was racing now. Facts, details, ideas, everything was there as soon as he thought about them. And he was processing information on several different levels at the same time. The room about him, Kubin and Randhawa, watching him cautiously and waiting for a response, the strength and power of his new body compared with the useless frailty of his old one, MarsMine, the election, the presidency, New Mars, Leo Fischer, Lillian Fischer, the death of Mr Archer, the discovery of the alien spaceship, the newly developed weapons, the threat from Earth, the possibility of conflict. All this, in a fraction of a second.

'Fischer is obviously a Terran agent. He's been trying to undermine our government for months with all his rumours of aliens and conspiracies, and when it became clear to him that his lies weren't having any effect, he decided to take a more direct approach. And with one failed assassination attempt, he's given us all the excuse we need.'

'Excuse for what?'

'For retaliation, Ms Kubin. Such a potentially devastating attack requires a suitable response, and by god I'm going to give them one.' He smiled, and felt the full power of his new body flowing around him. 'It's time for Mars to go to war.'

Leo and Skater return in *War Between Worlds*, the final part of the Mars Alone Trilogy, published by Lightning Books in 2024.

ACKNOWLEDGEMENTS

First of all, I would like to thank James Marshall, Kate Scott, Iain Hood, Melissa Fu, Adrian Sullivan, and the whole of the Angles Writing Group – all of whom were previously acknowledged in *The Arcadian Incident*, but whose advice, guidance and support certainly didn't end with my first novel and who deserve another mention here as well. I would also like to thank Pete Bull, who has encouraged, enabled and shared my love of all things science fiction and fantasy for so many years, and Geoff Wilson, who first showed me Saturn and Jupiter through a telescope and so awoke the stargazer in me.

And I would be remiss if I didn't give credit, and thanks, to NASA for the fantastic wealth of resources they provide, free of charge, via their website, *nasa.gov*. Science fiction is so much easier to write when you have the ability to study many thousands of images from across the Solar System, especially those sent back from the surface of Mars, and where you can watch countless hours of video of humans living and working in the microgravity environment of the International Space Station.

As usual, thanks must go to my tireless editor, Simon Edge, who continues to take time away from his own writing in order to assist me with mine, to Dan and everyone at Lightning Books, especially Clio and David, who have done such amazing work to produce and promote these novels, and to Ifan for yet another stylishly understated cover. I would also like to thank my unofficial publicists, Leigh Chambers, Susan Perry and Kate Coghlan, who have gone above and beyond in their efforts to help me find a larger audience for my novels.

And lastly, a very special thank you to my younger early readers, whose enthusiasm is matched only by their constant demands for 'the next instalment'. Some of them really are Young Adult, but others are even younger, and yet their imagination, their knowledge of my world and characters and yes, even their criticisms, never cease to amaze me. So thank you Struan Gardiner, Campbell Young, Fraser and Ruaridh Bennett, Lila and Freddie Coghlan, and Nathaniel Hampton- Milne.

If you have enjoyed *Escape to Midas*, do please help us spread the word – by putting a review online; by posting something on social media; or in the old-fashioned way by simply telling your friends or family about it.

Book publishing is a very competitive business these days, in a saturated market, and small independent publishers such as ourselves are often crowded out by the big houses. Support from readers like you can make all the difference to a book's success.

Many thanks.

Dan Hiscocks
Publisher
Lightning Books

Previously in the Mars Alone Trilogy

THE ARCADIAN INCIDENT

It's 2312 and Leo Fischer is a fifteen-year-old computer whizz on his first ever journey off Earth. He's heading to the moon colony to help his mother Lillian with her scientific work. But before he can reach her, she is kidnapped.

Determined to find and rescue her, Leo has no choice but to accept the help of his newest friend, Skater Monroe, the daughter of a shuttle pilot and already an experienced space traveller.

Dodging space pirates as well as a ruthless assassin in the pay of the soon-to-be president of Mars, they stumble upon a secret that could lead to all-out war in the solar system.

The first instalment of Andrew Stickland's Mars Alone Trilogy is a gravity-defying thrill-ride into the human race's all-too-believable future in space.